Yarn to Go

First in the Yarn Retreat Mysteries

"A cozy mystery that you won't want to put down. It combines cooking, knitting, and murder in one great book!"
—*Fresh Fiction*

"The California seaside is the backdrop to this captivating cozy that will have readers heading for the yarn store in droves."
—*Debbie's Book Bag*

"A nicely knitted yarn where the setting was idyllic."
—*Cozy Chicks*

"What a great start to a new series. But I would expect nothing less from the very talented Betty Hechtman—author of the Crochet Mysteries. This was a real page-turner."
—*MyShelf.com*

Praise for Betty Hechtman's National Bestselling Crochet Mysteries

"What fun—crochet and mystery."
—Vanna White, cohost of *Wheel of Fortune*

"Get hooked on this new author! . . . Who can resist a sleuth named Pink, a slew of interesting minor characters, and a fun fringe-of-Hollywood setting?"
—Monica Ferris, *USA Today* bestselling author

continued . . .

Silence of the Lamb's Wool

BETTY HECHTMAN

BERKLEY PRIME CRIME, NEW YORK

THE BERKLEY PUBLISHING GROUP
Published by the Penguin Group
Penguin Group (USA) LLC
375 Hudson Street, New York, New York 10014

USA • Canada • UK • Ireland • Australia • New Zealand • India • South Africa • China

penguin.com

A Penguin Random House Company

SILENCE OF THE LAMB'S WOOL

A Berkley Prime Crime Book / published by arrangement with the author

For information, address: The Berkley Publishing Group,
a division of Penguin Group (USA) LLC,
375 Hudson Street, New York, New York 10014.

ISBN: 978-0-425-25258-1

PUBLISHING HISTORY
Berkley Prime Crime mass-market edition / July 2014

PRINTED IN THE UNITED STATES OF AMERICA

10 9 8 7 6 5 4 3 2 1

Cover illustration by Patricia Castelao.
Cover design by Rita Frangie.
Interior text design by Kelly Lipovich.

Acknowledgments

I want to thank my editor, Sandy Harding, for once again doing a great job with this book. As always, her comments and suggestions were right on the mark. Thank you to my agent, Jessica Faust, for helping me navigate the changing world of publishing.

There is a lot in this book about sheep shearing, processing wool for spinning, and spinning. I had so much help from all over the country with that information. Christine Thresh sent me her wonderful booklet on spinning with a drop spindle. The Pierce College Farm Walk in Woodland Hills, California, offered me the chance to see Chris Vandiver shear several sheep. Thank you to Amanda Beck, Danielle Snowden and Billie Kariher for the information about sheep and wool. Los Angeles firefighter and paramedic Tom Rodriguez let me look around his rescue ambulance.

Across the country, the Maryland Sheep and Wool Festival gave me the opportunity to see how many different kinds of sheep there are and to purchase some handspun wool yarn from Snook Farm.

Thank you to the owners of the Village Spinning & Weaving Shop in Solvang, California, for telling me all about wool combs and urging me to use them in the book.

My Thursday group of Rene Biederman, Alice Chiredijan, Terry Cohen, Trish Culkin, Clara Feeney, Sonia Flaum, Lily Gillis, Winnie Hineson, Linda Hopkins, Debbie Kratofil, Reva Mallon, Elayne Moschin and Paula Tesler are always a great help and offer lots of support. A special thank-you to Linda Hopkins for acting as my tech editor. Roberta Martia always offers good yarn advice.

And I can't forget my cookie and muffin tasters, Burl, Max and Samantha!

1

THERE IS NOTHING LIKE BEING AWAKENED BY A ringing phone and finding a pair of yellow eyes staring back at you. I think Julius knew I'd never had a pet and he'd taken it on as his duty to train me in the art of cat cohabitation, which included sitting on my chest when he wanted breakfast. His yellow eyes blinked at me as if to say, "Would you get up and get me some food. Preferably that stuff in the can with the fabulous fishy odor."

The fluffy black cat let out a complaining meow as I tried to move him out of the way so I could reach for the cordless, which continued to ring insistently. He held on tight and jumped off only at the last minute with another meow as I clicked on the phone.

"What was that noise?" my mother said, skipping right past a "hello" or "good morning." "It sounded like a cat. Casey, don't tell me you got a cat. Not with your history."

This was exactly why I hadn't told her about Julius.

Besides, I didn't really "get" Julius. He showed up at my door, invited himself in and stayed. I could only guess at his back-story. I'd taken him to the vet, who gave him his shots and told me he was somewhere between one and five years old. Since he'd already been neutered, it appeared he had belonged to somebody and then was most likely abandoned. Along with the other cat supplies, I'd gotten him a collar with his name on it and had him chipped.

The history my mother was referring to was the fact that I had trouble sticking with things. How could I explain to her that the cat was different? I might have trouble sticking with professions, but Julius and I were going to be together for his forever, no matter what. But I needn't have worried about an explanation, because she didn't leave space for one. She just launched into her call.

"I didn't wake you, did I?" my mother said, before offering some excuse about the time difference. C'mon. My mother is a cardiologist who fixes broken hearts. Did she really expect me to believe she couldn't calculate that 9:00 a.m. in Chicago translated to 7:00 a.m. here in Cadbury by the Sea, California? Nor did I believe that she didn't remember that I worked nights baking desserts for the Blue Door restaurant and muffins for the coffee spots in town.

I sat up, reluctantly pulling back the snuggly lightweight down comforter I'd been cocooned in as my mother continued on with small talk. She always began our calls that way, as if I didn't know what was coming. My feet touched the cold wood floor and felt their way into the rose-colored plush slippers next to the bed. The light coming in the room was flat and I could see a snippet of the white sky. It didn't matter that it was May; the weather was the same as it had been in November. Cool, cloudy and damp.

Once I was well versed in what was going on with my

pediatrician father, she moved on to the real point of the call. If my mother hadn't been a doctor, she could have been an interrogator for the cops.

"So, have you had enough yet? Are you ready to leave?" she said. I bristled silently at her questions. But I couldn't argue. I had a certain reputation and I can't say it wasn't well earned. I'd gone through numerous professions—a semester of law school before dropping out, two years of substitute teaching at a private school before I faced the truth that it wasn't for me. Even my gig as a baker had lasted only six months, until the bistro closed. But at least I'd loved it, and in a way it had led me to a future. The rest of the time I'd done temp work—everything from handing out samples of breath mints to spritzing shoppers with perfume. The only temp job I'd really liked was working at the detective agency, but that had ended, too.

Hoping a fresh start would make a difference, I'd relocated to my aunt's converted garage/guesthouse in Cadbury by the Sea. With her help, I'd gotten a job baking desserts at the Blue Door along with the muffin-baking business. Thinking about my aunt Joan made my eyes get misty. Just a few months after I'd moved in, she was killed in a hit-and-run. I'd inherited her house and her business.

"Mother, it's different this time," I said. I could practically see her response. She was no doubt dressed in one of her many pantsuits and I'd heard one of her dangle earrings knock against the phone. I would bet her eyes had gone skyward as she'd shaken her head in disbelief.

I might have shared a little of her disbelief. It wasn't as if I had any experience in the business my aunt had left me. It was called Yarn2Go and involved putting on yarn retreats. The next question was always, What are yarn retreats? The retreat part is easy to understand. It means a group of people withdrawing for prayer, meditation, study or instruction under a director. I guess the director means me. There isn't any prayer or study involved, but since yarn work seems to be meditative, you could keep the meditation in. And there is some kind of instruction.

That's where the yarn part comes in. So far it has been only knitting. Another reason for my mother's disbelief was my basic lack of yarn skills, or so she thought. When I put on the first retreat I hadn't even known how to knit. I have to admit it wasn't exactly love at first clack of the needles, but something happened during the weekend and by the end I'd begun to understand why people loved working with yarn. You could say I'd caught the bug.

In the time since that retreat, I had upped my skills, though I still had a long way to go before I'd be close to my aunt's level. At least now I knew how to cast on, knit, purl and cast off. I hadn't discussed it with my mother, knowing there was no way she would understand.

I girded myself as I got ready to tell her about the retreat I had coming up the following weekend. "I'm doing an event Aunt Joan always wanted to do. It's a little bigger than the first one I put on with only five retreaters. Well, six if you count the one who died."

"If I were you, I'd never mention that anyone died again. Who would want to go on a retreat if they knew last time that someone didn't make it to the end? So, what's the big number of retreaters for this one? Seven?" It was as close as my mother came to a joke.

"More like twenty," I said.

"Twenty?" she repeated.

"This retreat is totally different from the last. Joan called it Sheep to Shawl. We're going to start off with some sheep getting sheared—humanely of course—then go through the steps of turning the wool into yarn. Finally everyone will knit a shawlette out of the finished yarn." Before my mother could say anything, I added that I'd found somebody in town who knew about the process of turning wool into yarn and was handling that particular aspect.

My mother didn't really want to hear all the details and cut in. "I'm just checking. The cooking school called to let me know that a new session is starting up next month. It's all set up for you. You could be spending the summer in Paris. And at the end, you'd be a professional chef."

I'd gotten the same call the previous month. When I'd first taken over my aunt's business, my parents—well, mostly my mother—had stepped in, sure that I was just going off on another temporary job tangent, and offered to send me to cooking school in France, which she regarded as a way to turn my interest in baking into a real profession. I gave her the same answer I'd given her the month before: "Not yet." I wanted to say "not ever," but one thing I'd learned about myself was never say never.

After a few well-placed sighs of disapproval, my mother asked about Sammy. Sammy was Dr. Samuel Glickner, a urologist and my former boyfriend. He would have had the title of husband if my mother had had her way. Although we'd broken up, we were still friends, and he'd recently relocated from Chicago to the Monterey Peninsula and joined a urology practice. He insisted he wasn't following me. He claimed to love the area and it was a chance to pursue his love of magic.

"He got a job doing card tricks at a bar," I said. My mother gasped and I had to fight the urge to laugh. And I hadn't even mentioned that it was kind of a tough biker bar in Seaside.

"Has he lost his mind?" she said finally. "What if his patients see him?"

If only Sammy could have heard my mother, he would

have been so happy. He was convinced that part of the reason things hadn't worked out with us was that my mother liked him too much. Well, not anymore.

"And the cop down the street, what's his name?" my mother said.

"Dane Mangano. What about him?" I answered, playing dumb.

"Casey, I have eyes. Your father and I were only there for a short time, but I saw there was something between you."

She was right about that. There was some kind of spark that flitted between us, but I was letting it fizzle out. He was a neighbor and this was a small town. I knew me. If things didn't last and most likely they wouldn't, I'd still have to live down the street from him. I wondered if I should mention the food thing we'd worked out.

Dane Mangano was a cop who cooked pots of pasta covered with mouthwatering homemade sauce. I made desserts, but when it came to regular meals, I was okay living on frozen entrées. Dane and I had worked out an exchange. He left me plates of the delicious pasta and I left him muffins and desserts.

I heard some noise on my mother's end and guessed her next patient was there. Just before she signed off, she said her trademark comment: "I don't get it, Casey. When I was your age, I was a wife, a mother and a doctor, and you're a . . . what?"

My reaction was automatic, too. No thinking, just my back going up while I searched for a snappy retort. But before I could say a word, her tone softened and she added, "It's only because I love you. Have a good day, sweetie." Then with a click she was gone and I was left with a lump in my throat only she could put there.

By now I'd made it into the room I used as an office. What

that meant was that I had left it the way my aunt had it arranged. Even to the point of keeping my knitting stuff in there. The knitted scarf I'd started during the first retreat hung from a doorknob where I could admire it. I was so proud of the fact that I had finished it completely, down to adding the fringe.

Because of my worry about finishing things, my projects after the scarf had all been items I could make in a short amount of time. I'd become a wiz at washcloths, small pouch purses and bandanna scarves.

The golden crocheted lion my aunt had made was still guarding the desk. And I'd left the seafoam green lap blanket hanging on the arm of the black leather love seat. I liked to think they were reminders of her and what I might make in the future.

I'd gone into the office to check the status of the tote bags for the early birds, as I called them. Three of the people who'd come on my first retreat were coming ahead of time for a pre-retreat retreat and would be arriving this morning. The three tomato-red bags still needed the drop spindles and the pattern for the shawlette.

Julius came in and popped up on the love seat, trying to get my attention. As soon as I looked at him, he jumped down and sauntered toward the open door, looking behind to see if I was following. I got the message and he led the way to the kitchen.

He went directly to the refrigerator in case there was any doubt of what he wanted.

"When this can is gone, that's it," I said, opening the refrigerator door. I'd wrapped the half-used can in multiple layers of plastic to contain the smell. I held my nose while I went through the layers, having gotten a whiff of mackerel when I first opened the can. A stink to me; heaven to him.

I realized I must love this cat. I'd fed him before I even thought about making coffee. He ate every morsel of his stink fish while I stirred some crystals in hot water. I looked at my aunt's coffeepot and thought I really ought to start using it, but this instant stuff was so much easier. I sat down at the table with the coffee and a container of yogurt while Julius searched the bowl for any pieces he might have missed. When he was done, he nestled in my lap and began to purr his thank-yous.

It was nice having all this space after living in the converted garage, which was really just one big room. I knew my aunt would be happy to see how I was changing things around to make the house my own. The kitchen had been the first order of business and I liked seeing my stand mixer ready for action on the sea green–tiled counter. All my baking pans were easily accessible and my cooking tools nicely arranged in the drawers.

Julius took time out from his purring to tap me on the arm for his taste of the yogurt. I gave him the last spoonful and then we both got up. I had places to go and people to see.

2

HERE ON THE TIP OF THE MONTEREY PENINSULA, the weather was the same year-round. The temperature bounced back and forth between the fifties and sixties, occasionally slipping up into the seventies, and I'd learned a whole vocabulary for describing white skies and fog because blue skies came and went in a hurry. I'd found the perfect outerwear was fleece and I now had a whole wardrobe of the soft nubby jackets in different colors. This morning I'd opted for the cream-colored one with a rosy pink scarf wound around my neck to add a little color. I zipped up the fleece as I stepped outside, letting the bracing air wipe away the last feeling of sleepiness.

When I had bought Julius his cat supplies at Cadbury Pets, the pet specialist suggested I make him an indoor cat. Right. He was an escape artist able to turn door handles and slip through windows left open only a sliver. The solution was to let him go in or out at his own discretion. He followed me down the step from the back door and took off into what passed for a backyard. I was relieved when he didn't follow me farther. He wasn't a welcome guest where I was going.

I lived on the edge of Cadbury by the Sea. Everything was wilder out here and people's yards had either whatever native plants (that's the politically correct way of saying *weeds*) that grew on their own or ivy ground cover. The only planted aspects at my place were the pots of red and white impatiens my aunt had set near the back door.

I'd never been an outdoor kind of person. Growing up in the hermetically sealed Hancock building in downtown Chicago had been all about looking at the view rather than being part of it. There, Lake Michigan was a few blocks away. Here, an even shorter distance took me to the sea. I could smell the salt in the air and hear the rhythm of the waves as I crossed the street to Vista Del Mar, the hotel and conference center where the retreats were held.

It was obvious why my aunt had decided to hold the retreats here. How much more convenient could you get than just across the street? And there was another reason, too. Something about the way Vista Del Mar was closer to a camp than a resort made it the perfect setting for yarn lovers to gather and work on their craft.

Two stone pillars marked the entrance to the driveway. The flat light made the dark weathered buildings appear even more moody, like they were hiding deep secrets. The buildings were spread over more than a hundred rolling acres surrounded by picturesque trees, and the hotel and conference center grounds were even more untamed than the rest of the area. There was no team of gardeners taking care of these grounds. The Monterey pines and Monterey cypress trees grew of their own accord, and if one of the lanky Monterey pines toppled over, it was left where it fell to return to the earth on its own.

Recently, I'd heard it wasn't just trees that were left to decompose on their own. When an animal died amidst the tall golden grass and brush, it was left where it fell as well. That thought kept me from looking too closely at the grounds as I proceeded down the driveway and followed the road as it curved toward the main building, called the Lodge.

I had done my best to sound confident about the upcoming retreat to my mother, but the truth was I was nervous. This was the first retreat I was doing from scratch and it was much more ambitious than just getting a few people together to knit. I was relieved that it was only Monday morning and the main group wasn't arriving until Thursday. I was looking forward to seeing the three arriving today. The early birds had become friends. They were the real reason for my first stop at the Lodge. I wanted to make sure their rooms were together and that there was a common area for them to meet and spend time with their needles.

The Lodge was a combination lobby, social hall and business area. To me it seemed like the heart of Vista Del Mar. I opened the double doors and walked into the cavernous room. This early on a Monday morning was probably the quietest time of the week. All the weekenders had checked out the day before and the people arriving for the coming week hadn't checked in yet. So, it was no surprise the seating area was empty.

It was funny to think that the gathering spot around the massive stone fireplace had recently been refurbished. Refurbishing usually meant something had been updated and looked new and modern. Not here. In the case of Vista Del Mar, it meant new things that looked old and were in keeping with the Arts and Crafts design of the building. The leather couches and mission-style chairs were pretty much copies of what had been there before. Even though it was daylight, the table lamps were on, adding a warm glow from their amber-colored glass shades.

The table tennis and pool table both sat empty at the far end of the room. The door was open to the gift shop, but I was betting there weren't any customers.

The rest of the room was equally deserted. The chairs were all pushed in on the two long wood tables near the piano. As I finished surveying the room, I glanced out the big windows and caught sight of the wooden deck and beyond the sand dunes that ran the whole length of the property. A deer was just crossing the boardwalk that led through the sand. After years of abuse, the white hills had been replanted and were now covered with native plants and tall bushes. The walkway looked like it was made out of old railroad ties, but in reality I think it was something like recycled plastic soda bottles.

Even with no customers, there was somebody manning the registration counter. It was really a big wooden barrier that separated the social aspects of the room from the business side. As I got ready to take care of my business, my nose perked up at the scent of freshly brewed coffee coming from the newly added café. It was definitely going to be my next stop.

I think the woman behind the registration counter was glad for the company and it was lucky I had come in to double check. They had it all wrong for my early birds and had put them in rooms in different buildings. It always made me feel good when I found a problem like that and took care of it. I suppose it was silly, but it made me feel competent.

"Ms. Feldstein, we were just talking about you." The voice came from behind me and startled me. I hadn't realized anyone else was there.

When I turned I was looking almost directly into Kevin St. John's moon-shaped face. He was the manager of Vista Del Mar and as usual dressed too formally for the rustic surroundings. The white shirt, conservative tie and dark suit combined with his serious expression made him look more like an undertaker than the person in charge of a place where people came to have fun.

I smiled weakly in response to his comment. I'm not sure if Kevin St. John just didn't like me or if it was all about the retreats. He had made it clear that he wanted to host any retreats held on the property and was unhappy that I had held on to my aunt's business instead of turning everything over to him. When I looked beyond him I saw that the "we" included Cora and Madeleine Delacorte and a man who seemed to be with them.

The Delacorte sisters were the last of the Delacorte family. Their family had owned fleets of fishing boats, a cannery and lots of property in Cadbury. The fishing fleets were long gone and the cannery had been turned into a shopping mall, and most of the property had been sold off and the money invested. The sisters had kept one of the Victorian houses for themselves, and Vista Del Mar. Though Kevin St. John liked to give the impression he was the lord of the hotel and conference center, as the owners, they were really his bosses.

The Delacorte sisters were in their seventies and their almost-matching navy blue knit suits seemed a little formal. They both had handbags hanging off their arms, Queen Elizabeth style. The man with them kept looking around the Lodge as if he were taking measurements.

"Casey, it's so nice to see you," Cora Delacorte said. She was the more vocal of the sisters and seemed to be the one in charge. I guessed they had both had early-morning appointments at the Cadbury Hair Salon. The giveaway was the slightly chemical scent of hair spray and the perfect bubble style each of them sported. No flat sides from sleeping on a pillow. And since the dark reddish brown color and the wiry texture of their hair didn't go together, I suspected the color was beautician enhanced. My old detective boss, Frank, would have been proud of me. During the brief time I'd worked with him, I had honed my powers of observation, even if most of the work I'd done was on the phone.

Madeleine was the silent sister. She kept a step back from the inner circle and looked toward the door like she wanted to leave.

"I was just telling Cora and Madeleine that your retreat was going to be one of the first under our new policy," Kevin St. John said.

I felt my stomach churn. Whatever the policy was, I was sure it wasn't going to be good—and I doubted that was all he'd said. I was willing to bet there had been some kind of disparaging remark thrown in about how I ran things. I was trying to get along with him, but he made it hard. Vista Del Mar was his domain and running it seemed like more than a job to him. He was possessive and protective, but most of all he wanted everything his way. Sometimes I thought he viewed the guests as a necessary evil. Kevin St. John nodded solicitously toward Cora and Madeleine.

"I was about to explain it all for Cora and Madeleine," he said. "I'm sure you remember when the cell tower that gave a signal to Vista Del Mar blew over during a storm. It's been replaced, but apparently it was moved to another location, leaving Vista Del Mar in a dead zone." To demonstrate, he took out his phone and pushed it toward me so I could see it had no reception. "At first it seemed like a negative, until I thought about it. The whole cell phone thing has gotten out of hand. I would look out into the Lodge and see nothing but people staring at their phones, tablets or computers. It never seemed to go along with the spirit of Vista Del Mar. So, I decided the best thing to do was simply to go completely unplugged."

"Completely unplugged?" I repeated. "You mean no Wi-Fi?" He nodded.

"It will make Vista Del Mar stand out. People come here to get away from the stresses of their high-intensity world. Now they truly will." As he spoke, I looked around the seating area and noticed the TV was gone, and he confirmed that was part of being unplugged.

"What about the radios in the rooms?" I asked. The rooms had neither TVs nor telephones and the only connection to the outside world were old clock radios. The kind where you didn't need a manual to figure out how to set the alarm.

Kevin assured me the radios were staying. "I didn't say our guests would be out of touch." He gestured toward a large corkboard next to the gift shop. "People can call the desk and we'll take a message and post it. Guests can leave messages for other guests there, too." He swiveled and indicated the alcove next to the large wooden registration counter. "I've had landlines installed and we're putting them in phone booths. The guests may balk at first, but by the end of their stay, I'm sure they will be thanking us. Imagine not having to listen to one side of endless conversations or watch people walk into trees because they are staring at their smartphone screen."

I could see his point, but I also knew that some of my group were going to freak when they heard the news.

"There's no reason for you to have to fill your pretty head with all these details," the man with Cora and Madeleine said. I noticed that Cora turned toward him with a melting smile and more than a few bats of her eyelashes before she shifted her attention back to me.

"Where are my manners, Casey. I don't think you've met Burton Fiore, my fiancé."

How had I missed that news? Neither of the sisters had

ever been married, so one of them getting engaged was big news. "You're getting married?" I didn't mean to blurt it out, but it wasn't that often that a seventy-something woman introduced you to her fiancé—her first-ever fiancé.

I heard Kevin St. John snicker at my comment. I'm sure he was hoping it would irritate Cora Delacorte and make her dislike me. Then she would renege on the agreement she'd made with my aunt. Cora had adored my aunt Joan and had been impressed that in her actor days she'd been the spokesperson for Tidy Soft toilet paper. The Delacorte sisters had loved the idea of my aunt putting on yarn retreats at Vista Del Mar and had offered her the rooms and facilities at a reduced rate. The same deal had carried over to me. I wasn't sure if it was really the money part that bothered Kevin St. John as much as having his power stepped over. It was clear that he liked to see himself as the lord of Vista Del Mar.

But to Kevin St. John's chagrin, Cora merely smiled at my comment. "I know it must seem surprising, but when Cupid's arrow pierces your heart, well, age doesn't seem to matter." She turned and looked toward Burton with adoring eyes as he seemed to reciprocate. "It's all so new," she said. "Burton just popped the question a few days ago." She held out her hand to show off a sizable diamond on her finger.

I regarded the man with new interest and wondered if Cora knew she was a cougar. Burton Fiore appeared a good ten years younger than she was. He had salt-and-pepper hair and a mustache that added a little interest to his round soft face. It was hard to tell if his eyes were shining with love for her or were just beady looking. Maybe it wasn't fair to judge him since we'd just met, but I immediately wondered if Cupid's arrow had been directed by dollar signs.

"Have you seen our new café?" Cora said with pride in her voice. Her pumps made a clicking sound on the floor as she led me to a wall plaque next to the café's open door. The plaque was definitely new. I'd been dropping muffins off at the café since it opened a month ago and had seen the interior a number of times, but I followed along anyway, since she seemed so anxious to show it off.

My breakfast had been pretty meager and I glanced at the glass case filled with fruit salad and cold sandwiches with a hungry eye. Jane Crawley, the café employee, was wiping down the counter and looked up at us, inquiring if we wanted anything. I felt like saying I'd take one of everything, but Cora said she was just showing off her namesake.

Cora's gaze stopped on the muffins in the glass-domed container on the long wood counter. "Are those your work?" she asked, directing her comment at me. I nodded and she asked what kind they were. I hesitated. The town council wanted everything in Cadbury to have straightforward names without any cutesy flourishes. They'd hassled me when I started calling my muffins fun names like Merry Berry or Heal the World with Chocolate, so I'd renamed the muffins with more practical names. But in my mind I still sometimes called them the fun ones. Cora was really part of the establishment, so I told her they were chocolate and vanilla muffins, but my name for them was Ebony and Ivory.

Jane seemed a little intimidated by Cora but still managed to mention that half the muffins had already sold and it was just a little after nine.

"In that case," Cora said, "why don't you pack a couple of them up for me. Burton and I can have them with our lunch." She patted my hand. "Everything you bake is worth every calorie."

While Jane packed up the muffins, Cora asked me about the upcoming retreat.

I described how it was going to start with a sheep shearing and then the group was going to prepare the wool and spin it into yarn. "The grand finale is knitting a shawlette with the yarn." Cora nodded with interest though I doubted she knew much about yarn craft.

Her expression dimmed a little and she leaned toward me. "I hope there won't be any deaths this time." I didn't know what to say. Should I correct her and say that only one of the actual deaths took place during my last retreat? It probably wouldn't help, so I said the only reassuring thing I could come up with and reminded her that I had found the killer.

"That's true," she said. "As I recall, you were quite the detective. Better than our own Cadbury Police Department." I was relieved when the subject was dropped as Jane handed her the package with the muffins.

When we rejoined the group in the main room of the Lodge, she held up the bag and told Burton she had treats. I couldn't help but notice that Burton Fiore and Kevin St. John had struck an adversarial pose. Madeleine had found a chair. I tried to remember if I had ever heard her talk, wondering if she might not be able to speak. As if to answer my thought, Madeleine asked her sister what was taking so long. "Everything seems fine to me," Madeleine said with a wave of her hand, apparently to indicate all of Vista Del Mar.

"How many acres did you say this place is?" Burton directed his question to Kevin St. John. The manager muttered an answer under protest and turned his attention back to Cora. It didn't stop Burton Fiore's stream of questions. When he asked if Vista Del Mar offered twenty-four-hour room service, Kevin sputtered and I stifled a laugh. Room service?

The manager mentioned the café, making sure he said the whole name.

"We offer a full line of drinks, snacks and coffee drinks. It's up to the guests to plan ahead if they're going to be hungry after hours."

Undaunted, Cora's husband-to-be walked over to an open area in front of the large window looking out on the wood deck. "Cora, this is the spot I was telling you about. It would be a perfect place to put in a bar." Kevin St. John immediately dismissed the idea, saying it didn't go along with the vibe of the place. "We have beer and wine in the Cora and Madeleine Delacorte Café. This isn't a cocktail or whiskey shots sort of place."

Kevin's usually placid face had taken on an annoyed expression. "This is a historic place, one of a kind. If guests are checking the thread count on the sheets and how plushy the towels are, this isn't the place for them. There are plenty of resorts in Pebble Beach if they want luxury. People come here for the experience."

I waited for Cora to say something in favor of one of the men, but she merely smiled. Madeleine made a *harrumph* sound and wanted to know if the meeting was over yet.

Cora's navy blue Chanel-style jacket had gotten askew and Burton straightened it and gave her shoulder an affectionate touch. The older Delacorte sister leaned into his gesture and thanked him with a few bats of her eyelashes, saying how nice it was having someone to watch her back. Kevin St. John viewed the moment with distaste, probably figuring it was only going to get worse once they were married.

The door opened from the deck side and a distinguished-looking man with silver hair came in with a quick stride. He was wearing cargo pants and a bomber-style leather jacket. I wondered if his face was naturally ruddy or if it was the cold air. He looked over the group with a friendly smile. "Virgil Scarantino at your service." He did a mock bow and I instantly liked him. Kevin took it upon himself to introduce us, though the only ones Virgil hadn't met before were Cora's fiancé and me. He seemed as surprised as I'd been at Cora's engagement news, but handled it better and just offered them his congratulations before he turned to me.

"So you're Casey Feldstein," he said with a big smile. "I wondered who was behind all the muffins and the wonderful desserts at the Blue Door." He went into detail about his favorites, which turned out to be the muffins he called "those rich chocolate ones." My name for them was Heal the World with Chocolate. As for the Blue Door desserts, it was apple pie all the way as far as he was concerned. When he finished, I was almost blushing from all the praise.

"Well, chief," he said to Kevin St. John, "should I tell them my duties?" The manager nodded and gave Virgil the floor. "I've lived in Cadbury all my life and love this area. Nothing gives me more pleasure than to share what I know so I've volunteered to do some nature walks and star hikes."

Cora loved the idea and thought it was very much in the spirit of the place. Madeleine surprised us all by adding her approval. I hadn't meant to get sucked into this dog and pony show for the Delacorte sisters and started to excuse myself until I saw that someone else had come in.

Dr. Sammy? In a tuxedo, no less. Sammy Glickner, my former boyfriend, was tall with a hulky teddy bear–like build. In the tuxedo, he reminded me of a panda bear. He was all smiles as he crossed the space to the group in a few long strides. His eyes were glued to the manager, but then he saw me, his eyes widened as his face lit up.

I knew we weren't a couple—and it was all my doing—but it was certainly nice to have someone seem so glad to see me. "Case, what do you think?" His hands rolled down displaying his outfit, the way models on game shows displayed prizes. I still laughed at his calling me Case. Really? Did taking one letter off my name make it a nickname?

Kevin St. John broke into the moment. "I thought it would

be entertaining having table magic on the weekends in the dining hall." The sisters both nodded their agreement. Virgil thought it sounded dandy, and Burton Fiore just muttered "Dining hall?" before excusing himself from the group, saying he had to make a call.

The manager introduced Dr. Sammy to the group as the Amazing Dr. Sammy. I got the message that Kevin St. John was running all this by the Delacorte sisters for their approval rather than presenting it as a fait accompli. Sammy was there to audition for them.

I felt instantly nervous for him and almost couldn't watch, but Sammy started his patter without the slightest stumble and took out a deck of cards. He had sized up the situation and played to Cora, who was delighted with his little show. She even clapped at the end. Madeleine seemed to have forgotten her rush to leave and added her own applause.

"The guests will love you," Cora said, beaming a smile at Sammy. Madeleine nodded her agreement and Kevin St. John told Sammy the job was his, provided the first weekend went well.

The only person not so sure about adding Sammy as a regular on the weekends was me. The retreats I put on were always on the weekend, which meant our lives would be intersecting when I was doing my best to keep some distance between us. So when the Amazing Dr. Sammy offered to do an encore to his audition, I extricated myself from the group. Cora and Madeleine were front and center and I heard them talking as I walked away.

Cora spoke directly to Kevin St. John, saying, "You're doing such a wonderful job with Vista Del Mar. I like all these changes. Edmund would so approve," she added with a bright sound in her voice.

Edmund?

3

"HEY, CASEY, LONG TIME, NO SEE," ALISON SAID AS
I sailed into the gift shop. I used to see her almost daily when
the shop had a coffee wagon, where my muffins had been
offered along with the coffee drinks and assorted other
snacks. But once the café opened, the gift store had been
rearranged and a display of T-shirts and fleece jackets with
the Vista Del Mar insignia had taken over the spot where the
coffee wagon used to sit. Two sides of the shop were almost
all windows, which gave a good view of the grounds.

As I greeted Alison, I looked through the window behind
her and noticed Burton Fiore rejoining Cora and Madeleine.
It was interesting watching him without hearing what he was
saying. His gestures seemed a little over the top as he greeted
the sisters.

"I'm here about the yarn," I said, turning my attention back
inside. When I'd first made the arrangements for the retreat,
I'd talked to Alison about carrying yarn and supplies for the

retreaters, but also for the other guests of Vista Del Mar. It turned out that when other guests saw the retreat group working with yarn, it inspired them to do the same.

"All taken care of." Alison came from behind the counter and walked me over to an empty gondola that already had a sign that read YARN. There were empty baskets just waiting to be filled with colorful fibers, and containers for needles and hooks. "Someone from Cadbury Yarn is supposed to come by today."

I was a little disappointed, because I'd been hoping the yarn would already be there. But my early birds weren't arriving until the afternoon anyway. "I'm stopping by Cadbury Yarn. I'll double check with them." Two men wearing matching red polo shirts came into the small store and began to look around. A moment later a woman in sandals and a pale green stretchy outfit walked in.

I left Alison to her customers and was startled by the change in the main room of the Lodge when I exited the store. There were more people in the red polo shirts milling around near the registration counter. There seemed to be a lot of others who resembled the woman in stretchy clothes as well. Kevin St. John was in the midst of it all and I figured out these must be two retreat groups he'd made the arrangements for.

I played my own game of "let's figure out what kind of retreat were they here for" as I got closer. The yoga mats were a giveaway for the people in stretchy clothes. There were a lot more of the red polo shirt crowd and they were a little harder to figure out. But after hearing a few bits of conversation, I got that they were from all over the country and were here for a managers' retreat. I wondered if the business group had heard that their cell phones were useless and it was ixnay on the Wi-Fi.

The morning was slipping away and I still had things to do before I got back here to greet my pre-retreaters. As I neared the café, the pungent smell of freshly ground coffee reminded me that I'd planned to stop there. I'd just get the coffee to go.

There was a hum of voices as I walked into the corner room and I noticed that Jane was talking to someone standing at the counter. The room was almost the mirror image of the gift shop, with the same two walls of windows, making it feel like it was almost outside. I noted the sky had turned a brighter shade of white. As I got closer I heard something about a problem just before the man standing by the counter turned toward me. When I saw that it was Will Welton I completely understood. He was the caretaker of Vista Del Mar and problems were his business. In fact if there were no problems, he wouldn't have a job.

"Morning, Casey," he said in a friendly voice. He was one of those people who seemed to always be upbeat. He even walked with a spring in his step. His longish blond hair was a little scruffy, but it made him look cute. He stepped aside so I could get right up to the counter, probably because the need for coffee showed in my eyes. Jane must have noticed it, too, because she was already reaching for one of the large white paper cups.

"So, you're back. What will it be? Cappuccino, latte or maybe just a straight cup of today's brew?" Jane was trying to be sparkly, but it came across as unnatural. It was terrible, but whenever I said her name, it seemed to be preceded by *plain* in my mind. She had pale brown hair that hung to her shoulders and she never wore makeup. Her clothes were always neat, but like the light blue top she was wearing, they were best described as serviceable. I'd heard that she'd taken care of her ailing mother and probably had never had anyone to show her how to enhance her appearance. While I waited, Jane told the caretaker about my earlier visit.

Will knew all about Vista Del Mar being unplugged. It was fine with him, as he was into the place being authentic.

"And it will be a lot safer. I've seen guests walk right off the paved path without realizing it. They have their noses stuck in their screens instead of looking at all this." We all looked out the window and agreed with one another that missing all this beauty was almost a crime.

"I hope my retreat group takes it well," I said. It was only one of the uncertainties I had about the upcoming weekend. It was a bigger group and an ambitious program. I said something to that effect and Will gave me a reassuring nod.

"There's nothing for you to worry about. Nicole is an expert and really looking forward to handling the fiber part." He spoke another five minutes about his wife's skills, bringing up that she had a master's degree in textiles and was an accomplished spinner, weaver and knitter.

"You don't have to sell me. She's the only reason I considered doing this retreat. It's nice that you're so proud of her." I turned to Jane and asked for a cappuccino.

"Isn't Nicole supposed to give your early people a lesson tomorrow?" Jane asked, trying to be part of the conversation.

"That's absolutely right," I said. "Right about this time."

"I really want to thank you for giving her this opportunity. She's kind of gotten off track. This could be just what she needs," Will said.

A deliveryman came in wheeling a dolly full of boxes. He slipped them off the cart and asked Jane to sign for the delivery. While she signed, he looked on the counter at the empty container where my muffins had been.

"Missed them again," he said with regret. Jane told him the last one had just been sold and introduced me as the baker. He gave me an appreciative nod and said it always felt like his lucky day when he managed to score a muffin. I suggested he might have a better chance at one of his earlier stops, since I provided muffins for a number of places in town.

"Will do," he said with a smile. "One question. What kind are you baking for tomorrow?"

I blushed at the compliment, but loved it all the same. Then I hesitated. Should I give the real name or the toned-down version the town council required? Out loud I said "blueberry," but in my head I called them by my name, The Blues.

The empty dolly made a squeaky racket as the delivery guy wheeled it out. "I better get back to work," Will said, picking up his coffee, but Jane took it from him.

"You'll spill it all over yourself." She snapped a white cap on the paper cup with the Vista Del Mar logo on it and picked up what looked like a long green cocktail pick. I was surprised when she dropped it into the opening in the cap. "It's something new we just got. It acts as a plug so the coffee doesn't splash out of the top." I looked closer and saw it had *VDM* embossed on the top.

"What's the problem today?" I asked Will. "The antique plumbing acting up?"

Will laughed. "It's always acting up. You just have to know how to finesse it to work." It seemed kind of odd. Will was barely twenty-five and yet he had such an affection for Vista Del Mar, most of which was over one hundred years old. He was an expert at replacing shingles and aging the replacements so you couldn't tell the old from the new. He mixed his own formula for polishing the brass doorknobs, dictated to the housekeepers what kind of cleaners they should use that wouldn't harm the old surfaces and he even made his own insecticide from a vintage recipe.

"It's the phone booths," he said before explaining that he'd found three that had been in the back room of an old pharmacy in Capitola. He'd brought them over in his truck and they needed to be installed so the phones could be put in. "I think they're going to be a nice touch from the past." He thanked Jane for putting the plug in his cup and went off to his work.

I said I had to go, too. Jane apologized for not having made my cappuccino and went to make it. She talked as she frothed the milk, saying she'd known Will for years, all the way back to high school. She insisted on giving my cappuccino the same lid treatment as Will's drink. "Now you don't have to worry about spilling any."

I intended to cross the main room of the Lodge without stopping, but Kevin St. John blocked my path. The pleasant demeanor he'd had when the sisters were there was now gone. "Three things," he said curtly. "Please keep that cat of yours off the grounds. He nearly came inside." I almost laughed. Obviously Kevin St. John knew less about cats than I did. What did he think I was going to do? Sit Julius down and tell him his boundaries? To keep the peace, I said I would do my best.

"The second thing is, let's not have any more bodies connected with your retreats. Let's have the same number of people leave who arrive." If Kevin's expression hadn't been so serious I would have thought this was a joke. First, wanting me to tell a cat what to do and now telling me to keep all my people alive. He couldn't really believe I wanted anyone to die. I couldn't wait to hear what number three was.

"And the last thing is, you can't have the sheep sheared on the premises."

"But, but," I stuttered, "it's the kickoff to the whole retreat. I've told all the retreaters." Then I looked him in the eye. "You've known about this for weeks, haven't you? Why are you telling me now?"

"Oh, I must have forgotten," he said in a feigned-concerned voice. "I hope it doesn't cause you any problem."

How about taking away the whole first section of the retreat? I thought. *It's called Sheep to Shawl. Not Bunch of Wool to Shawl.*

4

"I DON'T KNOW WHAT I'M GOING TO DO," I SAID TO Lucinda Thornkill. "How can I put on a retreat billed as Sheep to Shawl with no sheep?" Lucinda was probably my best friend as well as my employer. She was also going to be one of the retreaters. I had made a detour in my errands to tell her my news.

I must have looked a little crazed when I walked into the Blue Door restaurant because as soon as Lucinda escorted a touristy-looking couple to a table in the window, she put her arm through mine and took me to the back room.

The Blue Door restaurant was named for the color of its front door and was a converted house. Maybe calling it a converted cottage was more accurate. I was used to being there at night, when I had the place to myself, and was always a little surprised to see customers waiting in line.

The back room must have once been a small sun porch. There was room for only four tables, all of which were currently empty. The decor was almost all white and the only spot of color was a red cushion on a bench at the table where Lucinda gestured for me to sit. The tablecloth caught on my knee as I slid in, causing it to scrunch up. I glanced around for Lucinda's husband, Tag, knowing it was just the kind of thing to throw him into a tizzy. Tag was a little OCD and anything out of order threw him for a loop.

Before I could do anything, Lucinda had leaned over and quickly smoothed out the tablecloth, then she chuckled. "Oh no, Tag fanaticism is rubbing off on me." She cast an eye on the menu lying on the table next to us. "I really should change that."

I knew the "that" she was referring to was the story on the back of the menu. It was written in fairy-tale fashion and told how Lucinda and Tag had been high school sweethearts, but their lives had gone in different directions. Then years later when she was divorced and he was a widower they had reconnected, gotten married and lived their dream of opening a restaurant. The trouble was the real story wasn't quite so happily ever after. Both of them had changed during all those years apart. The biggest problem was Tag's need to have everything just so. Lucinda wasn't messy; she was just more relaxed.

"There has to be some kind of solution," she said, getting back to my problem, "but you can't do it on an empty stomach." She signaled to one of the waitresses and asked her to bring me today's special. I didn't even ask what it was because everything looked delicious.

Lucinda was right. After eating the polenta circles sautéed in butter and covered with melted mozzarella and a drizzle of tomato basil sauce along with the chopped vegetable salad, things didn't seem quite so terrible.

"I don't know why Kevin St. John waited until the last

minute to tell me," I said as I pushed my empty plate away. Before Lucinda could speak, I answered myself. "Of course— he was trying to trip me up, make me look bad so I'd give up the retreat business and let him take it over."

In all my rumblings about the sudden no-sheep-shearing policy, I'd forgotten about all the other news. I mentioned that Cora Delacorte had brought in her fiancé. When I described Burton Fiore, Lucinda knew who he was right away.

"That explains it," Lucinda said before describing the scene when he and Cora had eaten at the Blue Door a few nights earlier. "I thought he'd dropped something when I saw him on his knees," she said. "And then when Cora shrieked and grabbed her chest, I was afraid she was having some kind of attack."

"Who is he?"

"Tag probably knows more of the details about who he is than I do." She waved her husband to the table.

Tag didn't like being pulled away from his restaurant duty and probably didn't like that Lucinda was sitting with me even though the place was still mostly empty.

Tag's answer came out in a burst as he cruised by the table without stopping. "Lives in Monterey and works in real estate and has a daughter."

"I wonder how they met," I said. By then Tag was back in the main room.

"I can answer that. It's really all your fault," my friend teased. "They met right here a couple of months ago. They were at separate tables. He was dining alone, and she was with Madeleine. Burton ordered a piece of your banana cream pie. Then Cora ordered a piece, but Burton had gotten the last slice. He played the gallant gentleman and offered her his, but she refused and the next thing I knew he'd moved over to her table and they were sharing it. I don't know what happened to Madeleine. I guess she must have felt like a third wheel and left."

I mentioned seeing the sisters and how formally dressed they were in their Chanel-like suits.

"Chanel-like?" Lucinda said with a twinkle in her eyes. "How about those suits are the real thing. I agree it's a bit overdressed for a trip to Vista Del Mar, but I think it's their everyday wear."

Lucinda knew about anything with a designer label. Everything she owned had one. But she knew how to dress so that she looked good but not overdone. She'd recently cut her hair and was wearing it short now, which only showed off her dangle earrings and great makeup job. She had on a sunny yellow shift-style dress with a white shrug. The daisy pin was the perfect accessory. It was like she'd brought some sunshine inside.

The banana cream pie story was swirling in my brain. I didn't have a good feeling about Cora's fiancé and wished it had been tomato soup that had brought them together instead of something I'd baked. I hated to think I'd played any part in their matchup.

I left the Blue Door with no solution to the no-show sheep, but amidst kudos for my baking. A woman by the door was eating a piece of the apple pie I'd baked the night before and her companion was having the from-scratch vanilla pudding with the chocolate walnut shortbread cookies I'd made as well. When Tag mentioned I'd made all of it, they showered me with compliments. Hmm . . . and that was all without any certificate from a fancy French cooking school.

As I came down the short flight of stairs onto the street, the noonday sun bathed me with warmth. There was still a sharp edge of damp and cool to the air, but having the sun out changed everything. The tall trees that grew down the center strip between the lanes of traffic on Grand Street now cast shadows. The strong light brightened up the whole street and even the yellow Victorian house across the street that had been turned into a bed-and-breakfast seemed a brighter shade.

Downtown Cadbury was a mixture of styles. Many of the storefronts were built in a Victorian style with bright-colored paint, bay windows and things like fish-scale patterns on the sides of the buildings. Others, like the post office, had a Spanish look, with white stucco walls and a red tiled roof. The unifying factor was that the buildings were all old. Some of them had plaques showing they were built in the late 1800s and gave their history.

As I looked up and down the street at the cars parked on an angle, I noticed a Cadbury PD blue-and-white was one of them. Even from this angle I recognized my neighbor Dane Mangano as the officer standing at the front of the cruiser talking to a sullen-looking teen. The kid was all bad posture and an I-don't-care attitude.

Cadbury wasn't exactly a crime capital and I knew Dane spent a lot of his time being proactive to keep things from happening. It was a small town with a bunch of bored kids, which was a recipe for trouble.

I could tell by the upward movement of Dane's chin he was giving the kid some kind of pep talk. He pulled out a card and wrote something on the back before handing it to the boy. The teen looked at it for a moment before shoving it into his pocket. He kept looking away and it was obvious he wanted to leave. Dane touched him on the shoulder in a supportive move and must have told the kid he could go, because the teen suddenly pulled away.

Dane looked up as I headed down the street. His eyes lit with recognition and his angular face softened into a smile. All the jogging and martial arts he did served him well, and the midnight blue uniform fit him like a glove. In other words, he was definitely hot. "Are you a social worker or a cop?" I said, gesturing toward the receding figure of the teen. I knew that he had turned his garage into a workout studio and gave karate lessons to the local kids and let them hang out there.

"You caught me," he said. His eyes held my gaze a little too long and his smile turned into a teasing grin. "I'm always looking for a new recruit. I'd rather get them when there aren't any handcuffs involved."

Dane had told me that he'd been a bad-boy teenager and gotten into plenty of trouble. He was trying to save the youth of Cadbury from going down the same road. Not only did he give them a place to hang out where they could use up all their excess energy in a positive way, he fed them as well. I should be grateful that he cooked for them, because he always left a dish of whatever pasta he'd made at my door. Just thinking of his spaghetti sauce with the tomato-garlicky taste made my mouth water.

We made a little small talk, which was really mostly him flirting. There was no denying I was attracted to him. It wasn't just his looks, either. Despite all the teasing, he had character. He took the whole concept of protecting and serving seriously.

"You know," he said, resting his hands on the assortment of tools on his belt, "we could try delivering our care packages in person. Even eat them together. My main course and your dessert." He stepped a little closer and had entered my bubble of space. His eyes moved over my face. "I promise to show you a good time."

I felt a little breathless and took a step back. I think he was completely aware of the effect he had on me and it amused him, along with my usual answer.

"Maybe someday," I said, with an over-the-top bat of my

eyelashes. Flirting wasn't my strong suit, so I tried to make it look like a joke, figuring it would come out that way anyway.

"Promises, promises," he said with a laugh. Just then his radio squawked something about a problem at the aquarium and he said he was responding. "Duty calls," he said. "Somebody jumped in the tank with the sea otters."

He rushed to his car, flipped on his lights and siren, and backed out in one move before doing a U-turn and roaring away.

The cars on the street responded to the flashing lights and siren, and froze. When the blue-and-white was out of sight, traffic resumed.

I suppose I could have told Dane about my problem with the sheep shearing, but it seemed out of his realm of problem solving, so I'd kept it to myself. I continued down to the corner and turned on a side street that sloped down toward the water. Cadbury Yarn was located in a former house halfway down the block. It was really more of a bungalow, with a nice front porch complete with a wicker rocker and a rainbow wind sock.

Inside a number of customers were milling around the main room, which had a wall of cubbies filled with yarn organized by color. There were displays of tools and books for all different kinds of yarn craft as well. I looked toward a room behind, which must have been a dining room when it was a house. A number of women were gathered around the long oval table working on their projects.

The deal was if someone bought yarn there, they were welcome to hang out and work on their projects. And Gwen Selwyn or Crystal Smith, the mother-daughter owners, would help them if they had a problem. I knew all about it because they had nursed me through several projects.

I was glad to see the place was busy, as I knew it was a

struggle to make enough to keep them all going. Gwen was old-school Cadbury. She had short brown hair with streaks of gray she did nothing to hide. Her clothes were comfortable. Mostly she wore loose-fitting slacks in neutral colors paired with a cotton shirt. Since it was always chilly, she wore something on top that she'd made, like the chunky toast brown sweater she had on today.

Crystal went the opposite way. Maybe her fashion sense came from being the former wife of a rock god. She wore skinny jeans with interesting tops, her earrings never matched and she wore heavy makeup that somehow never looked overdone. Her hair was black and so curly, the ringlets looked like tiny Slinkys.

Crystal was free so I told her I was there to pick up the drop spindles and patterns for my retreaters. After a moment her mother joined us and I mentioned the yarn and related items for the gift shop.

"Thanks for the reminder, but believe me we'll remember to bring it over. And we'll check it a day or so later and add as needed. These events are a real boost to our sales," Gwen said as her daughter went into the back and brought out a shopping bag with the spindles.

I told them the news about Kevin St. John's ixnaying the sheep shearing. "What am I going to do? That's the beginning of the whole event."

"You could just make spinning the yarn the main event. Just change the name to Spinning to Shawl," Gwen suggested. "There's still time, we could get in roving." She went to a basket and took out a slender plastic bag filled with natural-colored fibers. When she removed the fiber, it came out as one long piece. She explained it was wool that had been washed, combed and carded.

"But that takes all the fun out of it," Crystal said. She

suggested taking the group to the farm to watch the shearing and get the fleeces, but then realized I'd need to rent a bus and that it would cut way into my profit, which wasn't that big to begin with.

I began to second-guess my decision to put on such an ambitious retreat. "I should have stuck to something safe and easy."

One of the women had gotten up from the table and joined us. "I don't know why you didn't contact me if you needed someone to teach spinning," the woman said. Gwen stepped in and introduced her as Wanda Krug. The woman added "spinning specialist" to her name.

"It was a mistake to hire that Nicole Welton," the short stout woman began in a matter-of-fact voice tinged with annoyance. "She might have some fancy degree in textiles, but let me tell you, when it comes to spinning, I can spin her into a corner—any day."

I was taken aback by Wanda's attack. As if to punctuate her comments, Wanda pulled a drop spindle out of her floral-print tote bag and grabbed the length of roving on the counter. She moved so fast, I couldn't see what she was doing, but after a moment she began to hit the cylinder part of the spindle against her leg and held the long strand of wool as it twisted upward. She wasn't silent as she did it, either. She almost did a little dance and kept yelling "Woo-ha!" every time she gave the spindle a whirl.

I was amazed at how fast she turned the long piece of roving into a length of yarn. At the end she seemed to come back to reality and realized what she'd done. She paid for the roving and then left in a huff.

After she'd gone, Gwen told me Wanda really was an expert spinner and her confidence was earned even if she was a little hard to take. The older store owner went back to the table to help a woman who was holding up a piece of pearl gray knitting with a big hole in the middle, hysterical because she didn't know what she'd done wrong.

I hung around the counter with Crystal for a while and she assured me that Nicole Welton would be able to handle the spinning just fine and I said I'd let her know if I decided to skip right to spinning. "No matter where you start, the group is going to end up knitting," she said, handing me an envelope with copies of the pattern for the shawlette.

Of course the bag with the spindles and the patterns wasn't the only package I left with. Even though my aunt had left me a closetful of different kinds of yarn, I couldn't seem to get out of Cadbury Yarn without buying something. I'd become particularly fond of making washcloths. They were small and required only a few skills—like the knit stitch, yarn overs, increasing and decreasing—and I was left with something useful. I picked up a skein of pink organic cotton, thinking I'd make one and send it to my mother to show off my skills.

Who was I kidding? I could hear her saying, "So now you're a towel maker?"

5

THE SUN WAS STILL SHINING AS I WENT BACK TO
the main street. There were an assortment of Cadburians and
tourists out enjoying the bright afternoon. I looked down
toward the aquarium and wondered if Dane had had to dive
into the otter pool to retrieve the overzealous visitor.

Nicole Welton's shop was just down the street. Instead of
calling her, it seemed better to go there in person and bring
up the no-sheep situation. Maybe, after Wanda's disparaging
remarks, I wanted some reassurance that Nicole really could
handle the retreat. And a visit to Nicole's was always a feast
for the eyes.

I dropped my packages in my car and walked up the street
to the old Cadbury by the Sea Bank. It was an imposing
structure situated on the corner, with two white columns
flanking the door.

One of the arched windows still had CADBURY BY THE SEA
NATIONAL BANK painted in gold across it, though time had

smoothed away bits of the letters. My understanding was that the building had stayed empty and abandoned since the Cadbury Bank had closed years ago.

A machine-embroidered banner with ANTIQUES emblazoned on it hung over another of the arched windows and made it clear it wasn't a bank anymore.

Bells attached to a leather strap went into a ringing frenzy as I opened the front door and walked in. It took my eyes a moment to adjust to the lower light inside, though with large arched windows on two of the walls, it was still quite bright. The temperature dropped, too. The high ceiling and abundance of marble kept the place cool. The bells served their purpose and Nicole looked up from the back of the open space and waved.

I thought it was clever how she'd turned the bank into an antiques store and textile studio. The old tellers' cages were hung with samples of old and new textiles, and they were a feast of color and texture. There were quilts, afghans and knitted blankets, along with some of Nicole's hand-woven creations. An antique dressmaker's dummy seemed to be standing guard, swathed in a light green shawl that sparkled with tiny crystal beads.

"I can't believe what you've done to this place," I said, looking at the open area opposite the old tellers' cages. Beautifully refinished antique furniture had been arranged into settings complete with plants and more quilts and blankets to add color. I admired a deep blue lap blanket that hung on the arm of an oak rocker. I couldn't help but touch the intricate design of the thread doily sitting on a wooden washstand. I thought the clear vase holding a bunch of crocheted red roses was the perfect touch for the round mahogany table.

The store seemed to have everything . . . except customers. It was really out of place in Cadbury, too arty and

sophisticated, and instead belonged in San Francisco, Santa
Fe or even down the road in Carmel. It hadn't helped matters
when Nicole had decided to call it The Bank. Just like my
muffin names, Cadburians liked things to be called just what
they were.

Nicole was working at one of the looms and took a moment
before she left her work and gestured for me to join her. She was
dressed casually in soft-with-age jeans and a long white shirt
with a darker T-shirt underneath. She had a beautiful aqua woven
scarf arranged around her neck, held in place with a silver pin.
There was a nonchalance to her whole outfit, as though she'd
merely added one piece after the other without much thought
instead of agonizing in front of a mirror trying to figure out if
something looked good, like some of us—well, I—did.

"You should have seen the place when we got it," she said
as I passed a U-shaped island of glass cases in the center of
the large space. "There was dust a mile high and boxes of old
papers from the bank. They must have just shut the doors and
not looked back. The only good thing is they left me lots of
papers to use as kindling in the fireplace." I noticed a stack
of blue ledgers next to the stone fireplace on the side wall.
"The only thing they seemed to have taken were all the desks.
Too bad, they would probably be a hot item now."

I noticed a pile of old pieces next to a stack of books. I
glanced at the titles and noted they were all about textiles and
fibers. Nicole saw me looking at them. She picked up a dingy-
looking woven rug. "Most of the woven and knitted pieces I
get don't come with labels, so I have to figure out what they're
made of and when. It's amazing what you can find out."

Nicole had made the back area into her studio. Beyond,
there was a half partition left from when it was a bank and a
couple of cubicles that had been used for privacy when checking safety-deposit boxes. It was odd to see the thick metal

door of the open vault showing over the top of the divider, with the selection of spinning wheels in front of it. She had both antique and modern machines. She'd demonstrated how they worked, but looking at them now with all their wheels, hooks and pedals, I had no idea how to use them.

I didn't mention Wanda, but asked Nicole if she was ready for the retreat.

"You look tense," she said to me. "Don't worry, I can handle everything. I'll be there tomorrow morning to teach your pre-retreat people how to use a drop spindle. And I'll have Will bring these wheels over later in the week."

"I need your advice," I began, and then told her about the no-sheep-shearing situation. I didn't have to explain. She knew right away it was Kevin St. John's doing.

"Kevin St. John is so possessive of that place. I know all about it. Remember, my husband works for him. Though Will never has a problem with him because he just does everything Kevin's way."

I brought up the idea of bringing in roving and making the spinning the center of things, but she said there was no need to change anything. "Why don't you just go to the farm and pick up the fleeces? You won't have your razzle-dazzle beginning, but we can go from there."

I nodded in agreement, even though I didn't want to give up the razzle-dazzle beginning. She sensed my concern about the retreat. "Don't worry. The group will get caught up in picking through the fleeces and washing and carding them. Everybody is going to have a great time. The first time I started with fleece and ended up knitting with the yarn, well, there was something magic about it."

She was going to show me some handspun yarn she'd made, but the sleigh bell went into a frenzy as the front door opened.

A customer? I looked across the large space and saw a man in a familiar sports jacket. Burton Fiore? I checked beyond him, expecting to see Cora Delacorte, but he was alone. He seemed intent on his mission and didn't look around enough to see me, walking right to the U-shaped glass counter in the center of the place. As soon as Nicole saw him she stepped away and went behind the counter. He looked down through the glass at something and they spoke for a moment or two. Apparently what he saw hadn't pleased him because a moment later he walked to the door. Even from where I was standing, I could see that he'd left an envelope on the counter. I was going to call out to him, but when I looked again, the envelope was gone.

Nicole seemed a little disconcerted when she returned. "He was just looking for a gift for his fiancée. You do know that Cora Delacorte is engaged."

I explained I'd just heard the news that morning. Though Nicole was new to Cadbury, her husband had grown up in the area so she knew all the local stories. I was curious about what Burton Fiore had been considering and walked to the counter and looked inside. The glass cases had an assortment of mini-treasures. Things like silver chafing dishes and old silver dresser sets. But below the spot he'd been standing, there was a pink velvet backdrop with some pieces of jewelry on it. I'd never seen anything like them. The one thing the drop earrings, the watch chain and several brooches had in common was they were all brown. The piece that really caught my eye was a wreath shape decorated with tiny brown flowers.

"What are these?" I said, looking again at the drab pieces.

"Interesting color, huh?" she said, coming to stand next to me. She slid open the back of the case and took out the pink velvet backdrop the pieces were sitting on. "They're made out of hair."

"Hair?" I said with a combination of fascination and distaste. She smiled at my reaction.

"I guess I thought of it more from a student of fiber's point of view." She took out one of the dangle earrings for me to get a closer look and I saw that the design was created by intricate braiding.

"It's called mourning jewelry and became popular during Victorian times."

I wasn't sure if I understood what she was saying. "You mean it was made after someone died," I said, putting the earring down rather quickly. She nodded and explained it was worn as a memento, similar to keeping a lock of someone's hair. The whole hair-jewelry thing creeped me out, but the idea of it coming from a dead person's hair was even worse. I wasn't surprised that Burton Fiore had left empty-handed if this is what she'd showed him as a gift for his fiancée.

"These must be very expensive," I said, and she nodded, lifting one of the price tags. When I saw it was in the five-hundred-dollar range I commented that maybe she ought to keep the counter locked.

"I don't worry about it. Besides, locking things up is a red flag that they're worth stealing. I'm more of a hide-things-in-plain-sight sort of person," she said, putting everything away and sliding the back of the counter shut. "Anything really important I keep where no one would expect to find it."

She walked me to the door and repeated the time she was coming to the retreat the next day. She had worked it out so she could be back at the shop to open at noon.

"I'll come by a half an hour early, so we can set up things in the meeting room. I have the roving all set to go," she said.

"Roving?" I said.

"Your people need something to spin with," she prodded with a smile.

"Of course, you're right. I didn't even think about that. I'm certainly glad I hired you."

By the time I got home, I barely had time to put the drop spindles and patterns in the three red tote bags with *Yarn2Go, Fun with Fiber* emblazoned on the front, and go across the street. The white van was pulling up to the Lodge just as I got there.

"Casey," an excited voice said. I recognized the short frizz of Bree's blond hair as she got out of the Vista Del Mar van. She still looked the part of the harried young mom in unglamorous jeans and a gray hooded sweatshirt.

"It's good to be here again." Olivia Golden lowered her head as she stepped out after Bree. Olivia's reddish hair had grown since I'd seen her last and now went below her ears instead of hugging her almond-shaped face. She looked around and took an appreciative breath of the cool damp air. She seemed glad to be here and looked very stylish in her dark slacks and rust-colored cowl-necked sweater.

"No secret what I have in here this time," Scott Lipton said, swinging his soft-sided briefcase as he got out last. *Bounded out* was more accurate. To prove his point, he unzipped the top and displayed his knitting. He seemed a lot less tense than he'd been at the last retreat and had loosened up from the button-down business attire he'd arrived in before.

The three swarmed me and we did a group hug before I escorted them inside the Lodge. I handed each of them a tote bag and helped them get checked in. Once they had their keys, the three of them looked at the surroundings and seemed surprised.

"Things have changed around here," Bree said, directing her attention to the seating area. She did a few minutes on how much she liked the new leather furniture and the rug underneath. She had a puzzled look as if she realized something was missing, but couldn't place what.

"It's the TV," I said. I left it at that, not sure how to break the news to her about Vista Del Mar going unplugged. She had spent the last retreat glued to her phone and tablet so she could stay in touch with her kids.

"A piano," Olivia said, walking over to it and hitting a few of the keys. "What a nice idea." I mentioned I'd heard there were going to be sing-alongs in the evening.

Scott had already set his briefcase on the long table and pulled out one of the chairs. "What a perfect spot for knitting." I know that I shouldn't have, but I still did a double take when he took out a ball of powder blue yarn and a pair of circular needles with something lacy hanging off. There was nothing wrong with a man knitting; it just wasn't the usual sight.

Still, when I saw the happy look on his face as he began working the needles, anything weird went away.

"I better tell them I arrived," Bree said. I knew the "them" referred to her young sons and her husband. She was better than last time, but I could see she was still nervous about being away from home. Before I could intervene, she had her cell phone out and her fingers were moving over the screen. She stared at the phone and started to move toward the window.

"It won't help," I said, putting my hand on her arm to stop her. I took a deep breath and explained the new policy of Vista Del Mar to the three of them. Bree's face crumbled. Olivia said it was no problem for her because there was nobody she wanted to talk to anyway. It took a moment to cut through Scott's bliss at knitting and then he seemed a little concerned.

"It's not that you can't make phone calls," I said, leading them around to the alcove where the three phone booths had been added. I unfolded the door to one and Bree looked in. I wondered if she'd ever even used a pay phone before.

Will walked across the large room with a hammer swinging from his tool belt. When he saw us hanging around the phone booths, he came over.

"So somebody is going to use them," he said in a good-natured voice. "I just finished installing them."

I introduced the caretaker to Bree, Olivia and Scott. "He keeps this place working."

He gave us a self-deprecating smile. "I love doing it. It's a pleasure to take care of something as historic as Vista Del Mar. I hope you appreciate how unique it is."

"Will's wife, Nicole, is supervising the fleece-to-fiber part of the retreat." I did a few minutes on her background and told them about her store-cum-studio downtown. Will seemed to be beaming with pride as he wished them a great retreat and went on his way.

"Nicole is giving you guys your own spinning class tomorrow morning," I said. I gave them the time of the class and said it was one of the few things planned for their pre-retreat. I mentioned there were also activities put on by Vista Del Mar. "I made sure you were staying in the same building and there's a cozy living room in it where you can get together and work on the projects you brought along."

"That sounds great," Bree said. "Remember how I was so stuck on only doing projects that were the same as everybody else's?" She pulled out something in different shades of red. As she unfolded it, she explained it was free-form knitting. "You just make it up as you go along, doing whatever stitches you want. It's going to be a scarf and probably kind of crazy looking." We all admired the interesting-looking piece as she said she was excited about working on it.

"Don't worry about us. If they run out of things to do, I

have something," Olivia said. "You all might remember I was a little upset about my husband getting remarried last time. I was doing a pretty good job of feeling sorry for myself. Then I realized the best way out of it was to stop thinking about me and think about other people." She had a very large canvas tote bag and pulled a knitted square out of it. "I started making squares to sew together. Then I give the blankets to people in need. I made up some directions." She looked at the other two. "Maybe you'd like to make some." Olivia also had a couple of works in progress with her.

"I can make squares or work on what I brought with me," Scott said. "All I want to do is knit." He said it was much better now that he'd come out and admitted to his wife and family that he was a knitter, but he realized he didn't need to tell everybody. There was no reason his boss or other people who wouldn't understand had to know he was a yarn lover. "But here, there is complete freedom to give myself over to it."

I was relieved with their attitudes. I showed them the Cora and Madeleine Delacorte Café and then walked them to the Sea and Sand building, where they were all staying.

"See you in the morning," I said as I turned to go. I didn't add what I was thinking. *This time no one is going to die.*

6

TUESDAY MORNING I AWOKE TO FIND JULIUS DRAPED across my chest, but at least there was no phone call this time. I didn't rush to get up and enjoyed the luxury of lying in bed for a few minutes more.

I'd finished off the evening doing my baking at the Blue Door. Even with the retreat, I had promised Tag Thornkill that I would keep to my regular schedule of baking. When I'd left the restaurant, a chocolate cake with buttercream frosting and a carrot cake with cream cheese frosting sat under glass domes looking delicious. I'd taken containers of The Blues muffins with me and left them at the usual spots around town. My last stop had been the Cora and Madeleine Delacorte Café. It had been late and the Lodge was empty when I set down the package in front of the closed door.

Julius made it clear that my extra minutes of rest were up when he went from lying on my chest to standing on it. I rolled on my side to push off his poking paws. "You can't be that hungry," I said, putting on my slippers. "I left you that cat food that smells like prime rib." Julius was already walking across the room, stopping in the doorway to see if I was following.

When I got to the kitchen I saw the kitty prime rib appeared untouched.

"You don't know what you're missing. This is high-quality stuff," I said, pushing the bowl toward him. He seemed to consider it for a moment then walked toward the refrigerator, looking up at me with a meow to be sure I understood what he wanted. I extracted the multi-wrapped stink fish and then held my nose as I pushed back the layers of plastic.

Julius rubbed against my leg as I went to his bowl and mixed a little stink fish with the other cat food to flavor it. Well, really to fool him. As soon as I stepped away, he was on that bowl like butter on popcorn.

I sat down with my instant coffee and instant oatmeal and thought I should have got going earlier and had my breakfast with the early birds. The dining hall excelled at breakfast. Visions of hotcakes with melted butter, scrambled eggs and crispy hash browns danced through my mind. My mouth was starting to water and I regretted not having at least brought home one of the muffins. I'd been so busy baking for everybody else, I forgot about me.

I drained my cup and finished the oatmeal. It was time to face the day. I had to laugh when I passed Julius's bowl. He had managed to eat all the stink fish and leave all the kitty prime rib behind. His meal must have tired him out, because I found him napping on my pillow as I went to get dressed.

An hour later I was on my way across the street to meet up with Nicole. I'd just gotten to the stone pillars at the entrance of Vista Del Mar when I realized I'd forgotten something. I was so focused on the early bird group and their tote bags, I'd completely forgotten I was getting a lesson, too.

Other than the three I'd made up for Bree, Olivia and Scott, the tote bags weren't finished. The bags and stuff to go in them were in the converted garage. I'd decided to keep them away from Julius after I'd found out the hard way that anything he could climb or jump in, he would. I could only imagine what he would have done with all those tote bags. Somebody might have gotten a surprise cat in with their drop spindle.

I stopped off in my former residence, grabbed one of the bags, put one of the drop spindles in it and retraced my steps. No surprise the sky was white. Though this morning it was a very thin white that was turning apricot as the sun melted the layer of clouds.

Once I was on the grounds, I passed a group of people carrying yoga mats and heading toward an open area. One of them turned and gave me a head bow and said "Namaste."

"Namaste back to you," I said, hoping it meant something nice.

I was a few minutes late and hoped that Nicole was already in the meeting room, setting things up for the spinning lesson. She had such limited time for the lesson, I wanted to make sure my people got the whole hour. The meeting room was really a small building set amidst the larger ones that had the guest rooms. It had been built more recently, but done in the same style of dark wood shingles so that it blended in.

A walkway led through an open area of dry grass. The door was unlocked, but when I checked inside the room, no one was sitting at the long table set up in the middle. I pulled out one of the chairs and sat down, expecting that any second Nicole would walk in with some kind of explanation.

After a few minutes, I took out my smartphone to call her, but remembered that there was no signal. Could there have been a misunderstanding about where we were supposed to meet? I walked out to the other meeting room I was going to use for the retreat and saw it was presently filled with the red-shirted group. I continued on, thinking I could use the phone in the Lodge. I was about to climb the stairs when I saw Bree running down the boardwalk. She reached the end and charged across the grassy area toward me.

"Call 911," Bree called breathlessly. She was holding her phone trying to explain she couldn't call. We rushed inside the social hall together and I explained to the woman behind the registration desk that there was an emergency.

It was a small town on a weekday, when there wasn't a lot of tourist traffic, so the Cadbury Fire rescue ambulance arrived in a few minutes. They cut the siren on the red vehicle as soon as they entered the hotel and conference center grounds, but they still managed to be an attention-getter as they stopped on the roadway next to the Lodge. It helped that the morning workshops had all ended and everyone was hanging around getting ready for lunch. As the two men in dark blue uniforms got out and grabbed their equipment, the bare-foot yoga group gathered around and a bunch of people in red polo shirts came out of the Lodge and stopped on the wooden deck to watch.

Bree was frantic, urging them to hurry as she ran toward the boardwalk to lead the way. The pair of paramedics rushed after her. I was a step behind. When I looked back I saw a whole crowd of people trailing along. I was sure Kevin St. John was somewhere in the pack.

Bree was running now, waving for the paramedics to hurry. Instead of going straight toward Sunset Avenue and the beach, she took a turnoff to the section of the boardwalk that twisted through the whole length of the dunes. The path went up a steep hill and then descended into a valley. Ahead, tall bushes obscured the view and it was only when we got close enough that I saw the bench next to the walkway. There was a woman sprawled on the ground. When I saw the aqua scarf artfully draped around her neck, I suddenly knew why Nicole Welton had never shown up.

7

"I'D GONE WALKING TO SEE IF I COULD GET A signal," Bree said, holding up her cell phone. "Then I saw the woman on the ground. At first, I thought she'd fallen." Bree still looked pale as we stood off to the side while the paramedics took over. "But when I asked if she was all right, she didn't answer." Bree's face crumbled. "It was horrible. She looked like she'd been sick all over herself." I could see that Bree was operating on nerves now and the words kept tumbling out. "I checked her pulse." Bree explained that she'd learned CPR recently at her kids' school. "I wanted to do something to help her, but you can't do CPR on someone who's breathing, can you?"

I let Bree continue to spew while my gaze went to the action on the ground, even though I was still feeling the adrenaline rush I'd gotten from hurrying to keep up with Bree, having no idea who or what we were going to find.

I knew I had only a few moments to get a look at the scene

before Kevin St. John threaded through the crowd, trying to take charge.

I'd learned from Dr. Sammy that people's area of focus is really very small. The whole reason Sammy's magic tricks worked was because of that fact. It was also why people missed all kinds of details outside their center of attention. I recognized that my eyes had locked on the two men in dark blue uniforms hovering over Nicole and I was missing everything beyond that. I forced myself to expand my focus and take in the bigger picture, making note of the details. I saw a smartphone sitting on the bench. Farther down almost to the other end I noticed a circle mark on the wood seat. I pushed my gaze to look at the ground, where a white-lidded red paper cup lay on its side. I noticed a small square-shaped glass bottle nearby. There was something else in the sand, but before I could step closer to see what it was, Kevin St. John stepped in front of me and blocked my view.

"Ms. Feldstein, I know what you're doing. There is no need for your amateur detective skills here. Now if you would gather your retreater and move along with everyone else and clear the area."

There was no choice but to follow his orders. I put my arm around Bree and joined the line of people heading back to the grounds.

Bree and I had barely settled on the soft leather sofa in the Lodge when I heard the engine of the ambulance start up and the flashing red light reflect in the building. A moment later the siren went on as it left the grounds. Bree reacted to the sound, but I gave her a reassuring pat. "It's a good sign that they're in a hurry to get her to the hospital," I said.

I hadn't broken the news to Bree about who Nicole was. I was barely facing it myself, convinced that she would recover quickly and be well enough to handle the weekend retreat.

But this was no time to think about my problems. I felt for Bree. She had come so far on the last retreat, learning to be away from her family and to be on her own for a little while. And this retreat hadn't even really started and already she'd been in the middle of an emergency.

I tried reassuring her that she'd really risen to the occasion. First trying to help Nicole and then getting help for her. My comments cheered her a little, but she still looked done in. "Can I get you something to drink?" I said, wanting to do something.

"A soda would be nice," Bree said, brightening. "I feel a little weak in the knees. Maybe one with real sugar."

I met up with Jane on my way into the café as she carried in a brown cardboard box and set it down next to the rack of chips. "I saw the ambulance drive in and everyone heading into the dunes. Did someone get hurt?"

When she heard it was Nicole, she sucked in her breath and stopped what she was doing. "Is she going to be okay?"

"I don't know what happened, but I'm sure they're doing everything they can for her," I said.

"Does Will know?" she said, sounding frantic. "Someone should get in touch with him." The words were barely out of her mouth when I saw him dash by and head for his blue pickup truck. It roared to life and pulled away.

"It looks like someone did," I said. Poor Jane seemed so upset, but then I'd heard that she'd gone through a lot taking care of her disabled mother and all this had probably hit a nerve. I took an extra minute to reassure her before I left with a chilled bottle of ginger ale made with real ginger.

When I came back, Olivia and Scott had joined Bree. They both seemed confused.

"I thought we were supposed to have a spinning lesson?" Olivia said. Scott and I went to the meeting room, but when nobody showed up, we finally went to the dining hall and had lunch."

"We heard sirens. Did something happen?" Scott asked. The two of them sat down and took out their knitting and began to work their needles while I tried to think of what to say.

Bree rushed ahead and told them about finding Nicole. Then I told them all who she was.

Bree got upset for me, but I urged her to take out her knitting, knowing it would help calm her. Frankly, I wished I had some yarn as well. I looked toward the gift shop and wondered if Gwen and Crystal had made their delivery. Telling the group I'd be right back, I went to the shop to find out.

Someone from the yarn shop had clearly been there because the gondola was full of yarn and supplies. It seemed foolish with all the yarn I had across the street, but I didn't want to leave my people just now, and besides, you can never have enough yarn. I picked out a skein of kelly green cotton yarn and a set of circular needles. I'd made so many wash-cloths and bandannas, I had memorized the pattern.

I rejoined the group and we all began to knit. Silently at first, but then the conversation started. Scott was thinking of joining a group of knitters back home. He was worried about being accepted since the group was all women. Olivia admitted to moments of intense anger toward her newly married ex, though they were fewer and farther between. Bree had been told she was a helicopter parent, which meant she hovered too much.

"But look, I'm here. If I was hovering so much I'd never leave, would I?"

After reassuring Bree she was right, they all looked at me. "My life is running perfectly," I joked. Then, being honest, I said that Cadbury had begun to feel like home to me and that I liked what I was doing and left it at that.

The ginger in the soda had a tonic effect and the color

returned to Bree's face. I think the knitting played a part, too. I sat with them for a while longer.

I was so busy thinking about taking care of the three of them, I barely considered there was probably going to be a problem with the retreat program. *Probably* was an understatement, but it was all I could handle at the moment. My aunt Joan would have been proud of how well I was taking care of the others. It was a skill I was learning from these retreats. Before, my whole MO had been that I was barely able to take care of myself. The thing I'd done best was drop things and move on.

When I saw Kevin St. John come from the office area behind the registration counter, I excused myself and went up to him. "Have you heard anything about Nicole Welton?" I asked.

His usually placid face appeared disturbed. "The news isn't good. She died shortly after she got to the hospital." I bombarded him with questions about how and why, but he said he had no details. "It's troubling that her death is going to be connected to Vista Del Mar. Any idea of why she was on the grounds?"

I was going to say there could have been many reasons, including meeting her husband, who was the caretaker, but I just came clean and said she was there to meet me. "She was going to run a program for my retreat. We were going to go over some things."

He shook his head with mock concern. "First the problem with the sheep shearing and now this. Some people might take all these obstacles as a sign that this yarn retreat business wasn't for them."

I waited, expecting him to offer to take the business over as he'd done before, but all he said was that he hoped I had some kind of backup plan. I think I understood. He was just going to let me fall on my face and then when I'd given up, he'd pick up the pieces.

"I'll manage just fine," I said defiantly. I sounded so sure of myself, I almost believed it. He tilted his head with a doubtful smile before he wished me a good afternoon.

I didn't relay the bad news to my people, but just told them I had something to do and would be back to have dinner with them.

As soon as I was out of their view, all my confidence evaporated. What was I going to do? I didn't even go into my house. I just hopped in my yellow Mini Cooper and drove into downtown Cadbury and parked in front of the Blue Door restaurant.

It was getting close to the time they opened for dinner. As I passed through the first dining room, I saw that Tag was in the kitchen and caught a snippet of his conversation with the chef about the proper placement of garnish on a plate. All the tables were covered in snowy white cloths and place settings, waiting for the dinner crowd.

In the second dining room I found Lucinda seated at one of the tables, inserting the dinner specials into the menus.

I bumped into a chair as I passed and the sound made her look up. Her first reaction was a happy-to-see-me smile, then she saw the trouble on my face.

"Come and sit," she said, patting the empty space on the floral cushion that covered the wooden bench. "Did something happen?"

"Did something happen?" I repeated with an intonation that made it obvious that something big had happened. I told her about Nicole.

"She's dead. I can't believe it. Was it natural causes or foul play?"

All I could do was shrug for an answer. "I heard the news from Kevin St. John," I said, and Lucinda nodded with understanding.

"Even if he knew, he probably wouldn't tell you. I suppose he's just concerned it happened on the grounds," Lucinda remarked.

"Exactly," I said. I told her how he was almost gloating over my problems with the retreat.

Tag heard voices and came into the room. Despite his fifty-something years, his hair was almost all brown and very full. If I hadn't known him better, I would have thought he was wearing a wig. But a wig or anything artificial wasn't Tag's style. Nor were any sort of blue jeans or shorts. The restaurant was casual, but he still always wore a blue blazer over gray slacks.

"Casey just told me that Nicole had some kind of seizure on the boardwalk at Vista Del Mar, and she died." The words were matter-of-fact, but Lucinda sounded like she could barely believe what she was saying.

Tag took the news with a hard swallow. He knew Nicole because The Bank was just a block away. Actually, Tag knew all the shopkeepers and coffee servers in the area. He took an exercise walk every morning at the same time and kept track of the goings-on of the street.

For a moment we talked back and forth about how horrible her death was and then Lucinda brought up the retreat.

"Not being able to get the sheep sheared at Vista Del Mar doesn't seem like much of a problem anymore," I said. "I should never have depended on Nicole so completely. I should have had her show me the process. At the very least, I should have made sure I knew how to spin yarn."

Tag listened and the idea that I had twenty people coming in two days expecting to learn how to make yarn and no one to direct it, made him crazy. "You'll have to refund their money," he said, shaking his head as he considered all the fallout. He was getting agitated and taking it all too personally. I knew I had to do something or he would end up driving Lucinda nuts with his worry.

"I'm sure I'll work it out," I said. "I think I know what to do about the sheep shearing. It won't have the same razzle-dazzle as having the sheep sheared in front of the bigger group. But I can just go to the ranch and pick up the wool."

Tag started to react again, thinking of all the wool I'd have and not know what to do with it. He had a hard—no, impossible—time being spontaneous. This time Lucinda stepped in and told him I had so much experience doing so many different things, I'd be able to pull off the retreat. She sounded so convincing, I started to believe it.

I took out my cell, glad to have a signal, and called the rancher. My suggestion was fine with him and we agreed on a time for the next day.

"Instead of the sheep coming to us, we're going to them. I'll take the early birds with me," I said to the couple.

"I'm coming, too," Lucinda said. The restaurant is closed on Wednesday, so any time is fine.

Tag straightened a knife on the table next to him. "Exactly how many of these so-called early birds are there?" he asked.

"There's Olivia, Bree, Scott, Lucinda and me," I said.

"You can't get five people in that little car of yours, and where would you put the fleeces?"

Before I could say anything, he continued. "We'll take the restaurant van. I can put the seats back in."

"You're coming?" I said, surprised.

"Yes, give me the location and I'll chart the course tonight."

I had never gone anywhere with Tag and wondered if I was making a mistake. But under the circumstances any and all help was appreciated, so I accepted and they said they would pick us up in the morning.

8

THE REALITY OF THE SITUATION BEGAN TO SINK IN as I sat in my kitchen. What was I going to do? In a couple of days, twenty people were going to arrive here expecting an organized retreat.

When I'd looked through my aunt's notes for the Sheep to Shawl weekend, it sounded like such a good idea, particularly since I'd met Nicole and she had been so enthused about it. But all that had changed.

Julius was sitting on the chair next to me, giving me a dirty look. I'd tried feeding him the leftover chicken breast Lucinda had given me before I left the restaurant, but he walked away with a plaintive meow.

Maybe my mother was right. Maybe I had made a mistake and taken on more than I could handle. I shook my head, trying to get rid of that thought. Had I just said, even to myself, that my mother might be right? No way. But still I had that feeling of wanting to take off.

But I couldn't cancel the retreat; it was in two days.

"When you get hungry enough you'll eat it," I said to Julius as I headed to the door. The early birds were expecting me to join them for dinner. The cat stared at me for a moment, flicked his tail and walked toward the bedroom.

How could Nicole have died? She was only twenty-seven.

The grounds of Vista Del Mar were quiet as I passed through on the way to the Sea Foam dining hall. The dinner bell had rung and almost everyone was already inside. I caught a whiff of the scent of hot food as I neared the building. Somehow in the mix of the day I'd forgotten about eating and my hunger had just shown up with a vengeance.

I recognized the frizz of Bree's blond curls as soon as I walked inside. She, Olivia and Scott were sitting at a table near the massive stone fireplace. Scott certainly wasn't hiding that he knit anymore. Something partially done in a masculine shade of brown was on the table next to his place setting and I saw he had the needles in his hands and was working them as he talked to his tablemates.

They all looked up as I pulled out a chair next to Olivia. I was glad to see that the color had returned to Bree's face and she seemed back to normal, but then she didn't know about Nicole's death yet.

"What's for dinner?" I said, glancing at their plates. Olivia pushed her plate closer to me.

"Mushroom stroganoff," she said. She showed me a card sitting on the table explaining that Vista Del Mar had adopted the plan of going meatless on Tuesdays. "It's quite the green thing to do now," she said. It must have been another of Kevin St. John's changes. I suppose he'd mentioned it before I'd joined them the other day.

Whatever it was made of, it smelled delicious and I went to get a plate. The plan was I'd eat and then break the news about Nicole. The only one whose reaction concerned me was Bree's. I was afraid she'd feel it was her fault. I didn't know the cause of death, but I doubted that Bree could have done anything to save her.

I'd barely set my plate down and tasted a forkful of rich sauce over buttered noodles when I saw Lieutenant Borgnine and Kevin St. John come into the dining hall. Lieutenant Borgnine was built like a bulldog and either had a whole wardrobe of grayish rumpled-looking sports jackets or always wore the same one. His hair was mostly a dark gray and cut short to lessen the contrast with his bald spot. Kevin St. John had a somber expression that matched the look of his dark suit, white shirt and tie. The two men passed through the roomful of animated people in casual wear like a pair of dark clouds.

I knew they were headed our way and reevaluated my plan. I dropped my fork and looked across the table to Bree.

"I'm sorry to have to tell you this, but Nicole, the woman you found, died." Bree didn't have time to react before the two men reached our table.

"I hope you are all enjoying your dinner," Kevin said, putting on a pleasant expression. He kept his tone light as he introduced Lieutenant Borgnine, apparently not realizing we'd all met before. The three early birds had been questioned by the lieutenant during the last retreat. And I had dealt with him a number of times. I heard Bree make a little gasp as Kevin St. John explained that she was the one who'd found Nicole. I was glad he didn't say "the deceased" or "the body." Referring to Nicole by name somehow didn't seem as bad.

"I'm going to need a statement from you," the lieutenant said to Bree. I'd never noticed what a growly tone his voice had. Her face went pale and she seemed befuddled.

"What's the cause of death?" I said, standing up. The

lieutenant glowered at me. He still hadn't come to terms with the fact that I'd bested him in a previous investigation.

"Here we go again," he said with an unhappy shake of his head. "I'm the one who asks the questions." Without taking a breath he turned to Bree and asked her to explain what had happened.

"Was she murdered? I didn't do it. I promise," the young mother said, seeming close to tears. Olivia put a hand on her shoulder to calm her.

"Bree, he just asked what you saw," the older woman said.

"Are you saying her death was suspicious?" I interrupted. Lieutenant Borgnine groaned at my question and paused as if considering his words. In the end, he ignored me, but explained a little more to Bree.

"Ms. Meyers, it's routine to get a statement under the circumstances," he said, but stopped there without any explanation of what the circumstances were.

Bree nervously repeated pretty much what she'd told me earlier. I interrupted and asked again about the cause of death. Lieutenant Borgnine rocked his head and looked skyward in a hopeless fashion.

"We're not ready to give out that information yet," he said tersely. He thanked Bree for her cooperation, which was a little dig at me, and gave her his card in case she thought of anything else. Just to be sure, he asked the other two what they knew about Nicole.

Scott shrugged it off and said the only thing he knew was that Nicole was supposed to have given them a spinning lesson. Olivia said pretty much the same thing.

Lieutenant Borgnine turned back to me. "And you, Ms. Feldstein. I understand that you hired her for your retreat. Did you see her this morning?"

"Why are you asking if I saw her? What kind of information

are you looking for?" I asked. It was an automatic response with me. When I'd worked for the detective agency, my boss had trained me never to give out information, only to get it. The policeman actually hit his forehead in frustration.

Then he pointed at himself. "I am the investigator here. Not you."

"I am just trying to be helpful," I said. "Do you want to know if she looked ill?"

It was clear I was trying his patience and he spoke brusquely. "Fine. Did she look ill when you saw her today?" He looked at me intently. "And don't you dare answer with a question."

"No problem," I said. "I didn't see her this morning."

Lieutenant Borgnine barely choked out a thank-you before he turned to go. I got a parting dirty look from Kevin St. John as he followed the cop toward the door.

Even with the cop and the manager gone, the mood stayed gloomy at the table. I didn't even feel like eating the mushroom stroganoff that had looked so luscious a few minutes ago. Bree seemed at a loss about what to do. She took out her cell phone and then put it away.

"This is like withdrawal," she said. "I wonder what she died of. Maybe she was choking. If only I'd known what was wrong." Bree's shoulders slumped and as I feared, she was beginning to worry she hadn't done enough.

"We don't know anything about her," Scott said and looked to me. "Casey, you're the only one here who knew her at all. Did she have some kind of condition?"

"It does seem strange that a woman so young would die of natural causes," Olivia said. I was trying to find a way to change the subject to something more cheerful and was happy to see Dr. Sammy come into the dining hall. The feeling seemed mutual because as soon as he saw me he bounded over to our table.

Sammy's natural expression was a smile that seemed to

come mostly from his eyes. I know that sounds weird, but that's the only way I can explain it.

"Hey, Case," he said, calling me by the nickname only he used. He glanced over at the people sitting around me and picked up on their glum mood. "What's up?"

I rose from the table and pulled him aside, dumping the whole story on him, including my problems with the retreat.

"Turning wool into yarn sounds like magic, but I'm afraid I'd be no help with that," he said. "But if you want to talk about your retreat person's death, I'm available any time, night or day," he added. The best thing about Sammy was I knew he meant that, but I had a more immediate problem.

"Can you do something to cheer them up?" I asked.

"Can I?" he said with a wink. "It works out perfect because I stopped by to check out the room. You know, get a feel for the space with people in it. Don't worry about it. I can take it from here."

He kept me next to him and addressed my early birds. "Allow me to introduce myself. I'm the Amazing Dr. Sammy and I'm going to be doing table magic here this weekend," he began. He looked down at his attire. "Oops, I didn't realize I was still wearing this." He whipped off the white coat with *Dr. Glickner* embroidered on it. "I'll be wearing a tuxedo," he said.

He put his hand on my back and pushed me forward. "And this is my lovely assistant, Casey." My group responded with smiles and I could feel their mood lifting already.

Sammy was tall and had an imposing build. People at other tables had begun to look toward our little group. He made a magnanimous wave and invited everyone to gather around.

When it seemed everyone who wanted to had joined us, Sammy reached into his pocket and pulled out a deck of cards.

Making eye contact with the crowd, Sammy began his patter. "You know there are people that think magicians are dorky," he said as if he were letting them in on a secret. "The kind of guys who never get the girl."

The crowd murmured in agreement. Maybe a little too much, and Sammy's smile dimmed for a moment before he continued. "Never underestimate the power of magic." He had me pick a random card from the deck. Once I saw that it was the six of hearts, he had me show it to the crowd. "My assistant will write her name on it," he said, handing me a pen. I'd never seen this trick and had no idea where it was going, so I did as he asked, including folding the card in quarters before he put it in my mouth.

He picked a card and showed the crowd that it was the king of spades before writing *the Amazing Dr. Sammy* on it. As he folded it up, he said now he was going to demonstrate the power of his magic. He put the card in his mouth and then before I knew what was coming, he kissed me. He had caught me completely off guard and while I was still reeling from surprise, he told me to take the card out of my mouth and unfold it.

"It's the king of spades—with your name on it," I said in amazement. He grinned as he took the card out of his mouth and showed off the six of hearts with my name on it.

Then he delivered the punch line. "It's all in the lips. A magical kiss. Pretty cool, huh? I tricked a girl into kissing me."

The trick had the desired effect and everyone laughed and rolled their eyes at the corny line. He even got a round of applause. He took a hammy bow and leaned into me. "Maybe we should practice that trick again."

Here was the problem with Sammy. There just wasn't any magic in his kiss on my end. He thought it was technique and that he could somehow learn how to fix it. I didn't share his opinion. Whether it was because he was too nice of a guy or my parents had endorsed him so strongly, there was something missing for me and I didn't think there was any way to change that.

"You told me that you never repeated a trick," I said with a laugh.

"I can always make an exception," he said with an overdone wiggle of his eyebrows. The mood of my little group had changed and the icing on the cake was when I told the early birds about our trip to the ranch the next morning.

As we parted company, Bree was telling Olivia and Scott they ought to meet in the lobby of Sea and Sand for their own knitting session.

"Thanks, Sammy," I said when they'd gone. "Your trick did the trick," I rolled my eyes at my too-clever comment. "Just a hint, though. You might not want to use that one over the weekend. Family crowd and all." Sammy nodded with understanding.

"I didn't do it in the bar in Seaside, either. Not the trick for a bunch of drunken sailors." Sammy laughed. "Actually, the only one I wanted to show it to was you."

What was I going to say? When someone wears their heart on their sleeve that way, you can't just walk away. I gave him a warm hug before I left.

Julius was waiting by the door. I checked his bowl and the chicken was still there. He did a few figure eights around my ankles and then went directly to the pantry, like I was supposed to follow him. He looked up at me with his yellow eyes and I swear his meow came out like "please." I was never good at tough love even when I was a substitute teacher. He did a happy cat dance when I took out a can of stink fish.

When he was happily eating, I was back to thinking about Nicole. It wasn't just because of my obvious problem. I wondered what had happened to her. Wouldn't the easy thing have been for Lieutenant Borgnine to explain they thought that she had died of heart failure or something? And why was he investigating unless he didn't think she'd died from natural causes? I was willing to bet there were some suspicious circumstances.

I looked at my watch and calculated the time difference in Chicago. It wasn't that late, I thought, as I punched in the number.

I didn't have to say who it was; Frank recognized my voice before I'd gotten all of "hello" out.

"Feldstein, it's been a while. What's up? You back in town or are you still in that town that sounds like a chocolate bar?" Frank had been my boss when I did the temp work at the detective agency in Chicago. It had been my favorite temp job and if I'd been offered a permanent position, I probably never would have ended up in Cadbury. But Frank's fortunes came and went with the clients who came and went, and he couldn't hire permanent help.

"I'm still in Cadbury," I said. "I just wanted to run something by you."

"Oh no, Feldstein. What happened this time?" Frank always sat in a recliner and kept trying to push its limit of recline, which made the chair protest. It was a loud-enough squeak to hear through the phone, but this time all I heard was silence.

"Where are you? I don't hear your chair." I heard Frank laugh.

"Good detective work, Feldstein. I'm not in the office. I'm doing a surveillance. Insurance case. A woman claimed she threw her back out picking up something at work. Her Facebook status said she was going for a dance lesson. I'm sitting outside the dance studio waiting to see if she's going to strut her stuff."

I apologized for bothering him while he was working, but he said it was pretty boring sitting in his car watching a bunch of people mangle the tango.

"You know how to tango?" I said, surprised. I always said Frank had more resemblance to the Pillsbury Doughboy than to James Bond.

"There's lots you don't know about me, Feldstein. Underneath my gruff exterior, I'm a romantic." He made some grumbly noises. "Forget I said that last part. You were going to tell me something."

"This woman I know died—" I said before Frank interrupted me.

"Not another death. Feldstein, it's a small town with a low crime rate. You come to town and people start dying. I hope they don't start connecting the dots."

"I didn't say she was murdered. I just said she died." I told him what I knew and then ran by how Lieutenant Borgnine was investigating. "Don't you think that makes it sound like there was something suspicious about her death?"

"Well, yeah," Frank said in slightly sarcastic tone. "Young women don't usually die sitting on a bench. What was she doing there anyway? Didn't you say she was supposed to be meeting you?" He didn't wait for me to answer, but went on. "Feldstein, I trust you know where to start."

"Yeah, flirt with the cop down the street," I said with a sigh. Frank had suggested that when I got involved with my first murder and was looking for information. Frank laughed.

"You can do it, Feldstein. A little hair twirling and eyelash batting and he'll tell you everything." Frank was teasing me. He knew I wasn't good at that girly kind of flirting, but what he didn't know was that I liked Dane. *Liked* was the wrong word. That was the kind of thing I said in elementary school about the boy who sat in front of me in seventh grade. There was a definite attraction thing going on between Dane and me, which I had been trying to ignore. I cringed, realizing the whole phone call had just been so he would tell me to do what I really wanted to do all along.

I thanked Frank for his advice, wished him luck with the lady dancer and hung up.

There was no time like the present to follow Frank's advice. I couldn't go to Dane's empty-handed, so I went to the refrigerator and took out one of the logs of butter cookie dough. I had made up a double batch and had them wrapped and ready to slice and bake for my retreaters. There would still be plenty with one less log.

While the cookies baked, I tried to spruce up my appearance. The long-sleeved black T-shirt and snug but comfortable jeans were a little dull. I tried to emulate Nicole's style and swirled an aqua cotton scarf around my neck. Even with the swirl, it looked forced to me and I took it off. Maybe a little more makeup, I thought, trying to do the Crystal thing with black eyeliner. It looked great on the yarn store owner, but I didn't have her touch and on me it looked like a cross between some Addams Family character and a raccoon. I washed my face and started again. When I'd put on what served as makeup for me and checked myself in the mirror, I felt better. I looked like me. The timer for the cookies was going off as I made another attempt with something around my neck. This time I dropped a cherry red cowl over my head and it felt natural. I finished by taking the scrunchy out of my hair and shaking it loose.

A short time later I left with a plate of hot cookies.

No matter how much I tried to tell myself that I was just going down there to find out what Dane knew about Nicole's death, I realized it was an excuse to go see him. Why fight nature. Even my mother had seen it.

I had the rest of the evening free. Since the Blue Door was closed on Wednesdays, I didn't have to go in and bake. Wednesdays were muffinless in town, too.

I needed my flashlight to guide the way since there were no streetlights in Cadbury. It was even darker here on the edge of town with all the trees. I was glad to see the street wasn't parked up, meaning there was no karate workshop going on in his garage.

As I got closer, I began to get nervous. When I didn't take

off like a scared rabbit, he'd get the hint. But was I opening Pandora's box? I could smell the wood smoke from his fireplace and had an image of the cozy room inside.

And then I was at his front door. I could hear a low hum of voices, the TV, no doubt. I took a deep breath and punched the bell. It took a few moments before he opened the door and I put on my very best beaming smile.

"Oh, it's you," he said. I should have gotten the message that there was something wrong when he sounded surprised and uncomfortable, but I was too caught up in what I was doing to notice.

I presented the cookies. "They're nice and warm," I said, trying to make it sound seductive. "You know how you're always saying I should come over and stay sometime. Well, here I am." He glanced toward the inside of the house, but instead of opening the door and inviting me in, he pulled it closed behind him as he came outside. He took the plate of cookies and snagged one. "Up to your usual standards," he said when he'd eaten it. He saw me looking at the door.

"It's kind of awkward," he said. "I have company."

From inside, I heard a woman's voice calling out and asking what had happened to him.

Oops. No, super oops. Of course he wasn't sitting around waiting for me to pick up on his teasing. He had somebody. I started to back away, but he grabbed my hand.

He started to say something and then seemed to give up. "It's complicated." He let go of my hand and seemed upset. "Whatever you think it is, is right."

I wanted to disappear. How embarrassing. But I wasn't fourteen, so I pulled myself together, remembering my other mission, and tried to pretend it was the sole reason I was there.

"No problem," I said, doing my best to sound indifferent. "I was hoping you might have some details about what happened to Nicole Welton." I mentioned that Lieutenant Borgnine had stopped by to question my people, but wouldn't tell us anything.

"I heard about that," Dane said with a grin. "I saw him taking a couple of aspirin when he got back. He complained that you refused to give him a straight answer about anything and just kept asking questions."

"I was only trying to find out what happened," I said, and Dane chuckled.

"I think he might have met his match with you." Dane made another glance toward his house and I got it: He was anxious to get back to his company.

"Sorry to keep you," I said, forcing myself not to sound sarcastic. "I'll take any and all details." I pleaded my case. "She was the center of my retreat and I ought to know what happened."

Dane must have felt guilty for the awkward circumstance because he was very forthcoming with information. The first detail was anything but what I was expecting. "We think it was suicide."

"Suicide?" I repeated.

"It isn't official until the medical examiner makes a ruling, but that's what it looks like." He explained that the paramedics had thought she'd been having some kind of seizure and rushed her to the hospital. "It was only later when Cadbury PD went to the scene to do an investigation that we found the note." I mentioned being there when the paramedics arrived and not seeing any note.

"It wasn't written on paper. When we checked her cell phone it was set to a note-taking app. I don't remember the exact wording of it, but it was something like she was doing something bad and couldn't live with it anymore." Dane shifted his weight and took another cookie. "After we read that, we looked at everything with a different eye."

"Right," I said. "I saw a red paper cup and a small glass bottle."

"The bottle had a homemade label on it. Basically, it said 'poison' and 'insecticide.' The results aren't in yet, but the ME thinks she dumped the insecticide in the coffee. Not that it matters, but you probably realized the cup came from the Coffee Shop," he said.

I nodded as if I had, but really until he'd mentioned it, I hadn't put the paper cup together with the coffee place on the main drag.

"Poison, suicide," I repeated, trying to put the pieces together in my head.

"The ME will probably make an official ruling on the cause of death tomorrow. Then that will be it. Case closed."

"You're not even going to do any more investigating?" I said.

"It's Lieutenant Borgnine's call, but I think he'll just take it at face value. It's common knowledge the shop wasn't doing well. She seemed to feel guilty about something. Who knows what she was involved in." A woman's voice called out for Dane. "I ought to go in."

"Of course," I said, backing away. "Thanks for the info. Even though it's a shock. Suicide," I muttered to myself.

"There's one other thing," he said. "I'm sure it doesn't mean anything, but we found a muffin on the ground."

"One of mine?" I said, feeling my brow furrow. "Are you sure?"

He nodded. "It was hard to miss the 'Muffins by Casey' on the bottom of the paper around it," he said. In an effort to brand my baked goods, I'd gotten the paper liners printed up. "Don't worry. She didn't give herself the poison with it. There wasn't even a bite out of it."

That information didn't make me feel any better.

9

THE RED-POLO-SHIRTED MANAGERS' GROUP
crossed my path as I headed toward the Lodge Wednesday
morning. Their retreat seemed to be going on as planned.
They probably didn't even know what had happened to Nicole,
but then it had nothing to do with them. Over their bright
shirts they wore matching navy blue fleece jackets adorned
with their company name. They were headed toward their
meeting room, probably just having finished breakfast.

This morning's version of white sky didn't have a hint of sun,
but was just a thick layer of opaque clouds. There was nothing
to reflect off a shiny surface and not a shadow to be found.

I was early and it was chilly standing outside waiting for
Lucinda and Tag, so I went inside to get a hot drink for the
road. I really appreciated Tag using the restaurant van to pick
up the group to take us to the ranch and I wondered if Tag
would have a fit if I brought a coffee into his pristine vehicle.

I was surprised—no, stunned—to see Will Welton, dressed

in his usual work clothes of plaid flannel shirt over snowy white T-shirt and loose jeans, coming out of the café, holding a white paper cup. I put my arms around him and said, "I'm so sorry about Nicole."

He swallowed a few times and we moved off to the side. "Are you sure you ought to be working today?"

"It's worse if I stay home," he said. Now that I looked at his face I saw that his even features looked drawn and his skin looked pale. He stared at the ground. "I had no idea . . ." He let the train of thought drift off before he composed himself and faced me. "I am so sorry for you. I know this leaves you in a lurch. If there is anything I can do."

I felt funny mentioning the retreat under the circumstances, but he had asked. "I'm sure you know I was pretty much completely depending on her to run the whole fleece-to-yarn part of the program. Do you think she had some kind of playbook? Something I could follow, since it looks like I'm going to be doing it now. And she was going to bring a number of spinning wheels?"

He fished in his pocket for a key and handed it to me. "To be honest, I don't know what she had. But go to her studio and take whatever you need." He looked away and seemed to be losing his composure. I thanked him and he walked away without looking back.

As I stepped into the café, Jane was standing with the delivery guy, signing a clipboard. He started to take it back, then flipped a page and asked her to sign the one she'd missed.

While she made my drink, I brought up Will and how surprised I was to see him. He'd told Jane that Nicole had killed herself. "The worst is, he's blaming himself. They think she used some insecticide he had in the shed. Some stuff he'd mixed up from some old recipe. The main ingredient is cyanide," Jane said, setting my drink on the counter.

I took my coffee and went back into the main part of the Lodge. I hadn't realized how early I was. None of my group was there yet.

While I waited, my mind wandered to my experience with Dane—which bummed me out. I wondered who the woman was.

But there was no time to dwell on that now. I looked out the window just as the Blue Door van pulled up. I looked at my coffee cup, glad that I'd let Jane put one of the plugs in the opening. There was less chance that I'd spill any in the van and make Tag go nuts.

Tag already had the side door open when I came outside. I saw him eyeing my coffee cup and he pointed out the drink holders and requested I keep my cup there when we were moving. Lucinda got out of the front seat and joined us. She was wearing a Ralph Lauren jacket that resembled an Indian blanket. She stepped close to me. "Any news about anything?"

Tag wanted to be included and stepped next to his wife. I looked around and saw we were alone. "I don't want to talk about this in front of Olivia, Bree and Scott. There is no reason to burden them with the problems of the retreat or anything about Nicole. They didn't even know her." I surveyed the area again just to make sure before I told them what I had learned about Nicole's death.

"Suicide, huh," Tag said. "I talked to her a bit now and then. I got the feeling she had begun to sour on Cadbury. Her husband is so popular with everybody but I don't think she was. She was too big for the room, as the saying goes. You have to work at fitting in, in a small town like this. Maybe it got to her."

I mentioned the contents of the note. Tag's interest perked up. "She was doing something bad? I wonder what?"

I saw Olivia, Bree and Scott walking together toward the van so I quickly changed the subject and asked Tag how long he thought it would take to get to the sheep ranch. Lucinda laughed silently and winked at me. She knew what I'd done. For all Tag's attention to detail, he sometimes missed the obvious, like me changing the subject. He was going on about his calculations as I greeted my group and we all got in the van.

Tag was still giving times based on traffic, stoplights and road work as we clipped on our seat belts. He only stopped long enough to make sure I'd "sheltered my cup," as he put it.

As soon as we got on the highway, I heard a squeal come from the seat behind me. When I turned, I saw that Bree was holding up her phone triumphantly.

"I got a signal," she said, showing the face of the phone to all of us. Olivia and Scott took out their phones as well. I heard them muttering that the line at the pay phones had been unmanageable.

As soon as we left the peninsula, as if by magic the weather changed and the scenery did as well. Suddenly the clouds got thinner and thinner until there was blue sky with sun streaming down and there were tall mountains on either side of us. It felt kind of like the movie version of *The Wizard of Oz,* when it went from black-and-white when Dorothy was in Kansas to Technicolor when she arrived in Oz. Soon, all that was left of the clouds were wispy fingers of fog that clung to the mountaintops. I watched as a hawk glided through the filmy white.

Everything was green. Not the dark green moisture-holding green of the Monterey pines and Monterey cypress trees. This was bright green, spring green. The mountains' sides were covered in grass and there were dots of black steers grazing. This was a different sort of rustic than where I lived. It was a more lush version of rural now that we were in the Carmel Valley. Organic lettuce farms, vineyards, horse farms and housing developments around verdant golf courses all whizzed by. We passed wine-tasting rooms and houses on big lots.

"I'm thrilled about this outing," Bree said, putting her phone down on the seat, "but the schedule you gave us yesterday listed the sheep shearing as Thursday afternoon at Vista Del Mar."

I'd forgotten I'd given them the folders with the information on the weekend when they'd arrived. "It seemed like a better idea to do it this way," I said. "Such a lot of bother to bring the sheep to Vista Del Mar."

"You listed it as the kickoff of the whole retreat. It sounded like a dramatic beginning," Olivia said. "But I suppose this is much nicer for the sheep. They don't have to leave home."

I heard Tag saying something in the front seat and Lucinda seemed to be trying to shush him. "I don't see why you just don't tell them the truth," Tag said. "It isn't as if it's your fault that Kevin St. John waited until the last minute to tell you he wouldn't allow the sheep on the premises."

"Is that true?" Scott said. The air was much warmer coming in through the open window and Scott took off his jacket. They knew that Kevin St. John wasn't exactly supportive of my retreats, so they understood when I explained, or really just repeated, what Tag had said.

I was glad when the subject got dropped as Tag turned off the road into a long driveway back toward a red barn. White fencing surrounded the grassy corrals on either side of the road. At the end we pulled in, in front of the barn. A black-and-white border collie ran up to the van as we got out. It started to try and corral us until the rancher came out and called the dog back. Nicole had told me that Buck Morrell's story was similar to Tag and Lucinda's. In his later life, he and his wife were living a dream of having a boutique sheep ranch. Buck, which I suspected wasn't his real name, greeted us all.

The rancher was dressed in jeans and a denim work shirt. I noticed he wore cowboy boots, the expensive custom-made kind.

"The sheep are hanging out in the pen," he said in a friendly manner. "Our shearer should be here any minute. Have a look around while you're waiting." He opened the door to the barn and led the way. I was expecting something full of straw and a little smelly. I was wrong on both accounts. It was more a museum than a barn. "This is the original," he explained. He pointed at a new-looking structure done in the same red. "We built a new state-of-the-art version."

Buck followed us as we fanned out. There were several old pieces of farm equipment that had been cleaned and polished to look like new. And some other stuff. A whole wall had been devoted to black-and-white photographs. As I began to look them over, the rancher joined me. "These are all from the old days. The ranch was much bigger and more of a working ranch than it is now."

I stopped at a photograph of a man sitting on a horse. He was dressed in work clothes, but there was something about him. The only word I could think of was *dashing*. The photo was black-and-white, so I couldn't tell the color of his hair, but I guessed it was dark brown with some waves. He was leaning forward on the horse as though he'd just come in from a hard day. A pair of leather work gloves hung from his jacket.

"That's Edmund Delacorte," the rancher said before explaining that the ranch had belonged to the Delacorte family. "Along with everything else, it seems," he added, punctuating it with a laugh.

The name rang a bell. Hadn't Cora Delacorte mentioned it the other day? "How does he fit in with the family?"

"He was Cora and Madeleine's older brother," the rancher said. "I gather he spent a lot of time out here. I think it was a hideaway for him."

Before I could get more information, the shearer arrived, pulling on his coveralls. He went to a small temporary pen. While the rancher got the first candidate, I asked the shearer if the sheep minded.

His face had the look of someone who spent most of his time outside and wasn't concerned with sunscreen. He stroked his chin. "I'd say it's like giving a five-year-old a haircut. They don't volunteer, but I think they feel better after." We gathered around the small enclosure as the rancher led in one of the sheep with a rope halter. It looked like the standard Little Bo Peep variety, but the rancher said it was a breed called rambouillet. He did a short talk on there being two kinds of sheep, the meat sheep and the wool ones. The ones used for meat had shorter hair. He dealt only with wool sheep.

"This is Clover and she's a ewe," he said. When Bree heard the word *ewe* she got all excited and mentioned that the Ewes was the name of her knitting group.

"It's a play on words," she said, in case anyone hadn't figured it out. She started snapping pictures on her phone, excited because she could send them right along to her boys. The shearer took the lead and got the animal in the middle of the pen, then he got the sheep on its side. He took out a pair of clippers that looked like the kind barbers used, only bigger. He positioned the sheep, then held it in place with his knee as he began to shear. I watched as all of her hair began to roll back on itself. The underside was shades lighter, but all of it looked soft and fluffy. It took only a few minutes for him to finish, coming away with the fleece in one large piece. He let the sheep up and it began to walk around the enclosure.

"You can pet her if you want," the rancher said. Clover

seemed to like the attention as I patted her head and looked into her eyes. Not exactly looked into. With their weird horizontal pupils it was hard to tell where she was looking, but when I stopped petting she leaned against the fence and pushed against my hip, wanting more. Buck mentioned that someone else had come out wanting the same number of fleeces recently. Clover was led back to the pasture and the next sheep brought in. Buck picked up the fleece and carried it out. Tag watched, taking in every detail, calling after the rancher when a piece of fleece fell free. I was glad to see my group seemed to be enjoying the outing. Olivia was taking pictures of Bree with the ewe so she could send it to her knitting group. Scott was interested in touching the fleece and was surprised at the slightly greasy feel that Buck explained was lanolin.

We watched them shear only two sheep. The rest had been done earlier and all the fleeces were loaded into the back of the van.

"That was great," Bree said when we were all in the van on the way back. She was busy making use of the cell signal, sending more photos and text messages while talking about the outing. I was about to agree when Scott looked toward the back of the van at the sheep fleeces piled on sheets.

"So how exactly do we turn all that sheep's hair into yarn?" he asked. I might have been able to wing it, if Tag hadn't stepped in.

"I was wondering about that myself," Tag said. "It would seem that there must be a number of steps, Casey. My understanding was that Nicole was the expert—"

"So the Delacorte sisters had a brother," I said, interrupting. I could see where this was going and managed to cut Tag off before he made it clear to the early birds about my predicament with all that wool.

Lucinda knew what I was doing and joined in. "Tag knows all about the history of Cadbury and its inhabitants. He can tell you all about the Delacorte brother. Can't you, dear?" she said, patting her husband's hand affectionately.

"I did spend quite a bit of time at the Cadbury Historical Society when we first moved here," Tag said. "I think that if you're going to live somewhere you ought to know about it. You probably don't know this, Casey, but Edmund Delacorte is the one responsible for Vista Del Mar." Tag seemed to have forgotten about his comment about the wool and became totally involved with talking about Edmund Delacorte. It was almost fascinating, except Tag tended to go into too much detail. It was interesting to hear that Vista Del Mar had started out as a camp and gone through several incarnations as a resort by the time Cora and Madeleine's brother had bought it. I don't know if the others were listening, but I didn't care as long as Tag didn't start asking me what I was going to do without Nicole and her expertise.

By the time we left all the blue skies and bright green of the Carmel Valley and entered a bank of fog drifting onto the Monterey Peninsula, I knew that Edmund had loved the outdoors and had wanted Vista Del Mar to stay a rustic spot for families to enjoy nature and for retreat groups to have a place to get away from it all. He didn't want it to be exclusive, like the posh resorts in Pebble Beach. There was talk of him running for office and it sounded like everyone viewed him as some kind of god.

Tag seemed to be running out of steam and I worried that we still had a ways to go. "So what happened to Edmund?" I asked, both out of curiosity and in an effort to keep him away from talking about the retreat.

"He died. He was in his prime, just forty-seven. I can tell you the exact kind of infection if you give me a day or so,"

Tag said. I told him it was okay and he went back to talking about Edmund's philosophy on the outdoors. The fog had grown thicker and it was hard to believe we'd been in such bright sunlight just a few minutes earlier.

We turned onto the street that bordered Vista Del Mar, and I started to relax as Tag's monologue continued. In a few minutes, the early birds would get out without knowing how worried I was.

The Lodge came into view and I was already reaching for the door handle, thinking I was home free. I had the door open the minute the van stopped.

"Where should we put the wool fleeces?" Tag said as we began to get out. Before I could say anything, he continued, "I hope you find somebody to—"

"To help you take in the wool," I said, interrupting him before he could bring up Nicole again. I looked at the three pre-retreaters and told them everything was under control and they could go off and enjoy themselves.

I just hoped that Nicole had left a lot of good instructions.

10

"THERE'S NO REASON FOR YOU TO FEEL STRANGE. Will gave you the key and told you to take whatever you needed," Lucinda said as we stood in front of The Bank. What she said was true, but I was still uneasy about going into the closed store. I was glad Lucinda had said she would come along.

The early birds had gone off to have lunch and Tag had gone on home after helping to get the fleeces to the Cypress meeting room. Just before he left, he pulled Lucinda and me aside and said he could research the wool-to-yarn process. Lucinda and I had shared a roll of our eyes.

Lucinda had sent him home and she'd driven into downtown Cadbury with me. "Tag needs to do his exercise walk," she said, shaking her head. "He always walks in the morning on the same route along Grand Street. You should take it as a high compliment that he chose to help you out this morning and delayed his walk." I did appreciate what he'd done. Tag was such a habitual person, making an alteration like that had to have been very difficult.

"I never noticed how ornate this building is," Lucinda said, touching one of the columns outside the front door of the corner building while I fished around for the key.

The leather strap with the bells attached let out a loud jangling sound as I opened the door. Lucinda jumped and then laughed at her nerves. "It's not like there are ghosts in here."

"Look who's feeling strange now," I joked as we went inside. The whoosh of air from the door opening had sent some papers sailing across the floor. I scooped them up, afraid we'd slip on them. Figuring they were just advertisements that had been slid under the door, I stuffed them in the canvas messenger bag I'd taken to using as a carryall. I looked around the interior. Even with all the windows, the light was low inside the old bank. This was so different from when I'd been there before. Now it felt eerie and quiet.

I found a light switch and turned on the inside lights. When I looked around I expected to see a fiesta of colors and textures, but instead my breath caught. Something was wrong. All the textiles hanging on the old tellers' cages were askew. Lucinda followed close behind as I took stock of the place.

The first things I checked were the glass cases in the middle of the shop. No surprise, the doors to the counters had been opened. The silver pieces were still there, but when I checked the pink velvet backdrop for the jewelry pieces, it was empty.

The spinning wheels were all in place, but a basket of yarn was dumped. I went behind the half partition and found what Nicole must have used as an office. The drawers on the desk were all open a touch, as though someone had pulled them open and been in too much of a hurry to close them completely. I went right past two cubicles and looked at the vault. The thick metal door was open and I got up my courage and went inside. As Nicole had said, she'd made it into a meditation room. A forest green cushion sat near a small low table with an incense burner. Not my idea of a place to meditate. The room felt claustrophobic as I looked at the gray metal walls, which I realized were actually rows and rows of safety-deposit boxes. Each had a round hole in the middle where the locks had once been. I noticed that several appeared to have been opened and carelessly shut, like the desk drawers. Lucinda had come in behind me and backed out, obviously reacting to the close feeling of the space. I walked farther into the vault and pulled out the ajar boxes and opened the tops, looking inside. Nothing. Not even lint. I guessed that whoever had checked those three and found nothing there had assumed the rest were also empty and given up. I considered looking through them all, but after opening another three and finding nothing, I gave up. But at least I shut them all the way.

I went back into the main area and took out my cell phone. "I'm calling the cops," I said, putting in the number. I explained to the dispatcher that it wasn't an emergency.

I was relieved that the dispatcher must have passed along the information because there were no flashing lights or sirens when the blue-and-white cruiser pulled in front of the store. A moment later Dane walked in, or should I say Officer Mangano, because he was in his midnight blue uniform with a canvas cop jacket on top.

Dane's demeanor softened when he saw Lucinda and me. "What's up?" He looked around the place as I explained Will had given me the key.

"But when we got here, it looked like this." I pointed out the blanket and quilt hanging askew on the tellers' cages and walked him to the glass cases.

"Is anything missing?" he said, looking inside one of the cases.

I explained about the jewelry made out of hair I'd seen the last time I was there.

Dane tried to keep his cop face on, but he couldn't help it, he wrinkled his nose with distaste and then asked me if it was valuable.

"The pieces weren't anything that I'd want," I said. I added that Nicole had mentioned that some of them were made out of dead people's hair as a remembrance of them.

After taking him into the vault, we all checked the back door. "This isn't the original door," Dane said. I remembered there was a fuss when Nicole had it installed, saying she wanted something to let in light.

He shook his head at the quality of the lock and pointed out that the door seemed to have been carelessly closed. What he said next came as a complete surprise.

"From the looks of things, I'm guessing Nicole made a last stop here. Maybe she was looking for something or wanted to wreck the place and gave up. In her mental state she probably didn't care about locking the door." I mentioned the missing jewelry.

"She might have just sold it between the time you were here and now," he said, gesturing toward the glass cases. "All those silver pieces are still there. If somebody was looking for valuable stuff, they'd have taken those."

Lucinda walked over to the glass cases and nodded with agreement when she saw what was still there.

"Even so, I think Will should be notified," Dane said.

I reminded Dane about the lack of cell service and offered to try to reach him. I called the café. Jane said he'd just been in and she'd try to catch him. A few moments later, he picked up the phone and I handed mine to Dane.

Dane didn't hide his emotions behind a blank expression and flat tone. He knew Will and began by telling him how sorry he was about Nicole and then eased into giving Will the reason for the call. When he finished the call, he handed my cell back. "He doesn't seem concerned about a break-in and agreed that Nicole probably just left it this way. Poor guy," he said with a sad nod of his head. "There doesn't seem to be any reason to write up a report."

He appeared to be getting ready to leave, but on second thought asked why exactly we were there. I reminded him about my upcoming retreat and that Nicole had been the center of it. "I came to look for some kind of playbook of the program and to look at the spinning wheels."

When Dane heard I was taking them to Vista Del Mar, he was concerned how I'd get them there.

"I was going to take them in the restaurant van," Lucinda said.

"I have a better idea," he said. "I'll pick them up later in my truck." He looked at me directly. "You're baking tonight, right?" When I nodded, he continued. "I'll stop by the Blue Door and we can come back here and you can show me what you want moved."

I almost said, "Are you sure your girlfriend won't mind?" but I smiled and agreed.

"It's the least I could do for a neighbor." His angular face lit up with a warm smile. After rechecking that the back door was shut tightly and reminding us to lock up, he got ready to leave. Just before he got to the front door he turned back. "About last night," he began.

I rushed in before he could say anything else. "You don't have to explain. I got it."

Lucinda and I went through the place, straightening the quilts and blankets hanging on the tellers' cages, closing the back of the glass cases and even straightening the stack of old ledgers that had fallen over next to the fireplace. At the same time, we kept an eye out for something describing Nicole's plan for the wool. She must have had it all in her head because we found nothing.

"It looks a lot less creepy this way," I said, admiring what we'd done. "Now let's get out of here."

"I don't know about you, but I need a nice cappuccino," Lucinda said as I flipped off the lights and led the way to the front door.

"Just what I was thinking," I said, suggesting where to go. Cadbury didn't have chain restaurants, big-box stores or Starbucks. But with the chilly cloudy weather, Cadbury was still a coffee town and the brew was dispensed in a number of small shops. My personal favorite was the Coffee Shop. In typical Cadbury by the Sea fashion, the name said what the place was without any fancy flourishes. My understanding was Maggie had been the first to serve gourmet-quality coffee.

The shop was located in one of the Victorian-style buildings and had such a deep fragrance of coffee it was as though the years and years of grinding beans like Sumatra, Costa Rican and Kenyan had been absorbed by the burlap-coffee-bag-covered walls. The walls that weren't covered in burlap were windowed and looked out onto a small courtyard next to the place.

Lucinda went to snag one of the small round tables. Several of the other tables were taken and there was a low hum of conversation. "Drinks are on me," I said. Lucinda had a hard time accepting, but after her help with the fleeces and dealing with Nicole's place, it was the least I could do. I held strong and she finally relented with a thank-you.

IT WAS A SLOW TIME OF DAY AND MAGGIE WAS working the counter alone. She was finishing up with the customer ahead of me. She popped the lid on one of the red paper cups with *Coffee Shop* in white writing and set it next to another cup in a cardboard carrier. As I stared at the cups, I had a flashback to the cup lying on the ground with Nicole. Of course, the cup had come from here. I wondered if Maggie was aware of it. I knew how uncomfortable and somehow connected to Nicole's death I'd felt when Dane had mentioned that one of my muffins had been found on the ground. And Nicole hadn't even eaten any of the muffin. I wondered if I should bring it up. I was afraid my thoughts showed on my face and I did my best to erase the clouds from my expression.

"This ought to do it." Maggie took a half straw and squeezed it before sticking it into one of the cup's sip holes and handing the man the carrier. He offered her a hearty thank-you before walking away.

I stepped up to the counter and her face broke out into a friendly smile. "Casey, I didn't see you hiding behind that guy." She leaned across the counter and gave me a hug. "What's your pleasure?" she said. She saw Lucinda and waved.

I'd barely said "two cappuccinos" when she said, "One with an extra shot, both with two-percent milk, am I right?" It was more of a statement than a question.

"Exactly right," I said in an amazed tone.

She seemed amused by my surprise. "I pride myself on knowing how my customers like their drinks." She saw me looking at the case of goodies. There was an empty basket where my muffins went.

"Nobody seems to remember that there are no muffins on Wednesdays," Maggie said, working her magic with the espresso machine. "You know, if you ever change your mind about baking Tuesday nights, my customers would be thrilled."

The Coffee Shop had been the first place in town to take my muffins and I was forever grateful. It was all thanks to my aunt, but then so much of my life in Cadbury was thanks to her. We talked for a moment about my aunt and how much we both missed her.

It turned out to be meaningless that I'd offered to buy the drinks because Maggie wouldn't take my money. "Consider it professional courtesy," she said, giving a nod to Lucinda, who mouthed a thank-you.

I set down the foam-covered drinks as Maggie attended to a new customer. The Coffee Shop proprietor was definitely striking looking, with glossy black hair she always tied with a red scarf. Red was her trademark color. She wore lots of it and even had cups that color. She was outgoing and vivacious and gave no hint to her own personal sadness. My aunt had told me that Maggie's daughter had died when she was in her early twenties. It had been some kind of accident. And then recently she'd been widowed. I think one of the reasons she always wore something red was to keep herself cheerful.

When Maggie finished with the customer, she grabbed a mug of her own brew and came to our table. "Mind if I join you?"

"As if you have to ask," I said, pulling a chair from another table. Maggie sat down with a sigh and said something about how all the years of being on her feet were getting to her.

Maggie wasn't a gossip as much as a news exchanger. The cheerful expression had faded from her face. "I suppose you've heard about Nicole Welton. So sad," she said.

Lucinda and I nodded in agreement. Maggie seemed upset. "I was horrified when I heard she put the poison in a cup of coffee from my place."

"Then the police talked to you?" I said, relieved that I didn't have to be the one to tell her.

"It seemed to be the customary type of investigation in the case of a suicide. They wanted to know if she seemed despondent when she came in." Maggie stopped to drink from her mug. "The thing is, I don't remember seeing her Tuesday morning. It was pretty busy and the girl I have helping probably waited on her. Poor Carol was so upset at being talked to by the police, she could barely remember her own name, let alone if she'd seen Nicole." Maggie paused and sighed. "I wish I had waited on her. Maybe I could have said something that would have made a difference."

"So then Lieutenant Borgnine told you it was suicide?" I said, thinking how he'd never divulged that when he was talking to me or my people. I was beginning to think that he just didn't like me.

Maggie nodded as an answer and I asked if Nicole came in often. "Her shop is just down the street. Not every day, but often enough that I knew she drank lattes with a double shot of sugar-free vanilla syrup. It's a wonder she even knew she was drinking coffee with all that milk and sweet syrup."

Even though I'd only done temp work for the detective agency, it had forever changed me and I automatically tried to gather information. I asked if Nicole had seemed unhappy.

"You know everybody who comes in here talks to me. I think of myself as being a coffee version of a bartender. She never said anything specific, but I think she was bored with Cadbury."

"She and Will seemed a little mismatched," I said. "Do you know how they met?"

"I think that was part of the problem. It was what they call a 'cute meet,' practically out of a romantic comedy. Nicole was living in Cadbury for the summer while she worked at the aquarium. She collected old textiles and used to hunt the local garage sales on weekends. Will had just gotten his own place and he was looking for cheap furnishings. They kept running into each other and then their hands touched when they both reached for the same Indian basket. He invited her out to breakfast and it went from there."

I was surprised at how many details she had, but Maggie reminded me it was a small town and she was in the center of it. "At the end of the summer, Nicole went back to school in San Francisco, but came back to Cadbury on weekends. Will's parents had just moved to Oregon and he was ripe for the picking, as the saying goes.

"They had a lovely wedding and made such a lovely couple. I think he wanted to start a family, but she seemed restless. I think when she opened the shop, he thought she'd calm down. But frankly, I always thought The Bank was too sophisticated for Cadbury. I can't imagine she had much business." Maggie rolled her eyes at herself. "Will you listen to me. I sound like an old busybody."

The door to the store opened and Maggie got up, anticipating a customer. A woman came in, but instead of heading toward the counter, she marched over to our table. The small stout woman looked familiar and I was trying to place her, but she saved me the trouble by sticking out her hand and introducing herself.

"Wanda Krug," she said, almost sounding like a drill sergeant. "I was walking by and saw you in here. I'm here to offer my services."

When I didn't respond right away, it must have occurred to her I had no idea what she was talking about. "We met before. In Cadbury Yarn. I'm here to offer to take over for Nicole Welton. For your retreat," she said, beginning to sound a little snippy that I wasn't picking up on who she was.

"It was just terrible about Nicole." The short woman said the right words, but they came across as hollow. "I told you I was a spinner and I know what to do with wool." She seemed to be getting frustrated. "I'm here to help you," she said finally. "So, what's the story? You want me to help you or not?"

Now all the pieces fell into place and I realized Wanda

was the answer to my prayers. She was better than any play-book describing the process, even if it was going to cut into my profit since I had paid Nicole half the money in advance.

"We have a deal," I said, shaking hands with her. The stern-looking woman's face brightened with a smile as I arranged for her to come to Vista Del Mar Friday morning.

"I should warn you. I only have one spinning wheel I can bring."

"No problem," I said, telling her about the tote bags with drop spindles and the selection of Nicole's spinning wheels at my disposal. Wanda turned on her heel and went out as fast as she'd come in.

Lucinda and I clinked our cups in a toast. The retreat program was saved.

Lucinda and I parted company after that. She and Tag had plans for a picnic in front of the TV. On their one night off from the Blue Door it was their favorite thing to do together. She had errands to run.

When I got back to my car and dropped the messenger bag that had become my purse on the passenger seat, some papers slipped out. As I retrieved them from the floor, I remembered they'd been on the floor of The Bank when Lucinda and I went in. I'd assumed they were some kind of coupons or advertising pieces and had ignored them. I glanced at them, getting ready to drop them in a trash can on the street.

They weren't at all what I'd thought. There was a brochure about a tour to Bhutan. A sticker was affixed to the top page with the information for the Cadbury Travel Agency. The other sheet seemed to be an itinerary and a cost breakdown. There was a note on the bottom thanking Nicole for the deposit for the trip.

I was struck by three things: how expensive the trip was, that the itinerary was for one person, and the fact that Nicole had paid the deposit the morning of her suicide.

11

INSTEAD OF GOING HOME I WENT DOWN THE STREET
to Cadbury Travel. It was located in a bland storefront that
had probably seemed ultramodern when it was built in the
fifties. The long window brought in a lot of light and the walls
were decorated with pictures of Hawaii, Paris and Rome.

The two desks in the front area were empty, but I heard
sounds coming from the back room and did a loud throat-
clearing a couple of times to let them know someone was there.

Two women came out. They looked familiar, but then
everybody in town did. I'd seen them in either the local drugstore or supermarket. I introduced myself, but it wasn't necessary; the older woman knew who I was.

"I'm Liz Buckley," she said, realizing I didn't know who
she was. "This is my daughter, Stacey."

So, there was another mother-daughter team working
together in Cadbury. But this pair was nothing like Gwen and
Crystal of Cadbury Yarn, who seemed like two distinct people

with different points of view and certainly different clothing styles.

Liz and Stacey looked alike. They both had chin-length dark hair and both wore similar-style suits. The only difference was that one was light beige and the other a darker shade of the neutral color. I listened to them as we made small talk, waiting for some kind of eye rolling to start or for Stacey to say "Mother" in that hopeless disgruntled tone I'd heard myself use. Neither one ever happened. It was too weird. They seemed in total agreement.

"Where is it that you wanted to go?" Liz finally asked, getting down to business.

"Nowhere, right now. I wanted to ask you about this." I held out the brochure and note. "I assume you heard about Nicole."

Liz nodded. She took the papers from me, and realized what they were. "I didn't think of it. I'll have to cancel everything."

My information-gathering talent kicked in and I brought up the expense of the trip and the fact that it seemed Nicole was going alone.

"We just make the arrangements, we don't ask any questions," Liz said. "But I thought about the same things. Nicole did mention something about a new source of income and said that Will was happy to stay in Cadbury and let her go off looking for exotic textiles." I noticed that Liz seemed to feel a little uneasy. "It was the way she said it that bothered me. As if there was something wrong with Will not wanting to go traipsing around the world."

There was nothing in her words, but something in Liz's tone made it sound like she didn't particularly like Nicole. "I'm guessing you weren't exactly friends with her even though her shop was just down the street," I said. Stacey spoke before her mother had a chance.

"She was an outsider," Stacey said with a subtle touch of hostility. "There were a lot of people around here who weren't so happy with her marrying Will. I went to high school with him and he was *that* guy. You know, friendly, good-looking, played on all the teams and was like the local hero. A lot of girls had crushes on him. Everybody liked him. They still do."

"Does that include you?" I asked, noting that she sounded very enthusiastic about him. The daughter tugged at her suit jacket, appearing uncomfortable. "That wasn't what I meant. It just seems like he could have found somebody local."

"I get it. Like you mentioned, Nicole was an outsider. I guess that puts me on the same list," I said.

Liz stepped in. "There are lots of new people who have moved to Cadbury and they fit in just fine. You, well, you went right to the heart of the town through their stomachs." When I seemed surprised, she said she was a big fan of my muffins and the desserts at the Blue Door. "But my waistline isn't," she joked.

"It's not that I didn't like Nicole," the mother said. "She just went against the grain of the town. Take that studio of hers. I know there are lots of places that think it's arty to turn churches and fire stations into businesses. But not in Cadbury. The old Cadbury Bank closed years ago. I know because my father worked there. You might have met him at Vista Del Mar. His name is Virgil Scarantino."

I had an image of a man in a leather bomber jacket who was going to direct a lot of the activities as the travel agent explained that the bank had been designated a historic building, so whoever rented it couldn't make any changes other than to, say, fix a leaky faucet. The only business that could use it the way it was would be another bank, but as branches of big banks moved into town, they wanted their own style building and weren't interested in the comparatively small bank building. The town council hadn't been keen on the idea of it being rented to Nicole, but because Will was so well liked and so persistent, they finally relented.

I wondered how the town council had felt when Nicole decided to change the back door, but I didn't bring it up.

I brought up my third concern. "It seems kind of odd that Nicole would give you a deposit for a trip on the morning that she decided to kill herself."

"I've thought about that, too," Liz said. "I don't have an answer."

Maybe Liz didn't, but I was pretty sure I did. I couldn't wait to go home and call Frank.

I suppose I could have sat in my car and called him on my cell, but I wanted to talk on a device that wouldn't suddenly get a bad connection or just cut out. I drove home quickly and pulled the Mini Cooper into my driveway. I rushed inside, almost falling over Julius as he came out to greet me.

I was punching in the number as I walked toward a chair. I barely got out a hello before Frank started talking.

"Okay, Feldstein, what now? Don't tell me someone else died."

By now I was used to his gruff response to my calls. I also was pretty sure it was all an act.

"No, Frank, it's the same body I called about before. I want to run something by you since you have so much experience."

"Feldstein, that sounds like you're saying I'm old," he said with a laugh. "'Cause if you're trying to flatter me, you'll have to come up with something better." He made a few grumbly sounds. "So, what's the story?"

"I told you about the woman who died," I said as Julius jumped into my lap. "I took your advice and talked to my cop neighbor—"

"Talked? I think I suggested flirting."

"Right, flirting." I didn't want to tell him that I'd actually had more than flirting on my mind and what a bust the whole plan had been. "Anyway, the medical examiner thinks it was suicide. They think she put insecticide in her coffee, and there was a note written on her cell phone."

I heard Frank groan. "Suicide notes on cell phones, geez. What did it say?"

I admitted I didn't know exactly, but it was something about how she felt bad about something she'd done.

"Let's cut to the chase, Feldstein, I hear a *but* coming in all this. So?"

I found myself starting to talk faster, knowing that he was getting impatient. "So, I found out she put down a deposit on an expensive trip to Bhutan that morning. What does your keen detective mind have to say about that?"

"Trying the flattery angle again," he said with a laugh. "Just a hint, Feldstein, a little bit sounds authentic, but when you start laying it on too thick—remember, I'm a PI and can see through things."

Julius was unhappy I was paying more attention to the phone call than to him and he started flicking his tail up and down. I was beginning to realize cats were in their own universe and wanted to call the shots.

"I get where you're going and yes, it does sound fishy to me, unless something devastating happened between the time she made the deposit and her farewell cup of java. If it was my case, I'd cross out suicide as the cause of death."

"Good, that's exactly what I thought. And if it isn't suicide, then it's got to be—" Julius had sat up and began using his head to butt my chin. He didn't stop until I started to pet him, but after a few moments he tired of that and jumped off my lap, looking at the refrigerator.

"Murder," Frank said, finishing my sentence. "Why do I think you're going to stick your nose in this case?" Frank let out a chortle. "Remember, Feldstein, cops don't like it when us PIs prove them wrong."

"Is that your attempt to show me how fake flattery sounds, or do you really mean it?" I didn't mention that I'd already started looking into her death without even meaning to. It had become automatic to start putting pieces together.

"You should know me better than that. I don't do flattery, fake or otherwise. I only say what I mean. So, yeah, I meant it, only you're not licensed and you're not getting paid. Maybe I should call you a VI, or volunteer investigator. By the way, the first thing I'd look into is whatever this *bad thing* is she was doing. It has motive written all over it."

"But that's from what we think is a bogus suicide note," I said.

"Feldstein, people often put some truth in their lies. Like the people who make up false names, but use their real initials."

"I get it," I said excitedly. "That part of the note could be true."

"Very good, Feldstein, you make me proud."

I mumbled a thank-you, not used to getting praise from him. By now I was sure his patience was wearing thin and I thought there should be a two-way stream of conversation, so I asked him about the surveillance he'd been on during our last call. Frank seemed to appreciate my interest, and if I wanted to get on his good side, it worked much better than my attempts at flattery. "I caught the supposed injured woman dancing her pants off. The insurance company even gave me a bonus," Frank said with pride in his voice. He threw in a few more details, before rather abruptly saying he had to go, and hung up.

"So, Frank and I are on the same page about Nicole," I said to Julius, who had done a figure eight around my ankles and then headed to the refrigerator as if he hoped I would follow.

"Okay," I said finally. I took out the multi-wrapped can and gave him a serving. Why had I ever bought that first can of stink fish?

It was already late afternoon. I left Julius noisily eating his smelly meal and went across the driveway to the converted garage. I finished filling the tote bags and came back to the main house. I had missed a bunch of meals and made up for it with a frozen dinner I microwaved.

The white sky was fading to dark when I went across to Vista Del Mar, pulling a couple of plastic bins on wheels that I'd filled with the tote bags. I deposited them in the corner of the Lodge, noting the table for registration had already been set up. I didn't feel so hopeless now that Wanda had offered her services. But I wasn't totally relaxed, either. I only hoped she'd live up to her own hype.

I noticed that Virgil Scarantino was talking to a group of people in the seating area. When I looked at him, I was reminded that he was related to the travel agent. Life in a small town. Everyone was connected.

The three early birds were sitting together on one of the leather couches. I stepped around the edge of the group and heard Virgil say he was going to give a little talk about the history of Vista Del Mar, starting in a few minutes. I would have liked to stay for it, but my real purpose was to talk to my group before I headed to the Blue Door.

"Just checking that everything is okay with you three," I said.

"You don't have to worry about us. We're happy to just be here and hang out," Olivia said. "Actually, we've sort of started something. The three of us were sitting in the living room area of Sand and Sea, knitting squares. A young woman saw us and asked about it. When I explained that we were going to sew them together and get them to people in need, she said she'd like to make one. I gave her some extra needles I had and a ball of yarn. Scott showed her how to knit. Bree wrote down the directions. Another woman came by and she wanted to join us, too. She went off to the gift shop and bought her own supplies." Olivia laughed and her dark eyes danced. "I think you better tell the people from Cadbury Yarn to check the stock in the gift shop." She went on to explain that the registration clerk had helped out and made a bunch of copies of the instructions in both knit and crochet.

"This is just wonderful," she said. "I had no idea how satisfying it was to inspire other people." She leaned toward me. "And, we told everyone about Yarn2Go and the retreats you put on."

Scott held up his knitting. He was working on a square in a bulky brown yarn. Even though he'd gone public, he still seemed a little apprehensive as he noticed one of the men in a red polo shirt staring at him.

Bree had her cell phone out, even though there was no signal. It seemed to give her some kind of comfort to be able to at least look at it. Virgil cleared his throat and announced he was going to begin his talk. I heard just the beginning. "This place was never meant to be some posh resort. It was supposed to be a place to step away from the busyness of the world, be in nature, give yourself over to the rhythmic sounds of the ocean, the call of the gulls, the barking of the seals. Reflect and renew."

No wonder it was such an ideal spot to hold the yarn retreats. It was as if it had been perfectly designed for it. I also understood why Kevin St. John had gone unplugged. It did go with the atmosphere of the place. I would really have liked to listen to more, but I had to go. There were desserts and muffins to be baked.

As I walked outside into the damp night air, I glanced around at the old weathered buildings that were barely visible in the darkness and I felt a deep appreciation for the place.

The Blue Door was locked up and dark, since it was the one day a week it was closed. I lugged the two tropical-patterned, recycled-plastic shopping bags full of the baking ingredients for the muffins up the short staircase to the porch that ran along the converted house.

Because the restaurant was closed I was able to get an earlier start on the baking. I flipped on the lights and glanced through the tall frame windows in the dining room as I went to the kitchen. I was used to seeing the streets empty, but at this earlier hour, there were still people coming in and out of restaurants and going into the movie theater for the last show of the night.

I turned on some mellow jazz and got into my baking groove. I was really in the zone, rolling out piecrusts and slicing up apples for the pie. I made a crumb crust to sprinkle over the pies and soon the air was filled with the scent of cinnamon, cooking apples and the buttery crust. I moved on to the cakes and in no time was filling tube pans with chocolate pound cake batter. When the pies were baked and cooling and the cakes baking, I started in on the muffins. They mixed up quickly and were baked and cooling when I heard a knock on the glass portion of the restaurant door. When I went to answer, I saw Dane's angular face in the semidarkness of the porch.

"I'm here to get the spinning wheels," he said as he came in, unzipping his black hooded sweatshirt. He stopped and sniffed the air. What's it today?" But before I could answer he started guessing. Probably as a result of all his martial arts training, there was precision and grace to his movements as he followed me through the dining room.

"I smell cinnamon," he said. "Apple pie, right?" I pointed at the dessert counter at the front of the restaurant. With the satisfaction of being right, he nodded at the lineup of golden crumb–topped pies in the glass dome–covered pedestals.

"And something chocolate, too," he said, admiring the two chocolate pound cakes under glass domes.

He continued with the game all the way to the kitchen. "More cinnamon with some other spice, maybe ginger." He closed his eyes. "Now what muffins have cinnamon?" I handed him a paper bag with some of the muffins I'd set aside for him. He held it to his nose and sniffed. Still with his eyes closed he reached inside and took one of the warm muffins out of the bag and took a bite.

"Hey, that's cheating," I said.

"Who said there were any rules?" he teased. "I've got it. You made the Fourteen Carrot ones." He opened his eyes and looked at the warm brown muffin with flecks of orange.

"I want you to know I appreciate that you know my muffins by their real names," I said, thinking "carrot muffins" sounded so dull in comparison.

"Anything to make you happy," he said with a twinkle in his eye. He was back to his flirty, playful manner, as if the previous night had never happened.

I had the muffins packed up in boxes, ready to be dropped off at the various spots around town. I offered to let him into Nicole's studio first so he could pick up the spinning wheels and be on his way, but he said he wasn't in a hurry and would help me drop off the muffins.

The movie theater was closed and the downtown street deserted as we walked to the various coffee spots. They all had alcoves at their back doors, meant for early deliveries. Our last stop was the Coffee Shop, which got us almost back to Nicole's place.

The way Dane was acting made me think that last night had been just a one-night thing. I itched to make a snippy comment, but forced myself to keep quiet. Besides, I had rethought the whole thing and decided friends and neighbors were all we were going to be, ever.

There were other things on my mind that I wanted to talk to him about. I was still trying to pick my moment when we walked into Nicole's studio. I turned on the lights and was relieved to see everything seemed as I'd left it. It had probably had been Nicole who'd messed the place up.

The interior looked lovely at night. The arched windows made a dark contrast to the natural color of the walls. The tiny hanging lights she'd added spotlighted the antique pieces, reflecting in their refinished surfaces.

"It's amazing how different this place looks now," Dane said. He walked over to the fireplace and picked up one of the old ledgers that were stacked next to it. He opened it and flipped through the pages. "The bank just closed and apparently left everything here. Except money," he quipped. He looked at the rest of the ledgers. "All that paper gave Nicole a lot of kindling for the fireplace."

Now that he'd brought Nicole up, I seized the moment. "I'm not so sure it was suicide." Dane's head shot up and he became a cop again.

"You're doing the Nancy Drew thing again, huh?" I told him about the ticket for one to Bhutan and the timing of her deposit. "Interesting," he said. "But it could have been some kind of last-ditch effort, which she immediately regretted. The medical examiner is about to make an official ruling that her death was a suicide. We took a lot of statements around town from people. The consensus was she was depressed that her business wasn't doing well and she felt trapped in a small town. Of course, Lieutenant Borgnine talked to Will Welton. He seemed to be in shock about her committing suicide. I think he is in shock about her death in general. Why else would he be going in to work?"

Dane stroked his chin and smiled. "I don't know if I should tell you this, but Lieutenant Borgnine put the word out that nobody should give you any information."

"That's ridiculous," I said.

"I think you can see I agree with your statement. I'm certainly not paying attention to it." He gave me a soft nudge to the shoulder. "So, if you have any thoughts about anything, you know my door is always open."

"Except last night." The words fell out before I could stop them and he looked surprised.

"Right," he said with no more explanation before he moved over to the back of the studio where the spinning wheels were lined up and went back to talking about Nicole.

"She must have been very depressed and she knew her husband had concocted an insecticide containing cyanide that was kept in the shed on the Vista Del Mar grounds. The suicide note on the cell phone. I have to admit that's something new."

"Did you check her cell phone for fingerprints?" I asked.

"You're unrelenting," he said. "We did and the screen was all smudged up." He hesitated. "Somebody might have tried to wipe off the prints. Lieutenant Borgnine doesn't see it that way. He thinks that woman with the blond hair who found Nicole probably picked up the phone and then freaked when she realized what she'd done and tried to wipe her prints off."

He started checking over all the wheels, looking to see what moving parts there were. "If you think about it, putting down the deposit could have been what pushed her over the edge. The note said she'd done something bad. Maybe that referred to the deposit, considering her business wasn't doing well." I mentioned that she had a job lined up with me and she had seemed anything but despondent when I'd last seen her.

"Not everybody shows their feelings," he said. "But say you are right. Then what? She was murdered? By who?"

He had me there. The only suspect I could come up with was her husband and that wasn't because of anything Will had done or said. It was totally based on the fact that murders were usually committed by those closest to you. It was an odd and disquieting thought. I let the subject drop.

Dane had parked his red Ford F150 next to the building. I helped him carry out the spinning wheels and he secured them in the back and covered them with a tarp. "Will is going to meet me at Vista Del Mar. He knows which meeting room to put them in."

I thanked Dane and expected one of his teasing remarks about how I could repay him for the favor. Instead he just thanked me for the muffins and apologized that there hadn't been any pasta care packages from him.

Despite my plan to keep things between us as they were, I couldn't leave well enough alone.

"Thanks for the help. Sorry for keeping you away from your *company*." Yes, I was hoping he would say something dismissive about it being over with.

"No problem," he said.

It was a little too cryptic for me and I pushed the envelope. "Then your company is still there?"

All he said was yes as he got in the truck and started the motor.

12

"CASEY, YOU SHOULD HAVE CALLED ME," WILL SAID. "I would have brought the spinning wheels over. It seems a shame to have bothered Dane." It was Thursday morning and we were in the meeting room on the ground floor of the building called Sandpiper. It was one of the original buildings left from when the place had been a camp and there were two floors of guest rooms above the meeting room, which felt like a dark and woodsy living room with a prominent fireplace. The windows looked out on a stand of Monterey pines, but since their foliage was all at the top, they looked more like a stand of poles.

Will wore his usual work uniform of well-worn jeans and a plaid flannel shirt over his tool belt. He looked a little scruffy in a Brad Pitt sort of way, with a day's growth of beard, but it was perfectly understandable under the circumstances. He began to move the furniture and arranged the spinning wheels along the windows. He was doing his best to act as if it was business as usual, but of course, it wasn't. I really wanted to ask him about Nicole, but wasn't sure how. Whether it was suicide or murder, either way he'd lost his wife.

Finally, I stopped him and put a hand on his shoulder in a supportive gesture. "This has to be a very hard time for you. Are you doing okay?" My words seemed to cut through the front he'd been putting up. I saw his whole body sag and he looked at the ground with a big sigh.

"We're waiting for her body to be released. Her family wanted her buried in San Francisco." He glanced toward the spinning wheels. "I hope you got everything you need for the retreat. I'm really sorry you were left hanging."

"Don't worry, I think I have things worked out," I said, not wanting to burden him with my concerns about Wanda. He again told me to take anything I needed from Nicole's studio.

Something had been bothering me since the other night at The Bank when it appeared to have been broken into. The empty velvet backdrop. I began to describe the pieces of jewelry made out of hair and asked if he knew if Nicole had sold them all.

"I don't think so. I don't think she ever intended to sell that stuff. Nicole looked at them as being pieces of fiber art."

Of course, I thought suddenly, seeing them in a new light. After all, what was a lot of yarn but animal hair. As Will continued with his work he kept talking about Nicole and how fanatical she was about collecting textiles and fibers. She bought old yarn and knitting tools at garage sales when they were looking for old pieces of furniture for the shop. It wasn't exactly the information I was after, but he seemed to need to talk. He sounded wistful as he talked about a particular sale they'd gone to.

"One of the bed-and-breakfasts was clearing out a storage area so they could convert it into a studio apartment. We picked up a highboy dresser that had possibilities. Nicole found a bunch of old clothes and stuff in it." Will wrinkled his nose. "The stuff reeked of mildew and I wanted to throw it all out, but she insisted on keeping it." As an afterthought, he mentioned there was a bag of yarn and knitting things in the back of the shop. "Nicole was going to offer them to you for the retreat."

I thanked him, but really wanted to find a way to steer the conversation toward the contents of the supposed suicide note. Will was giving the couches and chairs a final readjustment and I realized he'd be done soon, so I went the direct route.

"I suppose Lieutenant Borgnine questioned you to death," I said, suddenly regretting my choice of words. Will nodded and let out a weary sigh.

"He wanted to know about Nicole's mood and how the shop was doing. And if I knew that Nicole had booked a trip alone."

There was silence for a moment as I realized he was going to leave it at that. "Well, did you know about the trip?" I asked.

"Not exactly. She had talked about wanting to go on some exotic trip, but I had told her I wasn't interested."

"I suppose he asked you what Nicole was referring to in the note," I said, trying to sound casual, but Will's expression darkened.

"Whatever she was doing, it's over with now," he said with a surprisingly harsh edge. The friendly mood was finished and he seemed agitated as he looked around the room. "If you don't need anything else, I have other work to do." I thanked him for his help and wanted to apologize if I'd upset him, but he left before I could. I noticed there was no spring in his step this time.

I went on to the Lodge, where a table had been set up for registration. I set out all the lists of names and made sure the tote bags were lined up and ready to be given out. All the while I was thinking about Will. His mood swing shouldn't have been a complete surprise. It was only natural for him to feel sad and angry at the same time.

One thing I'd learned from working for Frank was not to necessarily take things at face value. Then another thought began to surface. Suppose he was angry for another reason altogether. Will was well liked and had a pristine reputation. If Nicole was doing something bad, he could have worried that it would reflect on him. I had an uneasy feeling as I realized that Will Welton had a motive for murdering his wife.

He certainly had the means. The poison in the coffee was the insecticide he'd mixed up. And he had opportunity. All he would have had to do was say he'd meet her for coffee.

Now I really wanted to find out what Nicole had been up to. I thought back to my trip to her shop with Lucinda. With Will's answer about the hair jewelry pieces, it was clear they hadn't been sold, which meant they'd been stolen. But why? Or, more important, by whom?

I didn't have to start registration for the retreat until the afternoon. And I'd promised to take the early birds into town. We were to meet Lucinda at the Coffee Shop and after, they were going to make a stop at Cadbury Yarn.

I found Olivia, Scott and Bree waiting for me in the seating area of the Lodge. They weren't alone. Olivia was showing two teenagers how to knit. Bree was explaining to one of the yoga people how to make the squares. And I did a double take when I saw Scott. The man in the red polo shirt I'd seen staring at Scott was sitting next to him. The man had a pair of big knitting needles and with Scott's help seemed to be trying to knit a row.

"Maybe you all don't want to go," I said, looking at how busy the three were, but they were all anxious for the trip to the main part of town. I heard them promising to meet up with their new friends later.

"Who'd have thought I'd be teaching someone how to knit," Scott said as he and the two women followed me across the street. "It turns out he'd been fascinated with knitting since he was a kid, but his grandmother told him it wasn't something boys did. When he saw me knitting, he realized his grandmother was wrong." Scott seemed to stand a little taller. "I told him my story and he was inspired and asked me to teach him." Bree and Olivia both gave him a pat on the back. They both had their own stories to tell.

Olivia went first. "Those girls told me knitting was 'the thing' now. It was so much fun being able to show them how."

"My person was a little different," Bree said as a bit of breeze caught her blond curls. "Somebody told her knitting might help her meditation practice. She admitted to me she was having a hard time with her yoga retreat. Everyone else seemed to be a super meditator, but she felt fidgety and kept thinking about her family." Bree went on that the woman's story was similar to hers, having young kids and not being used to traveling on her own. "She was so excited about making the squares. She knew how to knit, but had never thought of it as a calming thing or something that would 'focus her attention.' That seems to be important to meditating." Bree turned to me. "She wanted to know about our retreat. I bet she comes to the next one."

I was so happy with their enthusiasm and for that moment understood why my aunt had started the business. I felt a huge sense of fulfillment. I also had a sense of relief that they weren't talking about Nicole's death. Julius watched from the window as we all piled into the Mini Cooper.

"I understand the whole concept of not having cell phones at Vista Del Mar," Bree said. "But it is really a pain using those pay phones." She was sitting in the front passenger seat and I saw she had her cell phone out before I'd cleared my driveway.

"I wish I'd brought some of my extra yarn and needles. I

would love to have been able to give them to those girls," Olivia said. I was still getting used to the new Olivia. It was like the sun came out on a cloudy day. Her whole face was different. Her brows weren't furrowed and her mouth was no longer an angry slash. Scott brought up the guy in the red polo shirt and said he would have liked to have given him some knitting supplies, too, because he knew the guy would be too embarrassed to go buy them.

"I think I have a solution," I said, remembering Will's mention of stuff Nicole had picked up at the garage sales. I pulled my car into one of the angled spots on Grand Street. "But first we stop at the Coffee Shop."

Lucinda caught up with us just before we reached Maggie's place. My friend and boss was wearing the Ralph Lauren jacket again. She claimed she'd had it for years, but the Indian-like print and the classic design were timeless. An armful of silver bangles jangled as she reached out to hug me.

"I've got stuff to tell you," I said in a whisper. I saw that Olivia, Bree and Scott were all close by, and I whispered that it would have to wait.

The early birds were telling Lucinda about their impromptu lessons as we went inside the Coffee Shop. Maggie was presiding over the counter and the muffin basket was empty and it was barely past eleven.

We picked a small table and Scott grabbed some extra chairs. We'd just sat down when Wanda went past on the street. I saw her look in and before I could blink, she was on her way in the door.

She nodded a greeting at Lucinda and looked over the other three. "You must be some of the pre-retreaters I heard about," she said. "My name is Wanda Krug and I want you to know that I have everything under control and your week-end has been saved from disaster." I was going to step in, but

Wanda was unstoppable. "It's really going to turn out much better for your group. Nicole was clearly in over her head and never could have managed teaching you all how to spin fleece into yarn." Wanda's voice dropped. "It might be why she did what she did to herself." In case they didn't get it, she explained it meant that Nicole had killed herself.

Wanda seemed ready to go into more detail and I was glad when Maggie arrived at the table, interrupting the conversation. I pulled out a chair for Wanda, but she shook her head and marched out the door, saying she had no time to sit around with a coffee klatch.

Maggie waited for everything to settle before taking our orders. "Cappuccinos for you two?" the proprietor said to Lucinda and me. The tomato red of Maggie's top was an eye-grabber, but her smile was so warm, my eye slid right past the bright color and went to her face. We both nodded and she turned to the others and took their requests. When she had all the orders, she gave my shoulder an affectionate pat. "Now sit back and relax and I'll go whip up those drinks." It was a gift how she made all her customers feel like they were her guests.

As soon as she was gone, the three early birds looked at me for an explanation about what Wanda had said. Since she had opened up the topic, there was no reason to hold back anymore.

"I didn't want to bother the three of you with my problems, but yes, Nicole was the center of the Sheep to Shawl retreat." I tried to reassure them that Wanda would do a great job taking over for Nicole.

"And is it true that she killed herself?" Bree asked.

"That's what the official word is," I said. I watched as her sunny expression clouded over.

"If only I'd found her sooner, maybe I could have talked her out of it." Lucinda reached over and gave Bree a comforting pat before turning to me.

Lucinda's head tilted sideways while she studied my expression. "Why am I getting the vibe you don't believe it?"

Bree's brow got even more furrowed. "If it isn't suicide, what is it?"

The rest of the table looked at her and said "murder" in unison. "Oh no," she squealed. I waited to see if she was going to have a meltdown. But she was a changed woman from the first retreat and instead of falling apart, she pulled herself together. "What if the killer passed me on the boardwalk?"

"Did you see anyone while you were walking?" I prodded. She thought for a moment and then shook her head.

"It seems like everybody just takes the boardwalk to the beach. I've taken that path before and only passed a few people." She seemed to be straining to think. "Maybe I did see someone," she said suddenly. "Or at least their back. I remember now looking ahead and seeing someone in the far distance scurrying along." She raised her shoulders in an apologetic shrug. "It was before I found Nicole, so it didn't occur to me that it would be important or I would have paid better attention." The sound of the espresso machine made her jump. "What a scary thought. What if the killer had met me first? I could have been the victim." She seemed close to tears as she talked about her boys growing up without their mother. Then she wanted to know what had killed Nicole.

Hearing it was poison in Nicole's drink seemed to reassure Bree. "There's no way I would have taken a drink from a stranger. Stranger danger—that's what I tell my boys all the time. No, if a stranger had offered me a cup of coffee I never would have taken it."

"I don't think you understand," I said to the young mother. "I think Nicole was a deliberate target." I told them about what her husband had said about her being involved with something bad. We brainstormed for a moment about what it might be. It was hard since three of the people at the table had never even met the victim, though I described her shop.

We came up with counterfeit antiques. Smuggling drugs in the old quilts she had for sale. "Diamonds are always good," Olivia said. "Maybe she was fencing stolen jewelry."

"All good ideas," I said, "but I'd knock out the fencing-stolen-jewelry concept. The only jewelry in the place were some creepy pieces made with woven hair." I was going to mention that they'd gone missing, but Maggie arrived with our drinks.

"I heard you talking about hair jewelry." The proprietor began to set our drinks in front of us. "It's definitely not my taste. But Nicole seemed very fond of the style." When she had finished handing out the drinks, Maggie folded the tray under her arm. "She brought in a necklace to show me."

I asked Maggie what it looked like. "The chain was silver. The pendant had the woven hair." She held up her thumb and forefinger to indicate the size and said it was heart shaped.

"Was it a locket?" I asked.

"I think so. I do remember that it looked pretty beat-up. Nicole asked me a lot of questions about it. Like had I ever seen it before."

Maggie seemed about to walk away. I put my hand out to stop her. "Had you ever seen it before?" I asked.

"I'll tell you the same thing I told her. I have a definite memory of seeing someone wearing it all the time." She glanced toward the door as it opened and a couple walked in. "But no memory of who it was. Believe me, I racked my brain. Nicole was very persistent. It seemed to bother her no end that I could remember how my customers liked their drinks but couldn't remember who the necklace had belonged to."

The new arrivals were speaking German and taking pictures of everything. Clearly tourists. Maggie excused herself and eased back behind the counter. A moment later, there was a fuss going on.

It had something to do with confusion over their order as Maggie held a red paper cup with a sleeve around it in each hand while trying to understand what they wanted. One of the young men reached across the counter, took the cups out of her hand. Scott thought it was some kind of threat and jumped up to intervene.

The tourist ignored Scott and let the cardboard sleeves fall off the cup and hit the floor. Shaking his head vehemently, he made a big X out of his arms. Then his fellow traveler smiled as he took the cups and dropped one cup inside the other. Both men nodded with exaggerated approval.

"Now I get it," Maggie said with a friendly laugh.

"I'm glad *she* understood," Scott said when he returned to the table.

Lucinda looked at her watch as she drank the last of the foam on her coffee drink. "I have to go. I am going to work lunch in the restaurant and help Tag get ready for dinner, then I'll be at Vista Del Mar to check in for the retreat."

"We all have to go," I said. Scott, Olivia and Bree stood and said they were off to Cadbury Yarn.

"Some people collect snow globes when they travel. With me, it's yarn," Olivia said, and the others nodded in agreement. They asked me to join them, but I said there was something I had to take care of.

I walked with Lucinda as far as the Blue Door. There were already people standing on the small porch, waiting to be seated. As Lucinda rushed up the stairs to get to work, I realized I still hadn't had a chance to tell her about Dane and his company.

13

WHEN I WAS ALONE, I HEADED UP THE STREET TO
The Bank. I had the key and even with Will's mini-outburst,
he hadn't rescinded his offer for the bag of yarn and knitting
supplies, which would be perfect to use for making the
squares.

As I turned the key in the front door of Nicole's shop and
studio, I felt a wave of apprehension, remembering the other
night and the disarray I'd found. Once I was inside, I quickly
turned on the lights and looked around. There was a big empty
space where the spinning wheels had been, but other than
that the interior looked the same as when Dane and I had left
it the previous night.

I went to the back of the studio where the spinning wheels
had been and began to look around for the bag of yarn and
supplies. The basket of yarn seemed more for decoration and
had some samples of handspun yarn. I regretted not asking
Will exactly where it was. I went behind the partition into the

area Nicole seemed to have used as a private space. At first I
thought there was nothing there, but then I noticed the two
cubicles. I opened the door on one and noted that the small
room seemed to be a storage area. I saw a shopping bag filled
to the top with balls of yarn. Another bag sat next to it and
when I checked, I saw it held a hodgepodge of knitting needles, stitch holders and assorted accessories. Sure that this
was what Will had referred to, I started to pick up the bags.
My back hit something and when I turned, I saw a dresser
with the drawers pulled out. Hadn't Will said something about
a dresser they'd bought at a garage sale? As I stepped closer
to get a better look at the tall piece, I caught a whiff of a
mildewy scent. It was clearly coming from the cardboard box
on the other side of the dresser.

I looked over the top of it and saw it seemed to be full of
old clothes. Will had mentioned that, too. I thought back to
what he'd said. Something about wanting to throw it all out,
but Nicole wanted to keep the stuff. He thought she'd planned
to refurbish the fabric.

When I examined the item on top, I wondered how true
that was. Not only was it limp and a little slimy, the man's
dress shirt hardly seemed worth the trouble of saving. But
why else would she have kept the box of stuff? Then something Nicole had said to me floated through my mind. She'd
said locked cabinets were a red flag there was something
valuable inside and how she kept valuable things here no one
would look. This box definitely qualified as that. Who would
think there was anything of importance in a box of stinky
fabrics?

It was like dealing with Julius's stink fish all over again.
Holding my nose, I began to unpack the box. I took out the
man's shirt. It was hard to tell how old it was, as men's clothes
weren't as stylized as women's. Below it, I found some old

linen tablecloths and embroidered hand towels, then more clothes. The yellowing undershirts must have been white once. I picked up and dropped with a loud "ick" the yellowy pair of men's underwear. There was no clue to how old they were. That style of briefs had been around for years. The fabric felt clammy from years of absorbing moisture and I wished I were wearing some kind of gloves.

To speed matters up, I lifted everything out of the box and put it on the ground. I took the container closer to the overhead light and looked inside. Nothing. Maybe she had just kept the stuff with the hopes of dealing with it in the future. I started to lift everything back into the box, but had an idea.

I flipped over the stack of clothes and began to go through the contents piece by piece, putting each thing back in the box after I'd looked at it. The bottom items were definitely highest on the moldy factor. I quickly dropped them back in with only a cursory glance. And then as I peeled back a moth-eaten navy blue sweater, something fell out and hit the ground with a ping.

I checked the floor around me and found a key. After separating a few more items, I found a silver hairbrush and then a photograph stuck in an envelope with *Our Baby* written on the front. It was an old color print. Time and all that moisture had distorted the colors, but I could still make out the image of a baby. I continued going through the stack of clothes and a heart-shaped locket tumbled out. I had another *ick* response when I turned it over and saw that the front was covered in a pattern of woven hair. Even so, I opened it. The tiny black-and-white photo of the baby was still clear and seemed to be the same baby as the one in the faded photograph. Could this be the locket Maggie had mentioned? I could certainly see why Nicole wouldn't have displayed it in the condition it was in. Nicole probably had just been curious and that was why she'd asked Maggie about it. Nothing else showed up as I finished going through the smelly material.

I laid the items on the floor and examined them for some kind of identification. There was nothing to indicate whom they'd belonged to or, more important, what they meant. Or if they meant anything. Maybe I was seeing plots where there weren't any. The random items might have been in the dresser and ended up with the other stuff. Not sure what else to do with them, I took out some of the clothes and buried the items between the moth-eaten navy blue sweater and a pair of the men's briefs.

I'd lost track of time and remembered my group. I quickly rearranged everything to look like it had when I'd found it, grabbed the bags of yarn and supplies and closed the door to the small cubicle.

Finally, I turned off the lights and locked up before rushing to meet up with my group.

14

AS OLIVIA, SCOTT AND BREE CLIMBED INTO MY CAR, I showed off the stash of yarn and needles I'd gotten from Nicole's place. Olivia offered to take charge of it and hand things out as needed. By the time we'd driven back to Vista Del Mar, Scott had already extracted a pair of number 8 needles and a skein of gray worsted-weight yarn. I'd barely stopped the car in front of the Lodge when he hopped out and headed toward the dining room.

"I want to see this," Olivia said, getting out of the backseat. Without anyone explaining, I knew the "this" she was talking about was Scott presenting the knitting supplies to his red-polo-shirted friend.

"I hope it works out," Bree said as she got out of the other side. "Scott seems to have forgotten how secretive he used to be about his knitting."

I quickly parked the car and stopped the engine. I wanted to see what was going to happen, too, but for another reason.

If one of my retreaters made trouble with a retreater from another group, was I going to get the blame?

I started to sprint across the grounds toward the Sea Foam dining hall, imagining all kinds of scenarios. Just as I was passing the Lodge, the door opened and Lieutenant Borgnine walked out. I wanted to continue on to the dining hall, but I wondered what he was doing there.

I screeched to a stop and backed up.

"Ms. Feldstein," he said, nodding with a cursory greeting before walking on. He was holding up his cell phone, grumbling about not being able to get a signal. At least for him, the unplugged idea seemed to be having the opposite effect Kevin St. John intended. The cop seemed stressed. He looked even more stressed when he realized I'd changed directions and was walking beside him.

"Are you here about Nicole Welton's death?" I asked.

"Still with the questions," he said, looking at his phone one last time as if by some magic it might suddenly get a signal; then he jammed it into his pocket.

Undaunted that he'd ignored my question, I persisted. "I'm sure you checked the fingerprints on the paper cup found at the crime scene." I thought phrasing it as a statement rather than a question might sit better with him, but if anything it seemed to make him more on edge.

"Ms. Feldstein, I am very complete in my investigations. Of course we checked the fingerprints on the coffee cup along with determining where it came from. The fingerprints belonged to the victim and the proprietor of the Coffee Shop, just as expected." He seemed almost angry with himself for answering.

I should have quit while I was ahead. I had actually gotten an answer from him. But I couldn't resist. "The fact that you're here must mean the case is still open," I said. I saw his eyes go skyward and he started to walk faster, but so did I. His blue-and-white cruiser was just ahead. We were still neck and neck when he pulled open the door.

I thought he was going to get in and slam the door to punctuate his displeasure, but instead he looked me in the eye and spoke in a terse voice. "I was just here tying up loose ends. Nothing has changed. Nicole Welton's death is still being considered a suicide." He leaned down to get in. "So, then, there is nothing for you to investigate and there is no reason for you to ask me any more questions." He glanced back toward the Lodge as the Vista Del Mar van pulled up and began to empty. "Don't you have some kind of retreat to run?"

He mustn't have been expecting an answer, because before I said anything he was in the car, and a moment later he was backing out, coming within a hairbreadth of grazing me. It was too bad that he didn't realize we were really on the same side.

I had used up my time to check out the action in the dining hall. I just hoped that there hadn't been a big scene when Scott gave his friend the needles. Or if there was, that Kevin St. John wasn't there to witness it. I left the Mini Cooper parked on the grounds and dashed across the street.

It was time to take on the look of a retreat director. That was the title I thought best described me. I didn't want anything too authoritative-looking, like a suit, but a step up from my usual outfit of comfortably loose jeans and a stretchy top was in order. I had already planned the outfit, so it was just a matter of putting it on and doing my makeup and hair.

Julius slipped out as I left to go back across the street, wearing black pants with a white shirt hanging loose. I had made sure to add something from the accessories my aunt had knit and crocheted. The bracelet made of granny squares seemed perfect. The yarn seemed very fine and Crystal from Cadbury Yarn had explained it was crochet thread. I'd finished off the look with a black knitted wrap dotted with sewn-on small red crocheted flowers. One of my fleece jackets would have felt warmer, but I was learning that sometimes you had to give up comfort for the "look."

I let out a sigh of relief as I pulled out the chair to the registration table. I did a last-minute check. The tote bags were ready, the folders were complete with schedules, lists of activities at Vista Del Mar, a name tag and a meal ticket. A cluster of women were standing with their suitcases near the registration counter. As soon as they saw me at my table, they began to move toward it en masse.

"Showtime," I muttered to myself, putting on my most professional manner. This was a whole different situation than the Petit Retreat I'd put on with only a handful of people. The women formed a line. Before I could deal with the first person, the line had gotten longer. I realized my aunt probably would have had help.

The first woman stepped forward and I welcomed her, noting her rust-colored hair. Since I didn't think any of them knew who Nicole was, I had simply gone through all the programs and crossed out her name and written in Wanda's. There was no reason to mention what had happened to Nicole. It wasn't a happy note to start on.

"I'm so excited to be here," the woman said, writing her name on her name tag. She had already become "the Ginger" in my mind, whatever her name turned out to be. "I came up from San Diego." She was looking around as she pinned the name tag on. She stared at a sign by the door. "It says there's no cell service here?" Her expression began to crumble.

I pointed out the phone booths and she began to talk about how retro it was. Meanwhile I could see the women behind her beginning to shift their weight and look around—a sure sign they were getting impatient.

I tried to wrap things up, but she kept going on while I was mentally berating myself for not figuring out that everyone would arrive at once.

Out of the corner of my eye, I saw Olivia's almond-shaped face. She pulled a chair next to me and sat down. "I saw how swamped you were," she said, taking the sheets with the first part of the alphabet. She quickly made a card showing which letters she had.

"But this is supposed to be your retreat," I protested. I didn't say it, but I was thinking that she was paying me for this time.

"This is part of the retreat for me," she said. "It makes me feel useful."

Scott came in from the other side and took the last part of the alphabet and the line began to move and now I didn't feel bad spending time talking to each person as I checked them in.

Scott was beaming as he explained to each of his people that he was a knitter and would be attending the retreat right along with them.

Bree was working the line. I heard her apologizing for the wait and doing a pitch on what a great time they were going to have.

A young woman moved up to the table and looked at the three sections. "Fiore," she said with a question in her expression. I raised my hand and she stepped up in front of me. I looked down the page as I picked up one of the folders.

"Welcome, Ronny," I said when I found her name and information. I noticed that she listed an address in Monterey. "You're local. Most of the retreaters came from a longer distance." I looked at her name again. "I just met someone with the same last name the other day. Burton Fiore."

"He's my father," she said. It was hard to see any resemblance, since he had a mustache and she didn't. It suddenly struck me that she was going to be Cora Delacorte's stepdaughter.

While I handed her a tote bag, I gave her a once-over. The first thing I noticed was that she had an air of authority about her, as though she was used to being in charge of something. Her light brown hair was slicked back into a low bun with nary a loose wisp. Her clothes were casual, but there was almost a suitlike quality to the dark blue denim pleated slacks and the boxy-shaped sweater over a neat white shirt. She had the same manner as her father, looking around the cavernous room as if she were taking measurements.

It all began to make sense when she explained she was the assistant manager of a hotel in Monterey near the wharf. "I thought it would be nice to be a guest for a change," she said. "I've heard a lot about this property." She glanced past my shoulder through the large window that looked out onto the wooden deck and beyond to the boardwalk as it began to wind through the dunes.

"Is that where it happened?"

I was taken aback by her comment. "Then you knew her?"

Ronny seemed cautious with her words. "I wouldn't say I exactly knew her, but I have been in her shop. I can't believe she's dea—ah . . . not going to be here." The young woman looked around her to see if anyone had heard. "I was looking forward to learning how to spin from her. She seemed very accomplished." Something in the young woman's tone didn't go with her words. She didn't sound like she regretted Nicole's absence from the retreat or, for that matter, the world. She might not have known Nicole well, but it was clear she certainly didn't like her.

I pointed out the registration desk and said she could pick

up her room key. She gave the Lodge's main room another sweeping glance. "It's such an interesting place with so many possibilities."

"But you're here because you're interested in yarn craft, right?" I said. In answer she held up a small tote bag with a Hawaiian floral print. I could see some beige yarn with a pair of large-size needles sticking in it.

"Of course. Why else would I be here?" She stepped aside for the next person in line.

15

THE GREAT THING ABOUT HOLDING THE RETREATS at Vista Del Mar was that the hotel and conference center included meals in the Sea Foam dining hall, there were plenty of spots for impromptu knitting groups to gather, and they offered a number of activities that fit nicely around the actual yarn workshops.

I had hastily redone the first page of the schedule and taken out the planned parade of sheep and the shearing that was supposed to have kicked off the retreat that afternoon. For now the afternoon was listed as free time, with suggestions of activities and the official beginning of the program was to take place after dinner.

I had left the description of the program's beginning vague because I didn't know what it was going to be. As I passed the grassy circle between the Lodge and the beginning of the dunes where the gathering was supposed to take place, I was still trying to figure out how I was going to explain the lack of sheep.

I was so deep in thought I didn't realize anyone had come up behind me until Dr. Sammy spoke.

"What's up, Case," he said. I turned, expecting him to make flowers pop out of my hair or coins from my ears, but he had his hands in the pockets of his very formal-looking jeans. He had told me it was the thing now for doctors to wear jeans so they would seem less imposing, but the white coat they wore over the casual pants kind of blew the concept.

Sammy had left his white coat at his office and wore an unzipped dark red fleece jacket over the very new and stiff-looking pants.

"Not much, other than my main instructor isn't going to be here and the main event that was going to take place to start things off isn't going to happen."

Sammy took a step closer. "That's a good way to explain Nicole Welton's absence," he said. "Much better than saying she committed suicide."

"About that," I began. "As a doctor, if you wanted to kill somebody, how effective do you think it would be to add poison to their coffee?"

"Geez, Case. You sure have a way with small talk. First of all, I would never want to kill anybody. I'm a lover not a fighter," he said, looking at me with his soulful puppy dog eyes. "And since I'm a urologist, I usually deal with the other end." He considered what I'd said for a moment. "But if I did want to off somebody with poisoned coffee, I'd make sure to add a lot of a fast-acting poison like cyanide and I'd add a lot of milk and sugar to cover up any bad taste."

"Now a question for your magician side," I said. "How would you get this big dose of poison in the paper coffee cup without getting your fingerprints on it?"

Sammy answered quickly. "The most obvious answer is to wear gloves."

"Right, but would you take a cup of coffee from someone if they were wearing gloves?"

"That's if the killer brought her the coffee. Maybe she brought the coffee with her."

"And Nicole wouldn't notice someone wearing gloves monkeying with her cup?"

"You have a point," my ex-boyfriend said. "Why are you so certain it wasn't a suicide? Wasn't there a note?"

"On a smartphone. I didn't see the actual screen, but it said she was doing something bad and couldn't take it anymore." I took out my phone and started fiddling around with it. I found an app that was for notes. I wrote something as a test and then set the phone down to see what would happen. Eventually the screen went dark, but when I reactivated it, it went right to the note. I held it up to show Sammy. "I guess it could work." I mentioned that the fingerprints were all smudged, though I didn't tell him Dane had been the one to tell me. I knew Sammy would get all mopey about me spending time with my neighbor.

"Case, if a killer thinks enough to use gloves to handle a coffee cup, I'm sure they would think to wipe off a screen after they typed on it." His face brightened. "I like that you're asking for my help. Particularly my magician skills." His expression dipped when he said the last part.

"Okay, what's wrong?" I said, easily reading his face.

"You caught me. I'm trying to give off the illusion of confidence, but I'm nervous about this weekend. I'm not so sure about doing table magic. That's why I'm here. I want to walk through the dining hall and get an idea of who my audience is again."

"You're the master," I said. "I've watched you wowing people over and over. You'll do fine. At least you're in control of your tricks." I told him how my grand beginning had been ixnayed and instead of sheep, all I had was a pile of fleeces.

"Don't worry," he said, "I'm sure it will work out just like you said my magic will. Thanks for the words of encouragement. It's like I always say, Case, you're the only one who gets me." He had a hopeful look in his eyes. "I did a sample show at the B and B," he said. "I should have had you come."

Sammy's relocation to Cadbury was on a trial basis and he was still living at the bed-and-breakfast across the street from the Blue Door restaurant. I was glad I could reassure him, but worried that I was leading him on a road to nowhere. I cared about Sammy. I really did. There just wasn't that sizzle, and having my parents' stamp of approval all over him didn't help, either. We both had places to go and I got ready to go my separate way.

I always wondered how to say good-bye to him. Just the words weren't enough, but some big romantic moment was way too much. I settled by giving him a hug and like always he hugged back more than I gave.

As I went across the street to my place, I looked down toward Dane's. I saw him opening the passenger door on his truck. He helped a woman get out and then put his arm around her as they walked toward his house. I strained my eyes to get a better look, but they were too far away for me to make out much more than that it looked pretty serious between them. I tried to tell myself I didn't care, but the trouble was, I did.

When dinner ended, I was waiting in the grassy circle holding a sign saying YARN2GO YARN RETREAT, hoping for the best. I hadn't come up with anything more than giving a welcoming speech and trying to excite them about the upcoming workshops.

My group separated from the rest of the guests filtering out of the Sea Foam dining hall and began to gather around me. Lucinda came out of the Lodge and greeted me with a hug. She had just finished checking in and stowing her suitcase. I was glad for the moral support. Kevin St. John's golf cart arrived with its whiney sound. He parked on the paved small road that surrounded the grassy circle and got out. He stayed to the back and I wasn't sure why he was there. Did he think I was going to try to sneak in the sheep or was he just there to gloat over the dismal start of the retreat?

He seemed to have taken a new tack to getting me to hand over the retreat business. Instead of saying anything directly, he was doing everything he could to make it difficult for me, but not so unreasonably that I would go to the Delacorte sisters and complain.

When everyone was there, I put down the sign and did my best to speak loudly. "I want to welcome you to what I hope is going to be a fun learning experience, and a chance to get away from the busyness of your own lives and enjoy this rustic location." Okay, so I may have borrowed some of Virgil Scarantino's words, but I was looking for whatever I could to pump things up. "There will also be lots of time for you to work with yarn on your own projects," I said, trying to make it sound like a bonus.

"I had hoped to have some sheep here, so we could begin with an actual shearing, but due to some . . ." I stopped talking as something seemed to be moving through the group. I watched people step aside to let it pass. There was also some kind of noise that was somewhere between whining and singing. I began to make out some words. It sounded like a cock-eyed version of "The Whiffenpoof Song."

"I'm just a poor lost sheep who's here to give you my wool," a woeful voice intoned. The crowd parted and something wool-covered crawled through. But not totally covered. I saw the bottoms of Sammy's too-new jeans. As he lumbered into the circle, he launched full force into his version of the song. "I'm a poor little lamb . . ." (It was hard not to laugh at that line considering how big Sammy was. I could see now that it had taken two of the fleeces to cover him.) ". . . who's kind of a ham. Baa, baa, baa. Just a nice little sheep with wool you can keep. Baa, baa, baa." It was followed by a lot of *baa*s and ended with, "I'm just a poor little lamb, that's who I am. Baa baa baa."

Kevin St. John had started to react when the first sign of something woolly came through the crowd. He shot an angry look at me as he moved forward to stop the rogue animal. Did he really think I would ignore his command? But when the singing started, he stopped short and tried to make it look like he was doing something else.

"It looks like one of the sheep showed up after all," I said as the faux sheep stopped next to me and with a flourish took off the sheets with the fleeces on them with a loud "ta-da!"

Sammy winked at me before he took a bow. "Case, I wanted you to have a grand beginning."

Laughter broke out in the group, followed by applause, and Sammy took another bow. When I looked, Kevin St. John had gotten into his golf cart and driven away.

Sammy stayed next to me as I finished my speech and told them where we'd meet in the morning. He took the opportunity to remind them he'd be doing table magic in the dining hall over the weekend and took another hammy bow. Everyone seemed pleased with his performance and I heard someone shout out "Bravo!" though I'm pretty sure it was Lucinda.

When the group broke up, numerous people stopped and complimented me on the fun beginning. Bree, Olivia and Scott came up together and said the Sammy thing had come off as if it was planned.

Lucinda hung back with me as Sammy helped me roll up the fleeces in the sheets. I thanked him again and said he had saved the beginning. He seemed a little unhappy that I wasn't alone.

"I was hoping you could express your thanks with a drink." He gestured toward the café windows in the Lodge building.

"I'm afraid I'm going to have to give you a rain check," I said.

"When?" he asked so quickly even Lucinda chuckled.

"How about Sunday night. I'll be finished with the retreat and you'll have completed your first weekend of magic. We can toast our accomplishments."

"It's a date," Sammy said, looking so happy it made me want to cry.

There was a cheery spring in his step as he walked away. Lucinda watched me watch him. "I think Dane has some competition."

"Don't be silly. There is nothing with either of them," I protested. She tilted her head and gave me a knowing look.

"Okay, I admit that Sammy always coming through like this does get to me. But that's as far as it goes. And Dane"—I made something between a *huh* sound and an incredulous laugh—"he's too busy with his company."

"Company?" Lucinda's face lit up with interest. I finally got to tell her about my awkward moment with Dane.

"He's not even holding his karate workshops?" she said incredulously. Her expression changed to sympathy as she touched my arm. "I'm sorry." I tried to tell her it didn't matter and was for the best anyway, but she gave me another knowing look. She didn't have to say the words; I knew what she was thinking: I was protesting too much.

16

AS LUCINDA AND I PASSED THE SOCIAL HALL, I SAW
Ronny Fiore walking alone ahead of us. I quickly explained
who she was before we caught up with her. After I'd done the
introductions, I mentioned that Virgil Scarantino would be
talking about the background of Vista Del Mar and leading
a night hike. "And I'm sure there will be groups of knitters
and crocheters gathering in the Lodge." I pointed to the large
dark wood building we'd just passed.

"How quaint," she said. "It's just like my father said. This
place really is more camp than resort." Her gaze swept the
grounds to the small chapel up ahead, next to the beginning
of the dunes. "That's where they're getting married," she said.
When I didn't get it immediately, she explained she meant
her father and Cora Delacorte.

"Is she going to change her name?" I asked. Ronny shook
her head.

"On one hand she's old-fashioned and thinks married

women should take their husband's name, but at the same time the Delacorte name means too much in this town, so she's going to keep it. What's the difference? We're all going to be family anyway. I'm sure Cora will be glad to have our help with all her responsibilities. People think it's the sisters, but Cora is the one in charge."

Kevin St. John came down the stairs of the Lodge. His dark suit and tie still looked impeccable despite his long day. "Good evening, Ms. Feldstein and Mrs. Thornkill," he said in a managerial tone. I introduced Ronny Fiore, but didn't explain who she was. He turned on the charm and said he hoped she enjoyed her stay and asked if there was anything he could do. She responded with a knowing smile.

The manager and Cora Delacorte's stepdaughter-to-be both went on their way. He took off in his golf cart and she went in the direction of the dark wood-shingled buildings that held the guest rooms. With the cloudy sky there was no splash of orange and pink as it got dark. Instead it was like someone was slowly turning a dimmer switch.

"Do you think she's planning on taking over his job?" Lucinda asked when they were both out of earshot.

"That and more. Can Cora be so naive?"

"Maybe I should talk to her. I know a little about late-in-life marriage." Lucinda caught herself. "Did I really say 'late in life'? For her, maybe. My marriage was more like middle-age madness." Lucinda explained that she and Tag had drawn up a whole agreement before they got married since both had children with their previous spouses and stuff they had accumulated.

"You heard what Ronny said. Cora is old-fashioned and he's probably done a whole number on her about a husband's duties and sold her on the idea that he'll take care of her. She might be so starry-eyed, she'll hand over the control of everything." I thought a moment. "You're right, somebody should talk to her."

"But would she even listen if she's bought into the whole romance thing?" Lucinda brought up how her daughter had tried to point out some of Tag's quirks, like having to have everything lined up perfectly. "But did I listen? All I remembered was how I'd felt about him in high school and thought this was our chance at happily ever after. And I thought he would change once we were actually married." She sighed. "You would think I would know better by now. But even with the quirks, I'm still glad we're together."

The lights along the path came on. They were meant just to mark the edge of the narrow road and did little to light up the area. All the tall Monterey pines and bushy Monterey cypress trees blocked out the sky, making it seem even darker. There was a bite to the damp air and as usual it smelled of wood smoke from all the fireplaces. The last of the stragglers were gone and the lights from the Lodge shone through the windows with a welcoming glow.

"I guess we're done here," I said and made mention of stopping at my place before I went off to the Blue Door to do my baking. Lucinda pulled her Ralph Lauren jacket closer around her.

"I feel guilty going off to have a good time," she said. "We could have just done the ice cream desserts during the retreat, like last time."

"And go through Tag's tantrum again about the menu saying the desserts were homemade and the ice cream being store-bought? A promise is a promise," I said, though at the moment, I thought her idea sounded pretty good.

Lucinda hugged me. "Thank you, Casey. I didn't want to say anything, but people were upset during the last retreat when there weren't any of your desserts. We have people ordering their dessert when they make a reservation. They don't even ask what it is; they just want to be sure to get a piece of whatever before it runs out."

I must admit I loved the praise. Since I was a self-taught baker, it made me feel more confident. Lucinda went off toward her room to get her tote bag of knitting supplies. A group had agreed to meet in the lodge to do their yarn work and get to know one another.

I walked through the Lodge both because it was a shortcut and because I wanted to see this group she was talking about. I was surprised to see that Olivia seemed to be the center of it. The two long tables had been pushed together and she'd set out a stack of directions for the squares, along with some of the yarn I'd gotten from Nicole's.

Scott and his friend from the business group were sitting in a couple of the mission-style chairs, knitting. Several of the men in red polo shirts were stopped next to them, watching in amazement. I couldn't hear the words, but the body language said it all. Scott and his friend were pitching the guys on the wonders of yarn work.

Bree was sitting with the woman I'd called the Ginger. The redheaded woman seemed upset, but Bree seemed to be reassuring her. How nice to have them all helping out.

Virgil Scarantino was standing in the corner near a large sign announcing his night walk. I checked the group gathered near him to see if any of them were from my group. The yoga people were easy to pick out. They were all in stretchy pants and barely wearing shoes. The matching polo shirts gave away the business retreaters. The only person I recognized from my group was Ronny Fiore. She seemed to be listening intently to what Virgil was saying as if she was expecting to be tested on it afterward.

I stepped closer to hear what was so interesting. He was

in midsentence, but I quickly picked up that he was talking about the history of Vista Del Mar. I'd heard bits and pieces of it before, but was still curious about what he had to say.

My ears perked up when he began to talk about Edmund Delacorte. "He ran this place until his death." He gestured around the great room and commented on how the place looked very much the same as it had in the old days. He went on about how much the Delacorte brother had loved the place and wanted it to stay just as it was. He'd intended for his son to follow in his footsteps. Then he veered off to talking about Monterey Bay and what a mess it had been thanks to the Delacorte family and their sardine cannery. "Edmund felt personally responsible and helped spearhead the movement that turned the bay around."

I remembered how Cora had said Edmund would be happy with the "unplugged" idea. Now it made sense. I could tell Virgil was getting to the end of his talk by the rhythm of his speech, and moved in closer. There was a small round of applause when he finished and then the group began to make their way toward the doors for the actual hike. I snagged Virgil as he followed behind them.

"That was very interesting about Edmund Delacorte. I didn't even know he existed a couple of days ago and now his name keeps coming up." I mentioned our trip to the sheep ranch and Virgil commented on how it had been a favorite spot of the Delacorte brother's. I didn't mention what a hunk Edmund was, but as I was speaking I was picturing the photo of him on horseback as he leaned forward. His expression was what I think in model language was referred to as making love to the camera.

"Did you ever meet Edmund?" I asked. Virgil was well into his seventies, which made him close enough in age to the Delacorte brother that their paths could have crossed.

"I would say it was more a matter of knowing who he was."
Virgil chuckled. "We weren't exactly in the same social strata.
The Delacorte family has always been like our local royalty.
Of course, I saw him at the bank." Virgil reminded me that
he'd been a banker before he retired.

"There was a time when he came in every Friday, dependable as a railroad clock. Just before I went to lunch, I'd let him
into his safety-deposit box."

I started to ask for more details, but he looked down at his
pocket watch. "Showtime," he said with a happy smile. "I like
to think I'm as dependable as a railroad clock, too."

SATISFIED THAT MY GROUP WAS OKAY, I WENT
across the street for a breather before I went to the Blue Door
to begin baking. I had left a window open so Julius could
come and go as he pleased. The fluffy black cat greeted me
at the kitchen door when I came in.

He jumped up on the counter and rubbed against me. I
gave him some pets and he began to purr loudly. It was nice
to have someone welcome me home even if I was pretty sure
he had an ulterior motive.

The bowl of Tasty Treats dry cat food I'd left for him
looked untouched. Julius dropped to the floor and began to
parade back and forth in front of the refrigerator.

I pointed to the bowl of cat food and encouraged him to
at least try it. I even took out one of the pieces and tried to
feed it to him. He turned away as if I were offering him
poison.

In the end we had dinner together. I had a frozen version
of enchiladas and he had stink fish. What can I say? I was
putty in his paws.

I had noticed it was all quiet down the street. Another night

Dane wasn't hosting the karate group. I knew how he felt about those teens. Whatever was going on had to be really serious if he wasn't letting them hang out in his garage.

All the information I'd gotten in the past couple of days was floating around in my brain. I considered knocking on Dane's door. Hadn't he said he was always available for cups of sugar or investigative advice? Was I out of my mind? Since I couldn't talk to Dane, I called Frank.

"Feldstein, these calls from you seem to be turning into a regular event. What's up now?" Frank said. He was doing the gruff-voice thing, but I wasn't buying it. I heard the squeak of the recliner and pictured him straining to push it back farther as the chair protested. One of these days, he was going to push it too far. I always had this picture that somehow when it broke it would catapult him into space, but in reality it would probably drop him on the floor.

"It's the woman who drank the insecticide in her coffee," I said.

"The cops are still calling it suicide, huh, and you're still not buying it?"

"You tell me," I began. "First of all, why come to Vista Del Mar if she wanted to kill herself? She could have taken the coffee back to her shop and done the deed there."

"Except, didn't you say the insecticide came from some stuff her husband had in a shed on the grounds? Maybe that's why she did it there. That's where the poison was."

I slumped at his answer. "Okay, that's possible, but I still say someone isn't going to put down a deposit on a trip they really want to take just before they kill themself." Before Frank could say anything, I said it for him. "I know. She could have been so upset about putting down the deposit that it pushed her over the edge, but the travel agent said she seemed happy about planning the trip."

"So then, Feldstein, let's just assume it was murder. I kind of recall you said she was in some kind of trouble. Any news on that front?"

"The so-called suicide note said she was doing something bad," I said.

"Right," Frank said. "And I pointed out that even if it was written by the killer, it might be true."

"Whatever it was, it's over with, according to her husband," I said.

I heard Frank let out a big *hmmm*. "So obviously he knows whatever she was up to. And—"

"He could have killed her to make it end," I said, interrupting. I told Frank how well liked Will was. "There's a lot of weird stuff going on," I began. "I found some things hidden in a box of moldy clothes and it looked like her shop might have been broken into, but the only thing missing was a tray of jewelry made out of hair."

"Jewelry made out of hair? What happened to diamonds and gold?" I heard Frank let out a chortle.

"Burton Fiore was looking at that stuff," I said, suddenly remembering seeing him in Nicole's shop.

"Who's he?" Frank asked, sounding confused. It didn't get any better when I mentioned that he was engaged to Cora Delacorte and that his daughter was one of my retreaters. "Never mind," I said, cutting myself off from explaining who everyone was. "The important thing is Burton Fiore came into Nicole's shop while I was there. They seemed to be handling some kind of transaction," I said.

Frank still sounded confused. "And what's strange about a transaction going on in a store? Feldstein, nothing personal, but I think you might be losing it."

"I didn't explain it right. He gave her an envelope, but she didn't give him anything in return."

"I get where you're going now, Feldstein. The envelope that Burton What's His Name gave her could have had some cash in it. And if she didn't give him anything in return then it could have been some kind of . . ." We both said "black-mail" at the same time.

"And that would explain how Nicole had the money for the trip to Bhutan," I said.

"So maybe this Fiore guy gets tired of paying her or she ups the ante and he figures out a way to make that his final payment," Frank said. "Why don't you go down the street and tell that story to your cop friend," Frank said. When I didn't say anything, Frank continued, "What's up, Feldstein, are you on the outs with him? It's a fine line doing the flirting thing and then not letting it go anywhere. Maybe in the old days, but nowadays, I think they stop falling for it if no nookie follows."

"Forget about him and nookie. It's irrelevant," I said. "There's a major thing missing. Like any sort of proof. I never saw what was in the envelope."

"Feldstein, I'm sure you'll figure it out." There was a lot of background noise coming from his end. When I heard squeaking followed by footsteps, I figured he'd gotten up from his chair. "If you want my advice, I'd find out what she was black-mailing him about." I heard a door open and Frank said hello to somebody. Before I could thank him, Frank said he had to go. I heard a woman's voice in the background. Did she call him honey? Oh my God, Frank had a date.

I needed to get off the phone anyway. I was anxious to get going on the baking. Staying at the Blue Door till all hours and then distributing muffins around town while the town slept was much less appealing when I had to be back at Vista Del Mar early in the morning.

The restaurant was still open when I got there. Tag was doing the host thing and walking around the tables and checking on the last of the diners. I cringed when I noticed him rearrange the knife one of the patrons had set down on his plate. Lucinda would have had a fit if she'd seen it.

The chef looked up as I came into the kitchen with my bag of supplies for the muffins. He was pretty much done with cooking and was just cleaning up. He acknowledged me with a nod and reminded me that the kitchen was still his. We were both a bit territorial about the spot and I'm afraid we each viewed the other as an invader.

There was no way I could get started, so I sat at one of the empty tables and looked out at the street. I was trying to appear patient, but I was really antsy to get started. A couple was lingering over their dessert. Tag came over and sat down with me.

"Too bad you didn't bring Lucinda with you," he said with a hangdog expression. "I know she loves these yarn outings, but I hate it when she's gone." As he was saying it, he was absently rearranging the condiments in the center of the table so that they were in perfect alignment. "What was she doing when you left?" he said wistfully.

I thought it was sweet that he missed her so much already and she'd been gone only a few hours. He listened intently as I described her going off to find some knitters to hang out with.

Tag glanced toward the diners to see if they'd finished so he could collect the check and close the restaurant. I remembered that he'd seemed to know Burton Fiore. Why not see what I could find out about him?

Rather than building up to it, I just asked him directly what he knew about Cora's fiancé.

"What exactly do you want to know?" Tag asked with a perplexed expression. I forgot who I was dealing with. Tag didn't do well with anything that wasn't specific.

"How about how you met him?" I said. I was hoping for something short, but instead Tag went into a monologue about how that was hard to define. He'd known who Burton Fiore was when he'd proposed to Cora, but never really talked to him. Their first conversation had been when Tag was picking up his cleaning at Cadbury Cleaners and there'd been a line and Burton was in front of him. They made some small talk first. "Since I'd witnessed his proposal at the restaurant, I offered him congratulations. Then I pointed out the similarities in our situations."

It seemed Tag was going to leave it at that and I urged him to continue. "Burton seemed surprised by my comment and then he began to ask me questions." Again Tag stopped.

"And?" I said, trying to keep the impatience out of my voice.

"I was trying to remember his exact wording. It was something like 'It seems to have worked out for you. It's amazing what a woman will agree to in the name of love, isn't it?' After that he said something about wanting to get it in writing. I was going to ask him to explain exactly what he meant, but he just picked up his cleaning and left. I hate it when people are vague like that." My boss looked at me. "Why do you want to know about him?"

I made the mistake of bringing up the idea that Nicole Welton might have been blackmailing Burton. Tag's expression turned serious. "You're not investigating again. Please don't get Lucinda involved. She gets caught up in the excitement and then I seem dull in comparison."

I tried to be as noncommittal as possible, but Tag saw right through it and shook his head with disapproval. Luckily, the couple finally finished and left after paying their check.

The cook and Tag left and I had the place to myself and my thoughts.

17

"THIS IS IT," I MUTTERED UNDER MY BREATH AS I crossed over to Vista Del Mar the next morning. I checked the sky for today's version of cloudy. The clouds were spread thin and, instead of the opaque white, were tinged with gold. For the moment anyway. By the time I was walking up the driveway of Vista Del Mar, the warm color was already gone as the cloud layer thickened. So strange, all those cloudy skies and yet so little rain.

"Good morning," I said to Jane as I walked into the café. I asked for an Americano, hoping it would get my eyes to open a little wider. By the time I'd finished baking and dropped off muffins everywhere, I was left with only a short time to sleep. I could almost hear my mother's voice telling me that I had taken on too much and wasn't that a surefire way for me to end up dropping everything.

"There you are," Wanda Krug said as she marched into the café. The diminutive stand-in for Nicole seemed bristling with concern. "It's lucky we're meeting early. Not to speak ill of the dead, but I think Nicole left a lot of loose ends hanging." She looked at me with reproach. "You put way too much faith in her." She turned to Jane and ordered a black coffee and then added in that drill sergeant tone that she wanted it double cupped. I don't think it was the request as much as the manner, but Jane froze for a second before pulling out a second cup.

Wanda had an intimidating manner and Jane's hand shook as she handed over the drink. Wanda seemed like one of those people who always appeared middle-aged, even though I had the feeling that she was just a couple years older than me. Her clothing choice of a loose-fitting floral top over medium blue pants only enhanced the illusion.

"We can take our coffees with us," Wanda said, moving toward the door. Jane ran out from behind the counter to put one of the plugs in, but Wanda waved her off. I, however, accepted one and appreciated that I made it all the way to the meeting room without scalding myself with hot coffee.

As soon as we went inside the small building, Wanda started clucking her tongue. "This is it? Where are all the supplies?"

I looked around the room and saw that a long table was set up and the fleeces were stacked on it, with a sheet between each one. Someone had pulled the chairs from around the table and left them askew. I explained the tote bag with the drop spindles and the spinning wheels, and asked what else we needed. I knew I should be grateful that she'd stepped in, but she certainly wasn't easy to be around. She'd already turned the tables and was acting like I was working for her and not doing a good job, either.

Wanda turned to me with her hand on her hip. "Didn't Nicole explain the process? I would have thought she would have given you a list of what was needed."

I explained that Nicole had said she would take care of everything. I wanted to kick myself for not having had her demonstrate the wool-to-yarn thing. Wanda didn't seem to notice my upset and just made a lot of *tsk-tsk* sounds as she glanced around the room.

"I heard that you don't think it was suicide," Wanda said when she turned back to me. "What's your reasoning?" she asked curtly. I didn't really want to discuss it with her, since it was obvious by her tone she was ready to poke holes in my theory.

"Why don't you just tell me what we need for the first workshop and I'll see what I can do," I said, skipping over her question completely.

Wanda didn't seem to know how to handle having her question ignored. She sputtered for a moment and then acted like it was her idea. "It's really better if we don't get off track. First we'll have them wash the wool," she said. "We need buckets and hot water and some kind of soap. And we'll need something to dry the wool on."

"That sounds like something Will could help with," I said. We walked outside and headed to his workshop on the edge of the grounds. Wanda kept trying to get ahead of me, but I made sure we walked together.

The small building looked like it was one of the original buildings, which made it over one hundred years old. Like the others, it had weathered wood shingles and mullion windows. The front had a double wood door which was open and I could see that Will was doing something at his workbench. He must have heard us walking, well, more likely Wanda grumbling, and looked up.

Wanda pushed ahead of me and started to speak, but I stopped her. Drill sergeant voice or not, she wasn't in charge, I was. I stepped in front of her and put my hands on my hips, further blocking her. As the thought of being the one in charge went through my mind, I imagined my mother and everyone who'd ever known me hearing it. They would all be shocked. I was a little shocked that I was holding my own.

As I told Will that we needed a lot of big pails, something that would act like a drying rack and a lot of hot water, I looked around the interior of the shed. The shelves behind him held industrial-size containers and there was a supply of smaller empty bottles similar to the one I'd seen near Nicole. I thought of something, but it was touchy how to bring it up. I could feel that Wanda was getting ready to move in, so I launched into it directly and asked Will if he'd known that Nicole was going to be at Vista Del Mar the morning of her death.

He seemed to hesitate. "She seemed wrapped up in what she was doing and didn't always tell me her plans. There's no way I would have seen her. I was stuck under a sink in the dining hall from after they shut down for breakfast until I heard about her," he said. It sounded like he was offering an alibi. I glanced back at the shelves.

Will picked up on what I was looking at and swallowed hard. "After what happened, the ingredients for the insecticide and any I've made up are being kept in a locked cabinet." I nodded and said it seemed like a good idea. It was a terrible thought, but it occurred to me it was like shutting the barn door after the chickens ran out.

Will greeted Wanda, but his voice sounded strained and I guessed he knew how the short spinner felt about his late wife.

He brushed his scruffy sand-colored hair behind his ears. "I'm sorry. I forgot all about it. I got the stuff together for Nicole last week." Will said he'd bring the supplies to the meeting room.

No matter how fast I walked on the way back, Wanda got to the small building that housed our meeting room first. She barred my way as I tried to go inside.

"Didn't Nicole tell you this is an outdoor project?" Wanda said.

I thought back to what Nicole had said when we'd discussed what meeting rooms I should reserve. She'd just said the first encounter with the fleece would be messy. I remembered messy projects from my stint as a teacher and had chosen a room with a tile floor. Never again was I going to assume anything.

Will and another man arrived carrying a stack of big white plastic pails. Wanda directed them to set them up in the open space in front of the small building. Like the rest of the grounds of Vista Del Mar, the small area had been left to grow wild and was covered with dry golden grass and a few green plants. I dropped my messenger bag carryall on the ground and helped arrange the pails in two rows. Will took out an unmarked plastic bottle and explained it was a special wool wash he'd mixed up for Nicole.

Wanda stepped in and moved the pails so there was more space between them. I heard Wanda muttering under her breath that it was lucky for me that she'd taken over.

Will heard her and his whole demeanor changed. His friendly features were contorted in anger. "I'd appreciate it if you'd stop trying to bury Nicole. She would have done just fine."

Wanda acknowledged his comment with a dismissive huff and went inside to get the fleeces. This was not the mood I'd envisioned for the retreat. I could practically hear my mother bringing up her offer of cooking school in Paris. For a moment the thought of bailing sounded appealing. We hadn't even started and already I was wishing it was over and I could say good-bye to Wanda Krug.

"Hey, Casey," a woman's voice said behind me. I turned and was surprised to see Crystal Smith. She seemed to be from another fashion planet than Wanda. Crystal's favorite thing was to mix and not match things that came in pairs.

Today she had on one hoop earring and one shaped like a heart, along with an assortment of studs going up her outer ear. I saw the tops of her socks and one was spring green and the other was hot pink with spring green stripes. I suppose you could say they at least blended. One way or another she pulled off the look and made it seem fun. It was hard to believe she and Wanda were about the same age.

"I just dropped off another supply of yarn in the gift shop," she said before commenting on how much yarn they'd sold there. "I can't thank you enough for putting on these retreats. It really helps our business."

Crystal left it at that, but I knew what she meant. She and her two kids had moved back in with her mother when her rock god husband moved on to younger pastures. The yarn store was supporting all of them now, which had to be hard.

"I came to offer my services," she said. "I went through the wool process at last year's Monterey Wool Festival."

I thanked her profusely, feeling like I'd just been thrown a life preserver. I mentioned my concern about dealing with Wanda.

"She was hurt that you didn't ask her to handle the retreat to start with. She comes across a little harsh, but you have to understand she's always been upstaged by people. She has a younger sister who was the prom queen. Need I say more? I think she felt upstaged by Nicole, with her studio and her fancy degree. And then you hired her." She stopped talking abruptly as Wanda returned. After what Crystal had just said, I wondered how Wanda would take the yarn store owner's offer of help. To my surprise and relief, she seemed happy with it and noted that the retreaters were beginning to show up.

I had realized early on that I would never be able to keep their names straight. Instead I'd given them my own monikers as they'd registered. The woman I called the Ginger had joined Olivia, Bree and Scott, who were gathered around one of the empty pails. The other names were all connected to some kind of identifying feature. There was the woman who wore T-shirts with cat pictures, another whose big dangle earrings caught my eye, and a pair of women who stuck together like glue and I'd started thinking of as the Siamese Twins. You get the picture.

The one name I had straight was Ronny Fiore. She seemed to have toned down her clothes to almost casual, but she didn't seem to be mixing with the others. Whatever reason she had for signing up for the retreat, it certainly wasn't because she wanted to learn how to handle wool, or make new friends.

Wanda took center stage and gave them an overview of the wool washing. In her typical style she announced the water needed to be the right temperature and ordered that they absolutely could not agitate the wool or it might felt. The wool needed to be washed twice and then rinsed twice and had to be dried before the next step. She ordered them to form small groups around each of the pails, since she made a point that there wasn't enough for them each to have their own.

Now I understood Wanda's concern. Nicole had never given me any idea how long any of this was going to take. We only had until Sunday and they were supposed to be knitting their shawls by then.

Wanda instructed Crystal and me to hand out a handful of fleece to each person.

Will had rigged a hose from the restroom in the small building and was going around filling the buckets. As he finished filling each one with hot water, Wanda stuck a thermometer in it and then added a squirt of Will's special soap. She turned to the group around the pail and snapped, "Put your fleece in now." The women jumped as if a buzzer had gone off and dropped their wool into the water.

"Why exactly are we washing the fleece?" the woman in the cat T-shirt said. She seemed to be taking notes. Wanda stopped what she was doing and in a most cordial tone explained it was to get the dirt and lanolin out of the wool and told everyone to move the fleece to the next wash.

Crystal hung near me, waiting to jump in when needed, but Wanda seemed to have it under control. She already had Will filling buckets with rinse water. When he'd finished, she turned to us.

"You two can help with this," Wanda said and instructed us to help the groups move their fleece to the rinse water and on to a second one. It was a messy job and I was grateful we were outside. I was surprised at the murky beige of the wash water.

While Crystal and I worked next to each other fishing wet wool out of the pails, she turned to me. "I told you she'd be okay."

I shrugged in surprise. "I shouldn't say this, but I think Wanda is more qualified than Nicole. I guess I was wowed by her studio and all those spinning wheels." As long as I'd started to talk about Nicole, I brought up what had been sticking in my mind. "Did you ever hear anything about Nicole possibly blackmailing somebody?"

Crystal's head shot up and she put her finger to her lip. I hadn't realized it, but with all the background noise, I'd spoken a little loudly. I whispered an "I'm sorry" and then repeated the question in a softer voice.

"I heard she was asking a lot of questions."

"About what?" I asked

"About the town and the people. You should talk to Maggie. I think Nicole went there a lot and everybody knows Maggie knows everything going on in town."

"Ms. Feldstein," Kevin St. John said. I hadn't noticed the

whine of the golf cart and was startled by his appearance and the sharpness of his tone.

"What?" I said.

By now he'd stepped out of the golf cart and was standing so close to me I could smell the peppermint on his breath. "Who okayed doing your project outside? The yoga people are doing a morning meditation." He pointed across the walkway to a similar building. The doors and windows were shut and I could see the glow of candles and a circle of faces with closed eyes.

I took the blame and he insisted that we stop immediately. He waited while I approached Wanda. She wasn't happy with the idea, but finally agreed that the wool could be left in the rinse water. Crystal and I moved through the group, quietly telling them we had to vacate the area. Crystal came up with an impromptu plan and told them all to go to the meeting room where the spinning wheels were set up and she'd do a demonstration of some specialty yarns they'd just gotten in at the store.

Most of the group followed Crystal like she was the Pied Piper, but I noticed that Ronny Fiore went off on her own. I was about to join the crowd when I noticed that Kevin St. John was looking down and sounded perturbed. "Shoo," he said, waving his hands. Julius was sitting by the side of the path, ignoring the manager's commands. "Ms. Feldstein, will you please instruct this cat to stay out of the Vista Del Mar grounds."

I wanted to laugh. As if that was going to happen.

18

"LET'S FINISH UP WITH THE WOOL," WANDA
commanded when the group had reconvened in the washing
area. By now the yoga group was finished with their meditation and had moved on to the beach to do their poses. Crystal's
demonstration had been a big hit. The group was inspired to
try out the new yarns and had made a stop in the gift shop to
buy up the supply she had brought over.

Will had set up some drying racks he must have gotten from
the Vista Del Mar laundry. Wanda hadn't come to the yarn
demo and now I understood why. She had a huge plastic bag
and unloaded salad spinners for each group before pushing the
receipt on me. She shook her head in disapproval as she mentioned that Nicole had overlooked this step in cleaning the wool.

"I don't think this is a mandatory step," I said to Crystal,
sounding a little defensive as Wanda had someone in each
group take some fleece out of the rinse water and put it in the
salad spinner, explaining it would extract the excess water. I

wanted to believe what Will had said, that Nicole would have done just fine. "Now spin it, ladies," Wanda said, turning her hand to demonstrate. Crystal agreed it wasn't essential, but said it would certainly speed things up.

I saw that Lucinda was holding her dripping fleece, waiting her turn with the salad spinner, and I went to join her.

I could tell my friend the truth. "I feel like an idiot," I said in a low voice. "I trusted Nicole and now I wonder how qualified she was."

"This may sound callous, but it doesn't really matter anymore." She looked at Wanda checking the salad spinners to make sure they'd gotten all the fibers out before they were passed on to the next person. "I don't think any of the retreaters even know that Wanda is a stand-in, or care. She's a little rough around the edges, but I think she knows her stuff."

When Lucinda got her turn with the salad spinner, I went over to the drying racks and assisted Crystal as she helped arrange the wet fleece. I looked at the amount each of them was hanging out to dry.

"I realize I've never done this before, but it doesn't seem like they each cleaned enough fleece to make the yarn for a shawl."

Crystal's expression darkened. "I didn't even think of that," she said, looking as Lucinda hung out her fleece. "No, this can't be enough for a shawl."

Wanda was busy supervising and it took me a long time to get her away from the group. I brought up the fleece situation and she looked perturbed. "Do you think I don't know that?" she said. "I have it under control." She ended the conversation by walking away.

The truth was, I needed Wanda too much to take a chance on her getting annoyed at me and taking off, so I let it go. But I had my fingers crossed that she really did have things under control.

With the wool hung out, the first workshop ended and the group began to disperse. Except for Lucinda and my early birds.

I realized I'd dropped my messenger bag in the grass when we'd first been setting up. I picked it up as the lunch bell began to ring. The white sky had become filmier and bits of blue were showing through with some sun here and there. I hoped it would help the fleece to dry quickly.

"That was fun," Bree said. "I can't wait to tell the Ewes about it." She turned to me. "Are you having lunch with us?" she asked.

I nodded and said I thought it was a nice time to bond with the group. I invited Crystal to join us. I wanted to make sure Wanda got lunch, but she insisted on going home. "I don't think it would be a good idea if I was too familiar with the group," she said. "It would undermine their view of me as an authority, like letting them see behind the curtain of the great Oz."

Wanda grabbed my arm and pulled me farther away from the group. "After seeing how unprepared you were this morning, I thought I'd better be proactive. How many carders do you have?"

It took a moment for the word to register. "Are those the things that look like dog brushes?" I asked. Wanda nodded. I didn't want to tell her the truth, that I didn't have any. Instead I asked her how many she needed. I was, after all, the person in charge. So much for my plan to have lunch with the group. I sent Lucinda and the rest of them on to the dining hall.

I passed the yoga group on their way to lunch and apologized again for our noise. Their reaction surprised me. Instead of fussing the way Kevin St. John had, their leader said it was good for them to have challenges to their concentration and I had actually done them a favor.

I went looking for Will and found him back in his

workshop. He knew what carders were and assured me that
Nicole had a bin of them she'd planned to bring when they
were needed. He told me where to find them in his wife's
shop. Problem solved. I just had to pick them up.

I stopped at my place and found Julius asleep on my pillow.
I'd planned all along to bring over some cookies for the afternoon break. I wanted to bake them before my trip downtown.
By the time I'd preheated the oven, I had sliced up the rolls of
butter cookies and filled several baking sheets. They baked in
no time and were sitting on cooling racks as I got ready to go.

When I'd come across the street, I'd glanced down toward
Dane's. The red Ford F150 wasn't there and I figured he was
on duty. But I noticed a silver car parked in front of his house.
It had been parked there for days, or just about the whole time
his company had been there. It didn't take real detective skills
to figure out it probably belonged to his girlfriend.

There had been no care packages of his delicious pasta
since his company had come, but why not keep my end of the
bargain and leave him some cookies? And if I happened to
look in the window while I was leaving them, so be it.

I was really curious about Dane's company. Who was she?
What was his type? Whoever she was, she wasn't into cars.
The car had a nice dent in the front fender and definitely
looked like it had seen better days.

I walked up the driveway and headed to the back door of
the off-white stucco house. We always left our food offerings
at the kitchen door. The top part of his door was glass and as
I stood up from leaving the care package, I surveyed the
kitchen. I don't know what I expected. Did I think she was
going to be hanging curtains and dusting with a feather duster?
There was someone in the room. She was sitting at the table
with her back to me and it looked like she was wearing his

robe. All I could see was that she had wiry dark hair that hung below her shoulders and that her head seemed to be resting in her hands. Wasn't that universal body language for being upset about something? Maybe there was trouble in paradise. For a moment I considered knocking on the door so she would turn and I could get a good look at her, but I stopped myself. What was I going to say? "I'm here to check you out"?

I ended up just leaving the cookies.

I was glad to see the sunshine as I headed to my Mini Cooper. Wanda hadn't said anything, but I was worried about the fleece drying, even with the help of the salad spinners. Having some sun for a while would help.

I parked near the Coffee Shop and remembered Crystal's suggestion that Maggie was like information central for the town and might know something more about what Nicole had been up to. Getting the carders wouldn't take long. I certainly could stop for a coffee and maybe ask a few questions.

Maggie was behind the counter talking to a customer when I came in. The smell of freshly ground coffee alone was enough to give me a boost.

"Hey, Casey, are you here for one of my cappuccinos?" She handed a paper cup of coffee to the customer and got ready to take my order. As always she was smiling and friendly, dressed in a red bandanna-print top over a pair of work-quality jeans. A red scarf complemented her big hairstyle.

As long as I was there, a cappuccino seemed like a good idea. I'd never gotten to drink the coffee I'd picked up before the yarn washing. I really tried to insist on paying, but Maggie absolutely wouldn't hear of it.

Lunchtime wasn't a busy time at the coffee place and most of the tables were empty. There was just a couple in the corner with their backs toward me.

When Maggie had finished making the foam-covered drink, I hung around the counter instead of taking it to one of the tables.

I launched into talking about Nicole without any preamble. When I said I didn't think she'd killed herself, Maggie looked surprised, and then seemed to let out a heavy sigh.

"That's a relief," she said, reminding me that the poisoned coffee had been in one of the Coffee Shop's paper cups. The look of relief lasted only a moment before the reality of the situation sank in. "Maybe that's not any better. Are you saying you think somebody used a cup of my coffee as a murder weapon?"

"I probably wouldn't have put it quite that way, but yes. If she didn't put the insecticide in the coffee, then somebody else did."

Maggie's eyes darted back and forth and she was obviously thinking about something.

"What?" I asked.

She shook her head and the tails of the red scarf caught the breeze and fluttered. "I was trying to remember who came in that morning. It was Tuesday, wasn't it?"

I nodded and she suddenly looked stricken. "But the cops said the only fingerprints on the cup were Nicole's and mine." She looked straight at me with worry in her dark eyes. "You don't think I killed her?"

"No way, and don't worry, the cops aren't going to come knocking at your door. As far as I've heard they are still looking at it as a suicide." Poor Maggie seemed distraught and regretted letting the cops take her fingerprints.

"I was trying to be helpful."

I finally admitted that I was doing my own investigation on the qt. "I've heard rumblings that Nicole might have been blackmailing somebody. Do you have any idea what she might have known?"

Maggie poured some hot water over a chamomile tea bag. She glanced around furtively. "You won't tell anybody, will you? It's not a good advertisement of my wares, but your news on top of two double espressos I had this morning has left my nerves a little frayed." She pulled out the tea bag and snapped a cover on the drink and let out a sigh of relief. "I feel better knowing you're on the case." She did the thing with her eyes again and I knew she was thinking. "Nicole asked a lot of questions recently. I thought she was just curious about the history of Cadbury." Maggie stopped to think for a moment. "Blackmail seems kind of serious, but then it was obvious she had expensive taste and while I am sure the Delacorte sisters appreciate Will's hard work, I doubt they pay him that much."

"The Delacorte sisters decide about raises?" I asked, surprised. "Kevin St. John gives the impression that he is practically king of Vista Del Mar. I figured he handled the employees."

"When I said 'sisters,' I really meant Cora. Madeleine is like a rubber stamp for anything her sister does." Maggie let out a sigh. "The sisters were never supposed to end up with Vista Del Mar. It was never meant to be part of the family estate, but belonged solely to Edmund. His intention was to pass it on to his children. Though it turned out he only had one son." I was amazed at the detailed information Maggie had on Edmund's will, but then she was known as Information Central.

"He had a son? Why isn't he in charge of Vista Del Mar?" Maggie's cheerful expression dimmed. "It was a sad business. Barely a year after Edmund passed from an infection, his wife and son were killed in a car crash. The sisters were listed as next in line to inherit, but their mother, Antonia Delacorte, took over handling Vista Del Mar. She's the one who hired Kevin St. John. She died two years ago and then the sisters took it over and inherited everything in the Delacorte estate. Kevin has a lot of autonomy, but they still own the place."

I realized what she said was true. The sisters, or Cora, had been the one to offer my aunt a deal on the rooms. Kevin St. John hadn't been able to change it, which was one of the reasons I thought he was so anxious to take over my retreat business. Maggie looked at the couple in the corner.

"I think everything is going to change when Cora marries him." I followed her gaze and was surprised to see the couple at the table was Burton Fiore and his daughter. Maggie had lowered her voice. "I hope Cora hasn't lost her head. She has no experience in the love department. Her mother screened any suitors and no one was ever good enough."

We'd gotten far off the subject of blackmail and I brought it up again. I mentioned seeing Burton Fiore in Nicole's shop and the episode with the envelope. Maggie glanced in his direction a few times.

"Casey, I think you might be seeing plots where there aren't any. He could have been in there to buy a gift for his *beloved*. He probably thinks of her as an antique and so thought he should buy her one."

I didn't bring up the disappearing envelope again. I had begun to wonder if I'd seen it at all. Maybe it was just some kind of reflection on the glass. I did bring up Nicole's trip to Bhutan and Maggie seemed surprised.

"How'd I miss out on that bit of news?" She considered it for a moment. "An exotic trip like that? It does sound like Nicole must have come into some money. Maybe you're right about blackmail." The Coffee Shop proprietor started going through any damaging information Nicole might have known.

"There's the usual stuff that goes on. Who is having an affair with whom, but I can't imagine anyone paying money to keep it quiet." We got into an animated conversation and without realizing it, had raised our voices.

"Could there be something about the bank building she used for a shop?"

Maggie didn't think so. "It had been closed for years before she rented it."

When I looked up, Burton and Ronny were gone and I remembered I had to get back for the afternoon session. I thanked Maggie and tried to pay her again. She just laughed and pushed the money back at me and said she was looking forward to the next day's muffins. "It's always a surprise what kind you bring."

The sun was already disappearing behind a layer of fog that was drifting in. That was the thing I'd noticed about fog: It always seemed to be on the move.

I walked down the street toward The Bank, anxious to get the carders now and head back to Vista Del Mar. I let myself in the front door. With the sun making a hasty departure, the light inside was dim. My first thought had been to not bother with the lights, and just go to the area behind the partition where Will said I'd find the carders. But as I moved deeper into the store, it got darker and I accepted I needed the lights. As soon as I flipped them on and looked around the cavernous interior, my breath caught. Somebody had been in there. Everything seemed askew again and this time it couldn't have been Nicole.

I immediately checked the back door and it seemed locked, not that it meant anything. Dane had pointed out it took minimal skill to open the lock without a key. I considered calling Will but remembered that there was no cell service. I would tell him later and let him decide what he wanted to do.

I noticed that the stack of blue ledgers near the fireplace had fallen over and my first thought was to pick them up. One fell open as I tried to straighten them. It was just an empty binder. They all seemed to be. My next stop was the box of moldy clothes in the back cubicle. It was just as I'd left it. I debated about going through it and taking out the items I'd found mixed in with the clothes, but since it seemed like whoever was going through the place was ignoring it, I decided to leave it be. I also realized that if I ever needed to hide anything, a box of moldy clothes was the way to go.

I wondered what whoever had been in there was looking for. I checked the desk but all the drawers seemed to be shut. I was about to move on when I inadvertently knocked a catalog off the desktop. I jumped when I heard a rumbling sound, until I realized the catalog had just hit a paper shredder and made it come to life.

As I picked up the catalog, I noticed a sheet of paper stuck in the machine. I pulled it out and looked it over. It seemed to be a list of names, but what struck me the most was that so many of them seemed to have been written with a fountain pen. I thought back to the now-empty ledgers and figured out the sheet must have come from one of them. Curious, I opened the bin on the shredder and saw that it was full almost to the top. I saw enough tidbits of fountain pen ink on the strips of shredded paper to figure it all came from the ledgers. I considered what to do with the half sheet. Something told me to hang on to it, so I buried it in the box of moldy clothes. I started to walk away from the box, but on second thought decided to take it with me.

I was really out of time. I needed to find those carders and get going. Just as Will had said, they were in a container on the other side of the partition. As I leaned down to get them, my messenger bag fell forward and I regretted not securing it as the papers I'd jammed into it fell out. I went to retrieve the program folder and a scrap of paper fluttered out.

I picked it up and felt a shiver as I read the message on it. *Mind your own business or else.*

19

I PULLED MY CAR INTO THE ALLEY BEHIND THE BANK and loaded the bin of carders and box of moldy clothes into the trunk, trying not to think of the threatening note. The retreat had to go on. I stopped at home long enough to put the box of moldy clothes in the converted garage and pack up the fresh cookies. Then I rushed across the street and dropped them off, along with the bin of carders, in the meeting room. I did a quick check of the cleaned wool hanging on the drying racks and was glad to see the sun seemed to have done its work before it disappeared in the fog.

Next stop was finding Lucinda. She was the only person I could tell about the note. My friend had already finished lunch and was sitting with some other women in the area called the fire circle. The fire pit was empty and the women had made their own little knitting circle. They all had their jackets zipped and didn't seem to mind sitting out in the bracing air. When I saw how relaxed Lucinda looked, I hated to interrupt.

If ever I needed an advertisement for the benefits of the retreats, all I had to do was show a picture of her when she'd arrived and one a day or so later. All the tension had gone out of her body. Her shoulders were relaxed, and her squarish-shaped face looked peaceful. Probably the complete opposite to how I appeared as I rushed into the group. They all glanced up and before I could say anything, Lucinda had picked up her things and joined me. She led me away from the others like she was taking me to a table in her restaurant.

"Who had access to your bag?" Lucinda asked when I told her about the note. I waited until we were out of earshot of the group.

"It's more like who didn't?" I mentioned the bag had been on the ground during the entire time we'd been washing the wool. I'd taken it with me when Kevin St. John made us temporarily adjourn and then dropped it on the ground again when we came back.

"Did you look inside it during the break?" Lucinda asked. I knew where she was going. If I had and the threatening note hadn't been there, we could narrow down the time it was placed there. I tried to think back, but couldn't remember

"I was so busy with the wool washing, I never thought of my bag," I said. Lucinda had taken me to a bench on the boardwalk that was relatively private. A few people walked by on their way to the beach, but if they heard anything we were saying, it was only a word or two. "The whole group of retreaters certainly must have seen my bag lying there. Wanda, and even Will and Kevin St. John," I said. Then I remembered that other people had passed by on the path as we were out there.

"Maybe there's a clue in the note," Lucinda said, looking at the messenger bag. I fumbled through the bag and pulled out the purple folder. I opened the folder and showed her the sheet of paper in the front.

" 'Mind your own business or else,' " she said, reading the note out loud. "Too bad we're not handwriting experts. There's no way to tell who did it," she said finally.

"But don't you see what it means?" I said. It was really a rhetorical question and I continued without waiting for an answer. "It means I'm right about something." It was true that the note wasn't that specific, but maybe that was deliberate. "Maybe whatever Nicole knew, they wanted it to die with her."

"What are you going to do?" Lucinda asked.

"I'm not going to drop the ball," I said. Lucinda seemed worried and mentioned the "or else" part of the note.

"If what you're thinking is correct, someone has already killed once to keep it under wraps. They might try again." She fingered the black-and-white pattern of her knitting. "Maybe you should talk to Lieutenant Borgnine," she said.

I tried not to roll my eyes at her comment. "The note was too vague. Unless I have actual proof, he'd just nod and smile and push me out the door," I said. I closed the folder and slid it back in the bag. The motion knocked out a strip of paper and it fluttered to the ground. I rushed to retrieve it before the wind picked it up. "The last thing I want to do is litter this beautiful place."

I unfurled the strip to see what it was, preparing to crumple it up and drop it into the trash can.

I saw that it was a receipt, but the store wasn't familiar. It was only as I glanced down and saw the items purchased that it made sense. But when I got to the date of purchase, it seemed odd.

"It's for the salad spinners Wanda used to extract the excess water out of the wool fleece." I pointed to the last line.

"But these were bought last week. Last week Nicole was alive and all set to run the wool-to-yarn workshop. Why would Wanda have bought five salad spinners?"

Lucinda's eyes widened. "Unless she already knew something was going to happen to Nicole." I folded up the receipt and put it in an inner pocket.

"I could show that to Lieutenant Borgnine," I said. Then I thought it through and imagined his response if I did.

"You need something to help you unwind," Lucinda said. I hadn't realized it, but I clearly looked rather frazzled. She had me wait for her while she went back to retrieve her things and then we walked up to the café.

Since lunch had just ended in the dining hall, no one was looking for food or drinks and the new shop in the Lodge building was deserted. We found a table by the window and as soon as we were situated, Lucinda took a plastic bag out of her retreat tote. "Look what Olivia made up with the bag of supplies you gave her."

I looked inside and found a pair of plastic knitting needles with some stitches already cast on one of them from a small ball of yarn. A half sheet of paper listed brief instructions on how many rows to do to make a square. The title on the top called it the Win-Win. It was the perfect-size project to keep tucked with you. It was easy enough to be calming and in the end there would be a square to send off to her to be made into a blanket for a needy person.

"It's pretty amazing to see how she's changed," Lucinda said. "I like this happier version of her a lot better than the person she was on the last retreat." Lucinda pushed the kit on me and urged me to take it and do a few minutes of mindful knitting so I would calm down. In the meantime she took out her own work, a black-and-white-patterned scarf. It was hard to imagine that not long ago she hadn't even known how to purl.

Jane stopped next to Lucinda's chair to admire her work. "Even Tag will be impressed," my friend said. "And it isn't even hard."

"Maybe I should take up knitting," the counter girl said. She looked at my square and asked if I could show her how to make one. I agreed to do it after the retreat and then she asked if we wanted to order something.

Lucinda ended up getting a latte, but I said I was coffeed out and mentioned stopping at the Coffee Shop. "I had hoped that Maggie might help me figure out who really bought the coffee that Nicole drank."

Jane seemed confused and I said I was questioning if Nicole had really killed herself. Jane still didn't seem to understand and I let it go. The few minutes of knitting helped a little, but I decided what I really needed was a few minutes on the beach before the start of the afternoon session of the retreat.

Lucinda understood and I left her sipping her latte and happily working on her intricate pattern. I took the boardwalk and when I passed where the path through the dunes joined it, I instinctively looked up at the plant-covered hills of sand. I hadn't been up there since we'd found Nicole. Nobody had, since I'd heard that the area around the bench was still off-limits.

I reached the archway that marked the end of the boardwalk and the Vista Del Mar grounds and was about to cross the street that wound along the coast when a police car zipped by. It pulled to the side of the road up ahead with an abrupt squeak. The door opened and Dane got out. He crossed the street on a diagonal, which brought him next to me.

"Is something wrong?" I said, gesturing toward the cruiser. He cracked a friendly smile.

"Nope, all quiet in Cadbury for the moment. I saw you and pulled over. Where are you headed?"

I mentioned the beach and a few minutes away from all

the retreaters. "So, you're saying you want to be alone?" He
sounded disappointed. I was about to nod, but I thought of
the note in the folder. What harm would there be running it
past Dane?

"Not *alone* alone. More like a few minutes of fresh air.
You're welcome to join me." Before the words were out of my
mouth, he said it sounded like what he needed as well. I pulled
out the note and showed it to him.

He eyed me warily. "What exactly have you been up to?"

"I know everyone is content to think that Nicole's death
was a suicide, but let's say I'm still not convinced. I may have
been doing a little checking around." We crossed the street
and started down the pathway between the low fencing meant
to keep the planted area safe from footsteps.

"Have you been talking to your detective friend?" he
asked.

"Not friend, my former boss," I corrected. "We've talked
a few times."

Dane's smile faded. "You know you could run stuff past
me. Anytime."

I reminded him of his company and he let out a sigh and
looked at the ground. I was expecting some kind of snappy
remark, but instead all he said was "Right."

I couldn't resist. "So, you're tired of her already? What is
it, she won't leave?"

Dane's mouth was drawn in a straight line. "Something like
that." It was clear he didn't want to talk about it and changed
the subject back to Nicole. "This note seems kind of generic.
Could it be about something else? I saw all the evidence, the
coffee cup, the chocolate and vanilla muffin, the note on the
phone. Even the empty bottle of insecticide. There was nothing
that indicated foul play. I don't know what Nicole got herself
involved with, but it seems clear she felt bad about it. She must

have felt there was no way out." We'd reached the wide stretch
of beach and watched the waves roll in. I never stopped being
amazed at the color of the water as the waves broke. It was
absolutely seafoam green.

"It seems like this retreat is keeping you pretty busy. Why
don't you just concentrate on it and not worry about anything
else." Dane and I had walked to the edge of the damp sand
and we began to parallel the water. It looked odd to see his
dark blue uniform reflected in the water before it went back
out to sea.

I didn't think the note was about something else and I
didn't want to just accept her death as suicide and let it go.
Rather than say that, I changed the subject. "I can see why
you want to take a walk after the way things have been at
your place—" Before I could finish, his head snapped in my
direction and his expression looked anything but pleased.

"I was just going to say that you haven't had your karate
going all week." His expression softened a little, but we both
knew why he hadn't been having the town kids over in his garage.

I was still surprised by his demeanor. I was used to him
being flirty and cocky, but most of all upbeat. He seemed
almost depressed.

It was only when I was back in the meeting room, setting
up the coffee and tea and cookies I'd made, that something
Dane had said struck me. He'd been specific about the kind
of muffin they'd found. I had no doubt he was accurate
because he was somewhat of an expert on the different muffins I made. He said they'd found a chocolate and vanilla
muffin as part of the evidence. But here was the problem:
Nicole's incident happened on Tuesday, but I hadn't baked the
Ebony and Ivory ones, as I called them, for that day. I'd baked
them for Monday. I needed to talk to Maggie.

I backtracked and went into the Lodge, where the pay

phones were full and there was a line waiting for them. Instead I went into the café. Jane was more than agreeable to let me use the phone. Of course, I got Maggie's voice mail and left a message asking her to think about the day before Nicole died and mentioned the muffin.

The meeting room was still empty when I returned. I sat down and waited, hoping to get a moment alone with Wanda to ask her about the salad spinners.

I saw her coming up the path. It was hard to confuse her with anyone else. Her gait went along with her manner of speech. She didn't walk, she marched.

I came outside as she got near the drying racks and started checking the fleece. I called out a greeting. There was no quick segue from "Hello" to "Why did you know to buy salad spinners when someone else was supposed to be running the workshop?"

"That little bit of sun did the trick," she said. She pushed a pillowcase on me and told me to start collecting the wool off half the racks, but to make sure it was really dry.

"I just want to thank you again for stepping in. I don't know what I would have done without you." Wanda moved at lightning speed and had her share of the drying racks empty while I was still on the top rung of my first one. She went into the room and I stopped collecting the wool and followed her inside.

She glanced around. "Did you bring the carders?" I pointed out the plastic bin and she flipped off the top and began taking out some pairs of things that looked like large dog brushes, along with some actual dog brushes. I could tell by the *Fido's Friend* brand name on the back.

I followed her around the U shape of the tables. "There is no way we're going to get the whole group in here at one time," she muttered. She turned and almost tripped over me.

"You filled the pillowcase already?" she said, taking it

from my hands. When she looked inside and saw just a little bit of the fluff at the bottom, she pushed it back at me and tried to send me back outside.

I was good at talking to people and getting information, but Wanda was in a category all her own. You didn't have a conversation with her. She gave commands and you followed them.

When I tried to bring up the salad spinners, she brushed it off and said we were done working with them and I ought to concentrate on how we were going to divide up the group.

"Stand clear," she said as she unloaded two lethal-looking devices with long metal fingers. She seemed to be considering where to put them. Crystal came in just then and looked as Wanda set them on the table.

"You brought a pair of wool combs?" the yarn store co-owner said. "Maybe not such a good idea with such a big group." The two women made an odd pair. Wanda with her short stout build, in the floral top and lime green slacks, and Crystal, in her jeans and multilayered bright-colored tops with an armload of jangling bangles. Crystal held one of the wool combs by its wooden handle and showed me the rows of tines. "Make sure you don't touch the top of these. They're sharp. Deadly sharp."

Surprisingly, Wanda seemed to listen. "You're right. We wouldn't want somebody to back into one of these. It would be like being impaled on a bunch of tiny swords," Wanda said, eyeing the dangerous-looking tools. "Carding will have to be enough," she said as she packed them away. Any chance of asking more about the salad spinners ended when the rest of the group arrived.

Wanda had the group gather around her and said the next step was carding the wool. She did a little demo with two of the wooden paddles covered with short metal teeth. She might call it carding, but to me it looked like brushing the wool back and forth between the two tools. Whatever it was called, at the end of it, she rolled the white fuzz off the device and said the end result was called a rolag.

There were only five sets of carders and some of those were the dog brushes, which were smaller but worked just as well. We quickly divided the group up. Wanda had me be one of the first to try it and I thought I was going to be helping the others, but it turned out most of my time was spent moving groups of people in and out of the room. A woman who seemed to wear nothing but purple offered to do a demonstration on how to fix common knitting mistakes for the group not carding. I helped her set up in the other meeting room and then stayed to watch it as she repeated it for each new group. I was touched by her offer of help and apologized for not being better organized.

The woman in the cat T-shirt overheard and reassured me the most important aspect of the retreat was being away with a bunch of like-minded people with lots of time to knit.

"Tomorrow we spin," Wanda said when the last group had their turn carding. She scooped up all the rolags and put them in a container on wheels, saying she'd drop it off in the other meeting room. I tried to follow her and called after her, asking if there was going to be enough wool to spin. She answered with a dismissive wave of her hand.

20

"WANDA IS MAKING ME DOUBT MY SKILLS," I SAID to Lucinda. She had stayed behind when the group dispersed and helped me with the part nobody seemed to want to do—clean up. Even Crystal had bailed. Her kids would be home from school.

I folded up the drying racks and set them against the wall for Will to pick up. I packed up the carders and pushed the bin next to Wanda's stuff. Then it was just cleaning the bits of fleece off the tables.

I brought up the time I'd worked for the detective agency. It had only been a temp job, but it was my favorite and I'd been great at doing telephone interviews. My boss, Frank, always said I got people to spill all kinds of information. "People usually open up to me. But not Wanda," I said. I repeated what she'd said when I asked about the salad spinners. "I can just imagine how she would have reacted if I'd tried to find out where she was when Nicole died."

"Do you think she's a suspect?" Lucinda asked.

"I don't know if it counts as a motive, but the first time I met her, she presented herself as being the town expert on spinning and was angry that I had hired Nicole." I told Lucinda what I'd heard about Wanda being upstaged all the time. "Maybe my hiring Nicole instead of her was the straw that broke the camel's back."

Will came in and said we could leave everything and he'd finish up. His gaze rested on a pair of covered plastic bins. "I see you found the carders."

I mentioned my midday trip to The Bank and how it looked like somebody had been in there again. "I didn't do anything," I explained. "But I thought you might want to call the cops."

Will took the news with a stoic expression. "I'm glad you didn't bother the cops. I'll have to go over there and make sure the lock is secure."

I made an attempt to pursue the conversation and mentioned the fallen stack of ledgers. He blinked at me a few times and then completely changed the subject and asked me how Wanda was working out. He brushed off the top of one of the tables and began to fold it down. I decided not to mention the box I'd taken.

If I couldn't get an answer to one thing, maybe I could find out about another. "I'm grateful to have her," I said in my best diplomatic tone. "How well do you know her?"

It was very obvious that he felt much more comfortable with this line of conversation. He set the folded table against the wall and began on the next one. "I knew her sister a lot better," Will said. "We went to high school together." He stopped what he was doing and seemed embarrassed. "She was the prom queen, the year I was the king."

I remembered the travel agent's daughter talking about Will being the big heartthrob. He seemed to have no sense of

his own appeal, which only made him more likable. I asked
if Nicole had known Wanda. He balanced the folded table
against his hip as he wiped his brow with his shirt sleeve and
made a disparaging noise.

"If you mean were they friends, the answer is no. But they
each knew who the other was. Nicole did mention that Wanda
came to her shop last week. I don't know what was said, but
my wife seemed very upset with her manner. I tried to explain
it was just Wanda's way to be a little overbearing, but Nicole
didn't seem to care."

He went on to give us a little background on Wanda, most
of which totally surprised me. All the stuff with yarn was
more of a hobby or side business. Her real profession was as
a golf pro at one of the Pebble Beach resorts. "I know you
wouldn't think it by looking at her, but she's won a lot of golf
tournaments. They moved her down to teaching kids recently
after they hired another woman golfer." He seemed sympa-
thetic as he explained the replacement was younger and supposedly more the image they wanted to project than Wanda
was. "I don't think she took it well." Will said she was married
and, as could be expected, her husband was on the quiet side;
she also had two kids.

Lucinda looked at the plastic bins and asked if they should
be moved. I opened Wanda's and noticed the bag of salad
spinners. I guessed that she was keeping them until I paid her.
When I moved the bag to look underneath, Lucinda called
out for me to watch out. I understood why when I saw the
light catching on the sharp metal teeth of the wool combs. I
pulled my hand away quickly before letting the lid shut, shiv-
ering at the thought of what would have happened if I'd made
contact.

"How about we just leave the bins here for now," Will said,
taking out a broom. As he began to sweep, he grew thoughtful.

"Maybe I could have said something more to Nicole. I knew she was having a hard time here. I just didn't realize how hard." He let out a sad sigh. "She wanted to see the world and work in a big-city museum. Me, I'm happy here. I figure if you can't find what you want in your own backyard, you won't find it anywhere."

He cleared up the coffee things and ate the last cookie before handing me the empty plate. He was just about finished and was going to leave. Dare I push the envelope and bring up the word *blackmail*? He had opened up a lot, but from my experience talking to people, I knew if you crossed a line, they clammed up and stayed that way. I decided it was better to leave it that we were all on the same side, mourning the loss of his wife.

When Will left, I instinctively went to check my phone for messages, but then remembered about having no signal. I actually saw the point of everyone else being unplugged, but it was still a nuisance for me, since I wasn't there to get away from it all.

"Maybe there's something on the message board," Lucinda said.

"How could I have forgotten that option?" I said, rolling my eyes. "I bet that's what they used when Cora's brother ran the place." We walked together to the social hall. The Lodge was crowded with people. Lucinda noticed a group from our retreat and suggested we join them. I urged her to go on herself, reminding her that this was her vacation, but not mine.

The message board sat near the entrance to the gift shop. I was surprised to see how covered with scraps of paper it was. There was no order to how they were organized and it was a little dizzying reading them all. In the end there was one old message for me from Wanda telling me to turn the drying wool over during lunchtime. There was nothing from Maggie.

I went home to freshen up and get everything together for my baking later in the evening. The plan was I would bake that night for Saturday and Sunday at the Blue Door, so I wouldn't have to go back Saturday night. I'd bake muffins for Saturday, but the town would have to go muffinless for Sunday. I always baked those fresh for the next day only.

Before I went in, I checked the stoop outside the kitchen door. The plate I'd brought to Dane's with the cookies was sitting there with a note on it. I felt a little flutter as I opened it. He thanked me for the cookies and promised there would be pasta packages soon. He'd drawn a smiley face next to his name, but it almost looked like a heart. I didn't know what to make of it. The only thing I knew for sure was that I would never be the "other woman" in a relationship. He'd made his bed and now he had to lie in it.

I distracted myself from thinking about him by checking my landline and cell phone for messages. Maggie had left one on both of them. I was hoping for some sort of information, but all she said was that she was returning my call.

Julius was parading in front of the refrigerator.

"No stink fish tonight," I said. He'd finished the can in the morning and I found a can of kitty stew in the pantry. Julius rushed up to his bowl and waited until I doled some of it out, but he took one look at the little meatballs and flecks of vegetable in beige gravy and turned to me. I can't explain how the black cat did it, but something in the shake of his head and the flick of his tail made me think he was saying, "Really? You think I'm going to eat that?"

"When you get hungry, you'll eat it," I said. I cringed, realizing I'd just mouthed the words my mother had said to me when we had something I didn't like for dinner. Not that my mother had made it. She didn't cook. We had somebody who did that. I often thought that was why I had taken so to baking. It was making it clear that I was nothing like my cardiologist mother, who thought cookies came only from a bakery.

I changed into more formal-looking black jeans with a T-shirt in the same color. I added a rust-colored suede blazer-style jacket. There wasn't much to do with my hair beyond brush it and let it hang loose. I was beginning to learn from Lucinda that if you wanted to look your best, you needed to keep freshening your makeup. On a normal day, I wouldn't have bothered. The great thing about baking alone at night was that I didn't need to worry about lipstick and eye shadow.

But this was different. I was looking forward to having dinner with the group. I realized I might not know their names, but I still felt bonded with them. And especially to the early birds and Lucinda.

The Lodge was even busier when I came back. The business group was waiting with their suitcases to be taken to the airport. Funny, their retreat was considered work, so when Friday night came it was time to go home. It was easy to spot them because in their last move to be a homogeneous group, they were all still wearing matching polo shirts. I noticed Scott hanging with the guy he'd taught to knit. Scott waved me over and introduced me to Vinnie Pulaski.

"He wants to be on your mailing list," Scott said.

Vinnie nodded. "Scott here has changed my life. Who'd have thought someday I'd be working with sticks and yarn. He says your retreats really rock. I say count me in." Up close I got a good view of Vinnie's brown wavy hair and a set of rather large biceps showing under his polo shirt sleeve. I took down his information, thinking he would definitely be an interesting addition to a retreat.

The outside door opened and I was surprised to see Burton Fiore and Cora Delacorte come into the big room. The first thing I noticed was that Cora's fiancé looked like he'd raided

Kevin St. John's closet for a dark suit, white shirt and conservative tie. Cora wore an emerald green pantsuit, but then
she always dressed up. She'd gone a little heavy on the eye
makeup and I could see the green shadow from across the
room. In her typical Queen Elizabeth fashion, she was holding
a purse on her arm.

Burton had his arm around her in a protective manner and
she seemed to be loving it as they began to work the room. When
they got to the business group, Burton stopped next to the man
who appeared to be their leader. When Burton started to talk
to the man, I got nosy and moved closer, hoping to eavesdrop.

"I hope you enjoyed your stay," Burton said. He introduced
Cora as his fiancée and the owner of Vista Del Mar. He
brought up the unplugged concept and said that he understood
what an imposition it was. He tried to explain away the current
situation by saying there was a problem with a cell tower.
"But, it is being worked on. We believe our guests should
have the option to go unplugged or stay connected with their
electronics. I can assure you when you come back in six
months for your next management retreat, there will be a few
changes around here. Changes you're going to like."

The leader of the group listened with interest, then mentioned that the unplugged thing seemed to have worked out.
"Instead of my team being distracted with their screens, they
actually paid attention to our sessions."

Burton seemed a little disappointed by the comment, but
rushed to repeat that he thought guests should make their own
choices about going unplugged.

Cora stood there smiling through the whole thing. I was
shocked. Was she really going to just turn over everything to
him? I wasn't the only one listening. Kevin St. John had come
to stand almost next to me.

"I've gone through too much to get here to be pushed

aside," the manager muttered angrily. He turned toward me. "Has he been giving you trouble about your retreats?"

I was taken aback by the question and his demeanor. Instead of his usual adversarial manner, it was suddenly like we were on the same team. I told him the truth. Burton had said nothing to me about anything. "Well, let me know if he does," Kevin St. John said.

By now the van had arrived and the business group was filing outside. Ronny Fiore had come in the room from the other door. The manager and I watched as the younger woman joined her father and future stepmother, throwing her arms around Cora and kissing her on the cheek.

"Aren't they the happy family," Kevin said sarcastically. "Can't Cora see through them?"

"Maybe she doesn't want to," I said, still trying to get used to the idea of being on the same side as the moon-faced manager. Thinking I could take advantage of the situation, I asked him if he'd heard anything more about Nicole's death.

"What would I hear?" he said, his usually prickly side reappearing. "The police did their investigating and it's consistent with suicide."

"I was just wondering. I heard that Nicole might have had some information." I purposely let it hang to sound like I knew what the information was.

"Do you think I don't know that trick, Casey? I wouldn't say anything even if I did know something. When you run a place like this, discretion is your watchword." He looked back toward the threesome as the dinner bell began to ring outside and they made their way toward the door. "I hope this isn't going to be a regular thing with them," he said.

I had a feeling it was.

I went on to the Sea Foam dining hall and found my group. Lucinda had acted as hostess on the meals I'd missed and had taken over a group of the round tables for the retreaters. It was nice to see how they had all befriended one another. I made my way around all the tables and was pleased that everyone seemed to be enjoying the retreat.

I finally sat down next to Lucinda. Bree, Olivia and Scott had stayed together and were at the table, too. I barely ate, being far too busy talking to everyone. When dinner ended, I brought the group to the grassy circle outside the social hall. The sun had come out again, just in time for a last hurrah before it went down. The orange glow of the sky morphed into evening blue as Virgil met up with us and directed the group toward the boardwalk. I was determined to take part in this activity and walked at the front with the tall white-haired man. It was a real effort not to be looking at my watch, knowing my baking time was coming near.

"Let's go through the dunes," Virgil said, turning back to the trail of people behind him. I stayed alongside him and we took the turnoff on the boardwalk. Everything was beginning to blend together now and the silky white sand of the dunes had a bluish cast. In the semidarkness it was impossible to see all the shades of green on the white sand.

Virgil held up his hand to stop the group and then pointed toward some large bushes growing in the sand. Two deer came from behind them and stopped for a moment before moving off over the hill.

I stayed close to the older man as he commented that even after all these years, he loved taking evening walks, whether it was here in the dunes or along the water in town. He mentioned that even in his days working at the bank, he'd done it.

His mention of the bank stirred my mind and I thought back to my stop at Nicole's shop earlier in the day. I mentioned the empty binders and the sheet I'd seen in the paper shredder.

"Those binders sound like the ones we used for the safety-deposit box sign-ins," he said. "When Mrs. Welton rented it, she got it as is, with all the old papers left behind. I don't know why anybody would bother shredding the sheets now when they could just throw them out. Talk about out-of-date."

We walked on until we'd reached the highest point of the dunes. The lights had come on at Vista Del Mar and I could make out the assorted buildings. In the other direction the foam of the waves as they broke on the beach was still visible.

"Mrs. Welton wondered about those ledgers, too. She said she was going to use the pages for kindling in the fireplace and wanted to make sure what they were first."

Virgil started to speak to the group, pointing out the light-house up ahead, and beyond, how you could see the curve of Monterey Bay before we headed down into a valley. In the half darkness, I could see the silhouettes of the tall bushes. I knew we were approaching the area where Bree had found Nicole. "This is as far as we can go," Virgil said, pointing to the barricade across the boardwalk up ahead.

I heard Virgil sigh as we turned back. "It's too bad what happened to that young woman. I don't know what they're going to do about the bench. I suppose they'll take it out. If they leave it, it will always have a negative reputation."

When we'd gotten back to where we'd started, Kevin St. John came out and announced there was going to be marsh-mallow roasting at the fire pit.

21

"YOU'RE ALONE," TAG SAID WHEN I CAME INTO THE Blue Door. I arrived after the restaurant had closed and had expected to have to use my key, but when I had tried to door, it was still unlocked.

Tag rushed to help me carry the recycled bags full of muffin ingredients and followed me as I went into the kitchen. "I thought Lucinda might have come with you." The very precise man sounded disappointed.

I didn't want to tell him the truth—that Lucinda was having a wonderful time and was enjoying the time on her own. It wasn't really a reflection on him. I noticed a lot of the women talked about how glad they were to be away from their families. It wasn't that they didn't love them; they just needed time to regroup.

Tag sighed a few times and stayed in the kitchen as I emptied the bags. "I really miss her, you know," he said. "I know

I'm hard to live with, but I'd be lost without Lucinda. She is planning to come back at the end of the weekend, isn't she?"

I thought he was joking, but the forlorn look on his face told me he wasn't. I assured him that she was coming home and he appeared a little happier. But he still made no move to leave. Since it was his restaurant, I really couldn't say anything. He started talking about how much he liked living in Cadbury.

"After our trip to the sheep ranch, I got interested in finding out more about the history of this area. I went back over to the historical society. Those docents really know their stuff."

Tag had settled in as I went right into making the cheesecake. I was going to make extra so they would have enough for two nights. I began working on the crust, which was really just graham cracker crumbs and melted better.

"They have a model of the Delacorte Cannery. You'd never know by looking at Monterey Bay now, but it turns out the sardine cannery made a mess of it. All the stuff from the cannery was dumped into the water. If they hadn't fished out all the sardines and closed the cannery, the bay might never have gotten cleaned up."

I was only half listening, but when I heard him mention Edmund Delacorte's name, I paid attention. It seemed he'd felt guilty about his family's role in damaging the bay and he was determined to keep the Vista Del Mar grounds in their natural state and to restore the dunes by removing the gypsy plants that had taken over and bringing back the natural plants. Edmund had decided to run for governor and was in the process of campaigning when he died. I started to zone out again when he got too detailed with the Delacorte family tree and how it was ending with the two sisters, since neither had any children and Edmund's only child, a son, had died barely a year after his father had.

Tag noticed some buttery crumbs had landed on the counter. I could see he was staring at them and getting agitated. Finally, he grabbed a paper towel and wiped them up. He let out a sigh of relief when he'd tossed the paper towel, then he looked sheepish. "I'm sorry. I can't help it. Please don't tell Lucinda. I am really trying to relax, but you have no idea what it's like for me. Those crumbs were nagging at me. I had to get rid of them." His voice had grown tense.

Until he'd described it, I'd had no idea what it was like for him. I guess I just thought he was being difficult. "We all have our things to deal with," I said. For him it was crumbs on the counter and for me it was learning how to stick with something long term.

I had the cheesecake filling ready to pour over the crumb crusts. I lifted the bowl off the stand mixer and carried it over to the two big pans and prepared to pour it in. Tag was watching my every move and I could see he was ready to lunge forward and wipe up any spill. Even though I now had some understanding about why, it was making me nervous. I was doing my best to get all of the cream cheese mixture where it belonged, but when I scraped out the bowl and was ready to transfer what was on the scraper, a glop of it fell off and landed on Tag's shoe.

He looked down at his shoe and got more and more upset. I got a paper towel and wiped it off, but it didn't come completely clean. Tag was suddenly beside himself. I could see that having even the faint mark on his shoe was more than he could handle. He rushed out, saying he had to go home, where he had the right supplies to take care of it.

I was grateful for the peace and a little time to regroup. It had been nonstop action with the early birds' arrival, then Nicole's death, Wanda's taking over the retreat and me trying to keep up with my baking. Not to mention trying to figure out what really happened to Nicole. My mind went to Dane and then I laughed at myself. I had brushed off all of his flirting and friendly gestures. But now when it appeared he was taken, suddenly I had regrets. Wasn't that human nature? You always wanted what seemed out of your reach.

I had chosen to make the cheesecakes because it didn't require baking and I thought it would be faster, but Tag's presence had slowed me down. I picked up speed now that I didn't feel a pair of eyes on me just waiting for me to make a mess.

I poured on the blanched almonds and the layer of cherry topping and set the two finished pans of cheesecakes in the refrigerator. Now they had dessert for Saturday and Sunday. And I'd be free to spend Saturday evening at Vista Del Mar with my people.

I cleaned up from the cheesecakes and began to take out the ingredients for the muffins. I was just going to bake one day's worth.

I was going to make plain ones. I had originally called them Plain Janes, but after Jane had started working at Vista Del Mar, I'd dropped the name, afraid she might take it personally. I started calling them Simplicity.

I heard a knock on the glass part of the door. My first thought was that Tag had gone home, changed shoes and come back, but when I got to the door, I saw Sammy standing close to the glass, trying to look in.

When I opened the door, I was surprised to see that he was carrying a backpack.

"What's up?" I said, which was really a polite way of asking what he was doing there. Sammy was usually all smiles with an easygoing manner, but I was surprised to see him looking tense as he came in.

"Case, I've got so much on my plate right now. I needed

to talk to somebody and like I always say, you're the one who understands me." I led him farther into the place and offered a place to sit. I'd never seen him like this. It always seemed that he just let any kind of stress roll off his back.

He refused the seat. "Is it work?" I asked. "Something with one of your patients?" Sammy never talked shop, but since he'd temporarily joined a local urology practice and was probably still getting used to it, I thought that might be it.

"No, Case." He waved his hand dismissively. "I could do those exams with my eyes closed. Though I am a little stressed about my living arrangements. I have to make some kind of change."

Sammy was still staying at the bed-and-breakfast across the street even though he'd been in Cadbury for months now. "Are they pushing you out?"

He laughed. "No way. I'm the hit of the place. You know how they always have wine and cheese in the evening. I always do a little magic to liven things up." I had him follow me into the kitchen so I could get back to work. "It was fine just to have a room at first, but I need a little more space. They're adding on a studio apartment sort of thing, but I don't know if I want to wait until they finish." I had this feeling he was going to bring up the converted garage/guesthouse I had. No way did I want to have him as a tenant. I quickly changed the subject.

"So then what has you so stressed?" I said quickly.

"It's tomorrow night," he said, looking at his watch, then wailed it was almost midnight and then it would become today he was worried about.

I tried to calm him down and said it was just table magic for an audience who would be so glad to have any entertainment during dinner, it wouldn't matter what he did. It didn't seem to help.

"Case, you don't get it. The thing about magic is that it really is right before your eyes, and it's up to me to make sure your eyes are in the right place." I knew what he was going to say, but I let him say it again anyway. He began to explain that we really had a very small area of visual focus and as long as there was something going on in that space, we'd miss whatever he was doing outside of that space.

"Could you do me a really, really big favor?" he said. "Could I do all my tricks for you just the way I'm going to do them in the dining hall, close-up?"

I started to make a face, wondering if this was like his kissing trick and just a way to get close to me, but I quickly realized he'd meant exactly what he'd said. He wanted an audience of one for a dress rehearsal. What could I say, particularly when he gave me his best puppy dog look and said that I was the best.

Somehow I managed to finish the muffins while picking a card and having coins disappear and reappear and my wristwatch vanish. Sammy seemed a little off rhythm at first, but then he seemed to hit his stride and he did fine. I was surprised at how nervous he was. Somehow I'd always thought of him having a certain level of confidence. Didn't it take confidence to show up in Cadbury after we'd broken up and, calm as anything, say he'd decided to relocate? Even that close to him, I still never figured out how he did all the tricks.

Something he kept saying struck me. Everything was right in front of your face; you just had to know where to look.

22

"SORRY," I SAID AS I ROLLED BACK THE COVERS AND
Julius went rolling with them. He gave me a plaintive meow
and turned his fall into a jump. It was Saturday morning and
there was no time for even a few extra minutes under the
covers. This was the big day of the retreat. Time for the main
event. Although I'd called it Sheep to Shawl, it was really
about the spinning.

Sammy had hung around until I finished the muffins and
then followed me as I made my rounds dropping them off.
We ended up almost at his doorstep—the big yellow Victorian
across the street that had been turned into a bed-and-breakfast.
I was glad to see him walk away with a jaunty stride. His
dress rehearsal had given him a boost of confidence.

I was fighting with a thought as I walked to the kitchen. It
had taken all of Friday to wash the yarn, card it and form it
into long pieces that could be spun. How long was it going to
take for them to learn how to spin? And who knew if there

was enough wool? I had tried bringing up my concerns to Wanda, but anytime I said anything to her, she took it as some kind of reproach and blew me off.

Right then and there I made a decision. If I put on another retreat, I'd thoroughly learn whatever the theme was going to be. In my head I could hear my mother laughing at the concept that, number one, I would stick with this business long enough to put on another retreat, and number two, I would have the perseverance to go through a whole process that was unfamiliar to me.

Julius beat me to the kitchen and walked past his full bowl of kitty stew with disdain. "It's stink fish or starve, huh?" I swear it seemed like the black cat nodded.

"I must love you," I said as I took out a can I'd hidden at the back of the pantry. Julius jumped up on the counter next to me and licked his chops as I ran the electric can opener.

When he was happily eating, I hastily pulled open a carton of yogurt and grabbed the phone. I called Maggie and got her this time. There was the sound of voices in the background. I heard the steam from the espresso machine and someone giving an order for a nonfat, foam-only cappuccino. "This isn't the best time to talk," she said. Her helper, Carol, was there, but this was prime time in the coffee business. I quickly told her about the muffin that had been at the crime scene.

"Now I get what you meant in your message," she said. "That certainly changes everything. Whoever bought the coffee and chocolate and vanilla muffin must have come in on Monday. I know we sold out of those muffins before noon. It is kind of strange, though. If you're right and somebody gave Nicole the poisoned coffee, why would they use coffee from the day before? Let me think about it and see if I can remember anything about that morning."

My mind was still on Nicole as I showered and got ready. I was frustrated that everything seemed all over the place and there were lots of questions bouncing around in my mind. As I sat wrapped in a towel I picked up the phone and punched in Frank's number.

"Feldstein, is that really you?" he said in mock surprise. "I can't believe you're calling at such a reasonable time, though it is Saturday, which lots of people consider an off day."

"C'mon, Frank. You told me a good detective never has a day off."

"No, Feldstein. What I said was a detective's dream was to have enough work that he had to work weekends." I heard the squeak of his recliner chair, which he had told me he had in both the office and at home. "So what's up? More dead bodies? Something going on with the cop down the street? Your old boyfriend make himself disappear and can't find his way back?" Frank punctuated it with a chortle.

"This is serious," I said. "I have a whole lot of pieces of information like a jigsaw puzzle and I can't seem to make out what the picture is. I thought you could help."

"Uh-oh, you aren't about to start laying it on about what a crime-solving genius I am, are you?" I heard him laugh, so I knew he was joking, even though there was some truth in what he said. Only I'd planned to leave it at "superdetective."

"Okay, let's hear what you've got."

It turned out the first thing I had to do was bring Frank up to speed. "Feldstein, I haven't been sitting around here mulling about your last phone call. All I remember is something about some awful-sounding jewelry and maybe some blackmail."

I reminded him about Nicole and how we'd both agreed it didn't seem like suicide. I started to talk about the fact that Nicole hadn't been well liked and there were a number of people who might have wanted her dead. "There's a woman named Wanda who seems to have been the town's premier spinner until Nicole came along," I said.

Frank started to protest, saying he hoped I wasn't going to say she was trying to spin gold out of straw. I knew he was trying to be funny, but I persisted and told him how Wanda had ended up taking Nicole's place for my retreat. "And there's something odd—" I debated if I should tell him about the salad spinners she'd bought before Nicole was dead. It seemed like a lot of effort to explain what the salad spinners were used for. I finally kept it short and just said Wanda had bought some equipment for the retreat when Nicole still had the job.

Frank was having a hard time understanding how important being the premier spinner was to Wanda. I started to explain that she was rather plain and had been overshadowed by her younger sister, who had been the prom queen.

"It was the same year that Nicole's husband was the prom king," I added. "He was quite the heartthrob and I think a number of women were upset when he married Nicole."

"Maybe Wanda's sister was one of them and she decided to get her out of the way?" Frank said. "It wouldn't be the first time something like that has happened. But it seems to me you thought the victim was involved in blackmail. Doesn't it make sense to be looking at the guy you saw leave her an envelope? Any ideas what information she might have had on him?"

"I have no proof the envelope had anything to do with blackmail. I could ask Burton Fiore about it, but if it had to do with blackmail, I'm sure he would lie."

"Good thinking, Feldstein," Frank said, punctuating it with a chuckle. "People rarely fess up to stuff like that."

I brought up the bank that had become Nicole's store and how I'd found out it had sat vacant until she'd rented it. I described how she'd had to leave it looking like a bank, with the tellers' cages and the vault, and how there'd even been a stack of old ledgers, though she'd used the paper for kindling in the fireplace.

"A fireplace in a bank," Frank said incredulously.

"It's a small town and I guess it was the only source of heat in those days," I said, surprised by his comment. I mentioned how I'd thought someone had broken into the place earlier in the week, but it had been explained away. "But when I went in there yesterday, it looked like somebody had been in there looking for something again."

"Maybe it was the victim's husband," Frank said.

"I don't think so. He gave me free access to it and everything in there. I'm sure he dreads having to deal with the place. It is such a reminder of her."

"So cross him off the list. Any idea what whoever was after?" Frank asked. I made the mistake of bringing up the box of moldy clothes and the items I'd thought were hidden in the box. Frank had a good laugh.

"Feldstein, it sounds like a box waiting for the trash." I told him Nicole's husband had thought the same thing, but she'd insisted she wanted to refurbish the old fabrics.

"There's something more. It seems like someone was shredding the pages of those old ledgers." I could tell I was losing Frank's interest, so I quickly added more or less what Virgil had said, that the pages were such ancient history it seemed like a waste of time to bother shredding them when you could just throw them away. "The man who'd worked at the bank told me the ledgers had held the old sign-in sheets when people wanted to access their safety-deposit boxes."

There was silence on Frank's end and I wondered if he'd fallen asleep or hung up, but then I heard the squeak of the recliner chair and a grunt as he shifted his weight. "I was just thinking," he said, "I wonder what was on those sheets. Too bad you didn't have a look at them."

"Wait a second," I said, walking across the kitchen before going across to the guesthouse. I had forgotten the obvious— the way I knew what was being shredded was by the partial sheet I'd found in the shredder. I smelled the mildewy scent as soon as I went inside. I lifted the torn sheet off the top and looked at it.

"See anything interesting, Feldstein?" Frank asked.

At first my eye just went down the page and I was about to say that it just seemed to be a list of signatures and printed names, but then one of the names popped out at me. "Edmund Delacorte," I said.

"Who's that? Frank asked. I scanned the sheet again and I noticed something weird. "Feldstein, are you still there?" Frank demanded.

"Sorry," I said. I gave him a quick review of the Delacorte family and who Edmund had been. "But here's the strange thing," I said. "There's a box number next to Edmund's name and then a few lines down, the same box number appears again."

"So maybe he went into his box twice," Frank suggested.

"No. It's a different name. Or at least the beginning of a different name. That's just where the page is torn. All I can see is that it began with an *M*." Something from the back of my mind came to the forefront. "The man I met who used to work at the bank said that Edmund Delacorte came into the bank every Friday and went to his safety-deposit box." Julius had followed me into the guesthouse and sat down next to me and began cleaning himself.

"And then what, Feldstein," Frank said, sounding impatient. "Maybe the bank guy knows who this M was?"

"No. Virgil made a point that Edmund came into the bank

just as he was going to lunch." I stopped talking as I realized that it sounded like a plan.

"Are you thinking what I'm thinking, Feldstein?"

"Edmund was leaving something in the safety-deposit box and the M person was picking it up," I said, getting excited.

"How about it was money and some kind of payoff," Frank offered. "Very clever for him to time it so he got there just before this Virgil guy went to lunch, and then to have the mysterious M come in while somebody took over for Virgil. There was probably fill-in staff and different people all the time, so they wouldn't have noticed the same person coming in every week. Have you had a look at the safety-deposit boxes?" he asked. I told him the locks were all off and the boxes were empty.

"Nicole must have figured it out. She must have looked through the ledgers and seen the same pair of names connected to the same box," I said.

"But what did she figure out? What was this Edmund paying somebody off for? Feldstein, you got a lot of facts there, but there are still some missing pieces. You're smart. You'll figure it out." I hadn't even gotten to mention my threatening note. I barely had time to thank him for his help before he was hanging up.

Had Frank just given me a compliment? Or was it just a way to get off the phone? I tried to put the pieces together, but still all I got was that Nicole must have figured out that Edmund was paying somebody off. But why would anybody care now? There was no more time to think about it. I had a retreat to run.

23

I WAS 100 PERCENT FOCUSED ON THE RETREAT AS I cruised in at the end of breakfast and grabbed a plate of hot food. With no care packages from Dane and all my running around, it seemed forever since I'd had a decent meal. I set my plate down next to Lucinda's. I could always tell where she was sitting by the designer purse. She was making the rounds with the coffeepot. No matter how much she said she wanted some time away, she couldn't seem to give up playing host.

"Thank you for helping," I said as I passed her. I went past all three tables of my people, greeting them. I was relieved that everyone seemed to be having a good time and was looking forward to spinning.

I scanned the group hoping to see Wanda among them, but she wasn't there. Nor was Crystal. My mouth was sore from smiling when I finally took my seat, but I didn't want to let on that I had any doubts about the activities for the day.

Lucinda filled my coffee cup and slipped into the seat next

to me. I thanked her for the coffee and mentioned seeing Tag at the restaurant when I'd gone to bake. "He really misses you," I said.

"Really?" she said as a soft blush colored her cheeks. I told her about our conversation.

"Tag feels left out," she said. "I'm sure he appreciated being able to talk to you. It is hard for him to understand the kind of friendship we have."

"After he left, Sammy came by," I said. As I was telling her about the magic show, there was something nagging at the back of my mind. Was it something he said?

"He's a sweet guy," she said and I had to agree. "Anything new about anything else?" she asked, glancing around to see if anyone was listening to us. They weren't.

She didn't have to elaborate for me to know what she meant. I told her about my call with Frank. "I think Nicole figured out that Cora's brother was paying somebody off, but I can't figure out why anyone would care about that now." I brought up the shredded pages. "But it seems like somebody was trying to get rid of the evidence.

Lucinda hung her head. "I feel terrible. I've been hanging around here having a great time and you've been off trying to solve a mystery on top of everything else." My friend urged me to eat. People were already beginning to get up from the tables and, in the interest of speed, I slapped the scrambled eggs between the rye toast.

I knew what she meant by "everything else." "So you picked up on my concern about the spinning," I said. I went to take a hasty bite of my sandwich but everyone at the table was leaving. I wrapped it in a napkin and figured I'd just take it with me. I felt like I could be honest with her and I told her how bad I felt that I had left everything in someone else's hands. "First it was Nicole and now Wanda. If I ever put on another retreat, I'm going to know exactly what the program is going to be and how to do it. We only have today and a little of tomorrow. These people are just going to be learning how to spin. How fast does it go?"

Lucinda tried to reassure me that it would be fine and reminded me that I'm managed to overcome all the roadblocks so far, starting with Nicole's death, then not being able to have the sheep sheared in front of the group, and dealing with Wanda.

"If you call dealing with her letting her stonewall me," I said. As we passed one of the tables our group had taken over, I noticed that Ronny Fiore was still sitting down. I'd missed her during my early go-round and told Lucinda to go on ahead. "It's particularly important that she has a good time," I said. "It wouldn't help my case if she tells her step-mother-to-be that I didn't deliver what was promised."

My friend headed to the door and I stopped next to the young woman. "I hope you're enjoying the retreat, Ronny," I said, putting on my most pleasant voice, realizing this was also a chance to find out about her and her father with a few well-positioned questions. I had learned during my time doing phone interviews that the best plan was to keep it friendly and never make it seem like an interrogation. She looked up with halfhearted interest. When I got a look at her plate, it seemed like she was dissecting the food.

"I suppose working for a hotel as you do, makes staying at another one not exactly a holiday." She brightened at my comment.

"I can't help it," she said. I can't eat a meal without wondering about the quality of the ingredients. And the rooms here." The shake of her head made it clear they weren't up to her standards.

"If it were up to you, what would you change?" I asked.

"Everything. We already have—" She cut herself off. "My father has already talked to Cora about making the running of Vista Del Mar a family enterprise, meaning with my experience and his know-how, we can take the burden of running it off of her shoulders."

"I didn't realize it was on her shoulders," I said, seeing Kevin St. John come into the dining hall. Ronny saw who I was looking at.

"Cora is such a dear, but she has left entirely too much up to him." Ronny glanced around at the groups in the emptying dining hall. "You must realize how dated this place is. Imagine a bunch of modern buildings, rooms with flat-screen TVs, luxury bathrooms, and Wi-Fi everywhere. Knock down all these trees and put in a golf course." As she went on I realized she could have been describing any of a bunch of local resorts.

"But the whole atmosphere of Vista Del Mar would be gone and its unique beauty. That sort of place would lose all the retreat business," I said.

She turned and looked at me like I was crazy. "That's the point. We don't want groups expecting reasonable rooms that include meals. Instead of offering all these quaint little meeting rooms, we'll put in some luxury villas. If we decide to keep it as a conference center, we'd put in a big structure that could attract high-end groups for conventions and meetings."

The more I listened, the more horrified I got. I'd had the feeling both she and her father were taking mental measurements of the place and thinking about changes. I had no idea they were that far along. I half expected her to pull out some blueprints.

"And Cora agrees with all this?" I said.

"I'm sure she will. There's no reason to worry her with it now that her head is filled with wedding plans. I'm going to help her with everything."

It seemed like an opening and I mentioned that I'd seen her father in The Bank talking to Nicole. "Cora's so lucky to have him. I suppose he wanted to get her something really special. Everything Nicole had was one of a kind," I said.

She gave me a strange look. "You must be mistaken. I'm sure he's never even been in there."

Sometimes my attempts to get information didn't work out. Either Ronny was lying or she didn't know why her father was in the store. I reminded her that the workshop would be starting soon. I probably should have been glad that she didn't seem enthused. At least I didn't have to worry about her being disappointed.

People were milling around outside before the different morning workshops began. I rushed on ahead and went directly to the room where the spinning wheels were set up. The wood paneling and brown carpet made it much darker than the other room we'd used. There were plenty of windows, but they looked out into a thick stand of trees. As soon as I turned on the lights it seemed a lot more inviting. Folding chairs had been arranged around the couches and easy chairs to accommodate the whole group. A fire had been laid in the fireplace, but not lit.

Wanda came in at almost the same time I did. As she went to open the bin she'd left the day before, I mentioned that there didn't seem to be very much wool. She turned and glared at me. "There wouldn't have been even that much if Nicole had been running this." The little woman in lavender slacks and another blah sort of floral top didn't wait for a comment from me, but grabbed a handful of the rolls of wool, and like a whirlwind began to distribute them.

Will came in and lit the fire. Afterward he came over to me. "I just wanted to stop by to make sure you had all the supplies you needed," Will said. There was something sad in his gaze as he looked at the spinning wheels and I imagined that he was thinking that Nicole should be the one there now. I brought up my last trip to her store and asked if he'd made sure that the lock was secure on the back door. He shrugged off the question with a heavy sigh. "That place is just a heartache to me now."

I didn't want to let on that I'd figured out the importance of the ledger sheets, but wondered if he knew. I took a chance and mentioned it seemed like someone had been shredding the sheets and asked him if he had any idea why. I was curious about his reaction.

When I checked his expression, he seemed unmoved. Finally his blue eyes flared. "I know about your sleuthing, but please just let it be." He sounded tired and drained. Trying to keep going as if nothing had happened had to be wearing. Could Will be hiding a dark side under those scruffy good looks?

I mumbled an apology as someone from the kitchen staff came in looking for him and said the sink had backed up again. He sighed and went to follow the woman.

In the meantime, the retreaters had begun to come in and all my attention went to them. Lucinda waved as she walked in with Olivia, Scott and Bree. Crystal and Ronny Fiore came in last. Wanda had finished her task and was patrolling the front of the room. When Crystal and I tried to join her, Wanda made us both join the group. This was her moment and clearly she wasn't going to share center stage with anyone.

If I hadn't been so worried about the job she was going to do, I might have enjoyed the workshop. She had everyone take out their drop spindle and pick up the strand of yarn she'd left on each of the chairs to use as a lead.

Wanda glared at Crystal and me. "What are you two waiting for? Get your spindles and yarn."

I was hoping just to be an observer, but Wanda was unmoving until I found the tote bag I'd made up for myself and one of the extras for Crystal. We took out our spindles and found the length of yarn we'd been sitting on.

Wanda surprised me by giving easy-to-follow instructions

on how to attach the yarn. She moved right on to the actual spinning and ordered everyone to take out a roll of the washed and carded wool. She demonstrated how to fold the wool over the end of the yarn. Then she gave her spindle a whirl and showed how the bit of wool twisted into a strand. Of course, it wasn't as easy as it looked. I wished I'd paid more attention when Nicole had first demonstrated how to do it so that I could have helped the others instead of struggling myself. Luckily, Crystal was experienced and in no time had a long length of yarn coming off the spindle.

Wanda moved around the room like a force of nature. When she saw the quality of Crystal's work, she sent her off in the other direction to aid the fledgling spinners. Then Wanda began to go through the group, taking people to the spinning wheels. They were already set up with some spun yarn, so it was more about adding than starting from scratch. It also seemed to be more about the experience than producing much yarn.

Spinning was second nature to Wanda, but she was able to break it down to teach it. I imagined she taught golf the same way. She kept repeating the instructions and the group started getting the hang of it.

The time flew by and in no time the lunch bell was ringing. I urged everyone to leave their newly spun yarn and go eat. Wanda went with them, but Lucinda and I stayed behind. I was shocked at the paltry amount of yarn that had been produced.

"The whole point of this was to end up knitting with hand-spun yarn," I said in dismay.

Lucinda tried to be encouraging. "Now that everybody knows how to spin, they'll probably make a whole bunch this afternoon."

We looked at each other and neither of us believed what she'd said.

24

WANDA WAS STANDING BY THE DOOR AS THE
retreaters came back after lunch. The trouble with stopping
for the meal was that they had all lost momentum, or really
the rhythm of spinning. It wasn't quite as bad as starting all
over, but it wasn't too far off. Could everyone really forget
what they had learned that fast?

Undaunted, the small stout woman demonstrated how to use
the drop spindle all over again. She asked Crystal to handle the
spinning wheels. I was glad that I seemed to remember how to
use the drop spindle. I kept feeding more tufts of wool onto the
strand coming off the spindle and giving it a turn. I wasn't
exactly doing a jig while I did it like Wanda did, but I was
making progress.

When Wanda came by, I pulled her aside. I started with a
compliment. "Thank you for stepping in. You're doing a great
job." Okay, maybe I was buttering her up before I brought up

the yarn situation. "I really see your point. I don't think Nicole would have been able to handle this." Wanda's face lit up.

"Finally you're beginning to see the light," Wanda said in a triumphant voice. Just then Will went by the window. "In a town like Cadbury we appreciate old-fashioned values and he personifies them."

"I get the feeling that Will is kind of the town gem," I said. She watched a gust of wind blow open his flannel shirt. "You know, the guy who was a high school hero and has hung on to the title. I understand he was the prom king and your sister was the prom queen that year." I left it hanging, curious what she'd say.

"Half the girls in the school were hoping he'd ask them to prom. In the end he picked out a girl who probably wouldn't have had a date otherwise. That's the kind of guy he is." She made a face like she was considering whether to continue or not. "I know I shouldn't speak ill of the dead, but when he could have had any girl in town, why did he marry an outsider?"

"I suppose you consider me an outsider," I said. Wanda looked me up and down.

"Not completely. You seem to get along." She put her hand out toward the group. "You're bringing business to town. You seem to play by the rules."

"What rules?" I asked, surprised at her comment. I'd always thought I followed my own drumbeat and she was basically saying I was a conformist.

"You fit into the parameters of the town. Even what you call your muffins."

"Oh, you mean because I stopped calling the blueberry muffins The Blues?"

She nodded, but I wasn't there to talk about me. I went back to her sister and the prom and asked how upset she was that Will didn't ask her.

"She was the prom queen and she thought he liked her, so she sort of expected it. The trouble is Will acts like that to everybody. You know, when he talks to you, it seems like you're the only person in the world and what you have to say is the funniest most interesting thing he's ever heard."

"It sounds like you have a crush on him," I teased. A bad move. Wanda's demeanor stiffened as she announced she had a husband and wasn't into romantic fantasy. She was about to move on. I looked at the off-white wool that was turning into a creamy-colored yarn. There wasn't enough yet for the women to have to take it off the spindle and make it into a ball, and I seized the moment.

"I think we need a plan B," I said, showing off the small amount of actual yarn on my spindle.

"Don't be ridiculous," she said in a snippy voice. "Everything is under control."

"But if you could just let me in on your plans, it would help. I don't know if you remember, but they're supposed to at least start work on a shawlette."

I looked her in the eye, expecting her to see my point. Instead she put her hand on her hip and held the other one out. I couldn't help it, I immediately thought of those song lyrics about a little teapot that was short and stout.

"I just signed on to help prepare the wool and spin it," Wanda said. Then she suggested that if I was so concerned about how much yarn was being spun, I should make better use of my time and start working my spindle.

Lucinda had heard it all and had a raised-eyebrow worried look. By the end of the session, it was clear I wasn't the only one who'd noticed how little yarn we'd all produced. I heard someone say we'd be lucky to have enough yarn to make a shawl for a Barbie doll.

Around three, we took a break. Lucinda went on ahead to

the café. I stopped at the message board to see if there was anything from Maggie. The big board was covered with small pieces of paper and though they had the recipients' names written in large letters at the top, there was no order to their arrangement. The only solution was to start at one side and go through them all. Somewhere in the middle, I saw one with my name on it and pulled it off.

It seemed like everyone at Vista Del Mar had had the same idea about taking a break in the café. The line snaked all the way out the door. When I looked inside, I saw that more tables had been added and were quite close together now. Lucinda was almost the next person to be waited on and I quickly joined her, getting a few dirty looks from people who must have thought I was cutting the line.

Hoping to calm their fury, I pointed to my friend and said we were together.

While we waited I took out the note. "I finally heard back from Maggie," I said.

"What did she say?" my friend asked.

I held up the small piece of paper. "Not what I was hoping for. Just that she'd remembered something, but no details. I really need to talk to her. I did tell you that because of the muffin type, it seems like the items were purchased on Monday morning instead of Tuesday." I was purposely vague, not wanting the people around us to know what I was talking about.

We got a couple of passion fruit ice teas and started to walk back. The rest of the group trailed along with us. I couldn't help it, but I started to walk on ahead with a bad feeling.

When I got to the meeting room, it seemed to be as we'd left it. There were retreat tote bags spread all over the floor and drop spindles sitting on most of the chairs. The spinning wheels had been left in midspin. Everything seemed okay except for one thing: Wanda wasn't there, and when I looked for her tote bag, it was gone.

I waited as the rest of the retreaters returned, and when Crystal came in I pulled her aside.

"You know Wanda better than I do. Is it her MO to just take off?"

For all of Crystal's fun earrings, heavy eye makeup and corkscrew curls, she looked around the room with a serious expression. "She's gone? Are you sure?" I pointed out that her tote bag was missing and Crystal finally agreed.

I shook my head, thinking of what Wanda had said about having everything under control. Right. Under control because she was going to disappear.

Lucinda joined us and realized who was missing. "Maybe we should make other plans," Crystal said. "I could call my mother and see what yarn she can get together at the store that looks like handspun. The only thing is, she wouldn't be able to get it here for this session. But maybe for the one tomorrow morning."

I cleared my throat to speak. There was no reason to hold off on the truth anymore.

"I'm sure you've all been looking for Wanda Krug," I said. "She's been unavoidably detained. The schedule says you're supposed to start working on your shawlettes. We'll have to table that until tomorrow," I said, "because . . ." I was winging it now, hoping some words would come to me. Olivia stepped to the front of the room.

"What Casey is trying to say is that, instead of starting the shawlettes now, we're all going to work on a charity project." Olivia held up a handful of squares. "We need more if we're going to have enough for a couple of blankets." She asked if anybody needed yarn or needles. A ripple of laughter went through the room as everyone pulled out both items from their tote bags.

"Thank you," I said to Olivia when everybody had started knitting.

She knew that Wanda was a stand-in and had figured out what had happened. "It's the least I can do. You and the group helped me look at things in a new light. I feel like I owe my happiness to that retreat. After dinner we can start putting the squares together." Her eyes were shining and her smile lit up her almond-shaped face.

Olivia pushed one of the kits on me and said I looked like I needed some knitting therapy. She was right about that.

The group seemed to have no problem with the change in plans and soon there was the soft click of needles as a bunch of conversations started. I envied how they could talk and knit. I still needed to concentrate on my stitches and the best I could do was listen.

There was a lot about their husbands, children and grand-children. A reminder of all that I didn't have. One woman seemed particularly perturbed about a baby blanket she'd made for her grandchild. Her daughter-in-law had called the pink blanket sexist.

"There are some traditions that shouldn't be messed with. Pink is for girls and blue is for boys." Apparently I could also knit and think. Her comment stirred something in my mind.

25

IF THE GROUP WAS DISAPPOINTED NOT TO BE spinning or knitting with their spun wool, they kept it to themselves. But I felt I'd let them all down. Maybe this business wasn't for me. To keep going I'd need good word of mouth and recommendations, along with repeat customers. I could just imagine what they'd have to say about this retreat when they went home.

The last part of the workshop ended and most of them headed off for some free time before dinner. This was the part of the weekend where I should have been feeling a sense of accomplishment that the main part of the retreat was done. First it was the sheep and now it looked like there'd be no shawls. The name of the retreat had been hacked away at until now the only word left of Sheep to Shawl was *to*.

I walked to the Lodge with the early birds and Lucinda. The Ginger had joined us and seemed to be hanging close to Bree. We all stopped at the message board, but by now with so many messages piled on top of each other, it was simply too overwhelming to sort through them.

The Ginger and Bree looked at the line waiting for the pay phones and shook their heads. Too long. I wanted to do something to make up for all the problems and suggested a drink in the café, my treat.

"I'm not even going to try calling Maggie again," I said as we came into the café. "I'm just going to go to the Coffee Shop in the morning and talk to her in person."

"That sounds like a good plan," Lucinda said. We found an empty table and I got a round of homemade lemonades for everyone. Of course the conversation turned to Wanda's disappearance. I really appreciated how they rallied around me and tried to convince me that no one really noticed. Ha!

Bree and the Ginger kept glancing at the door so many times, I finally asked her what was up.

"I know it's sort of cheating, but I was thinking about walking out into the street . . ." Bree said.

". . . until you get a signal," Olivia said, finishing her sentence. We all agreed it wasn't cheating and they bounded off with their cell phones in hand.

Finally the rest of us went our separate ways to get ready for dinner.

As I headed toward my place, I saw Bree and the Ginger standing in the middle of the street. A car drove slowly toward them and they seemed to be playing chicken with it, only dashing out of the way a moment before it reached them.

"Drat. Lost my call," Bree said, giving her phone an angry look. I hadn't realized the signal was that fragile and invited them to come to my place. It seemed like the least I could do after all the problems.

Julius was waiting outside the door and I half expected him to look at his paw (in my imagination he had a watch on) and ask where I'd been for so long. He gave Bree's sneakers the once-over as we went inside.

I didn't even waste time fussing with him and just unfurled the can of stink fish, though I saw Bree make a funny face from across the room. Apparently the scent traveled.

I sent them off to the living room to make their calls while I considered whether to change my clothes. I heard a pounding on my door.

When I opened the kitchen door, Dr. Sammy was standing outside holding his tuxedo on a hanger. "Case, okay if I change here?" he said. He mumbled some explanation that he'd been looking at apartments all day and he didn't want to go back to his current place to change.

Julius was too busy with his stink fish to notice another visitor. I sent Sammy off to my bedroom to change. When he came out, he was a wreck. I had to remind him to tuck in his shirt and put on the cummerbund.

"Case, what would I do without you?" he said nervously. "You're going to be there, right?" I nodded and he gave me a grateful hug. "I guess I better go," he said. I walked him to the back door and watched as he walked past the converted garage toward the street. Poor guy looked like he was on his way to the guillotine.

Bree and the Ginger finished their calls and thanked me profusely. "It's the first real conversation I've had with them since I got here," the Ginger said.

"I told you it would be okay," Bree said, giving her a supportive pat. They left to change for dinner and the evening program. I was glad to see that at least something had worked out.

I still felt rather glum, but I had to pull myself together. I needed to put on a front for the group, and this was Sammy's big night. If nothing else, I could at least get dressed up. I picked a clingy black dress and flats. To brighten it up, I made

a design of my aunt's crocheted and knitted embellishments
along one of the shoulder straps. I changed my earrings to long
dangles and did a whole makeup job, but no raccoon look this
time. And I wrapped myself in a black mohair shawl that had
little sparkles. I mouthed a thank-you to my aunt Joan for
leaving me all these beautiful handmade items.

The sun had come out and was hanging low in the sky.
Maybe the sunset would be visible. It felt strange to be walking
up the driveway of Vista Del Mar in a dress, but at the same
time, it felt nice to feel the air swirl around my bare legs under
the ballerina-length dress. When I walked into the Lodge
shafts of golden sunlight were coming in through the window,
giving everything an inviting glow. There was a different feeling about the social hall. I thought perhaps it was that everyone
seemed to have gotten dressed up for dinner. I suppose I
shouldn't have been surprised to see Burton Fiore holding the
door for his beloved. They seemed to be spending a lot of time
at Vista Del Mar. When they passed Kevin St. John, it looked
like he and Burton were practically twins in their matching
dark suits, white shirts and ties.

Cora was dressed to the nines, too. Instead of her usual
suit, she wore a knee-length black dress. It had a scoop neck
and short sleeves and looked like the classic black dress every
woman used to have in her closet. She'd adorned it with a
string of big pearls and earrings to match. Going with the
more formal look, she carried a satin clutch purse. As usual,
she'd gone heavy on the eye shadow and I could see the iri-
descent blue from across the room.

I could almost hear her sigh with pleasure as her fiancé
put his arm around her waist. Ronny joined them. I had to
hold back a gag as she embraced Cora and called her
"Mother." Cora seemed to like the title and gave Ronny's arm
an affectionate squeeze.

I should have figured Madeleine was with them. She came out of the gift shop carrying a bag of something. She was wearing a similar dress to her sister's, though no pearls, and she'd gone way less obvious with the makeup. She looked toward her future brother-in-law and her lip curled into distaste. The expression lasted only the blink of an eye and she put on a forced-looking smile as she approached the family group.

I don't know why, but I suddenly felt very protective of Cora Delacorte—maybe because she'd liked my aunt so well, or maybe because of how she'd helped with the retreats. Seeing her with that smarmy man was like an accident waiting to happen. I needed to figure out what was going on with Burton Fiore and I needed to do it now.

Somehow I thought it was all connected with Nicole's shop. No matter what Ronny Fiore said, I was sure of what I'd seen. Her father had come into Nicole's when I was there and there had been some kind of exchange. It was clear now that someone had been in the shop several times. Could it have been he? And what was he looking for? What could Nicole have found out about him that he'd pay to keep quiet?

When I saw Madeleine head toward the ladies' room, I followed her. Something that Sammy had said popped into my mind and I thought she might know about it. Another thing I'd learned while working for Frank was that sometimes the people I was calling for information were lonely and glad just to have someone to talk to. I almost felt guilty when I got off those calls. The old saying "like taking candy from a baby" went through my head.

I fussed at the sink until Madeleine came out of the stall. I was glad to see she was the fastidious kind who washed her hands. Starting a conversation was easy. "That's such a lovely dress," I said.

The comment didn't register on her face for a moment,

then she broke into a small smile. "I didn't realize you were talking to me." She looked around and saw that no one was there but the two of us. "Of course you were talking to me. There's no one else here." She hesitated a moment. "Where are my manners? Thank you for the compliment. It is really quite old." Just as I suspected, she was glad to have someone to talk to and now that she'd started, she went on.

I listened to the whole history of the dress, which was really quite interesting. It was from the early sixties, when everyone wanted to look like Audrey Hepburn.

"That must have been when you were all living in the big house on Grand Street. The one that's the Butterfly Bed-and-Breakfast now," I said. Sammy's comment about his living arrangements coupled with seeing the Delacorte sisters had made me think of something. The dresser and the box of moldy stuff had come from a bed-and-breakfast that was clearing a storage area to build a studio apartment. Sammy had mentioned the B and B where he was staying was adding a small apartment. The yellow Victorian house was across the street from the Blue Door and more than once I'd stopped to read the historical plaque outside giving the house's history. It had been the family home of the Delacortes until the death of Cora and Madeleine's mother, Antonia.

Madeleine seemed thrilled to be having a conversation and talked on. She confirmed the bed-and-breakfast had been their parents' home and went on and on about what a grand house it was. They'd sold it only when their mother died. I was only half listening, thinking about the contents of the box of moldy stuff.

When Madeleine finally took a breath, I asked her if she'd ever seen a locket covered in woven hair.

"Do you have it?" she said quickly. Her tone made it clear she knew exactly what I was talking about. She barely let me get out that I knew where it was before she told me about it.

"My mother had that made when my brother died. With his hair," Madeleine said, making a face. "I think having that memory of him around her neck only made it worse. Personally, I thought it was grotesque and expected her to start wearing his finger bones as a pendant or something."

She asked again if I had it. I said Nicole had had it. Madeleine sucked in her breath and asked what else she had. When I described the dresser, she confirmed it had been her brother's. The door whooshed open and Ronny Fiore came in and locked eyes on Madeleine. "There you are. Mother Cora was worried you were taking so long."

"It was lovely talking to you," Madeleine said. Her smile was genuine as she reached out and took my hand in hers. "It would be nice if you came to visit sometime. I used to knit. Maybe you could refresh my memory."

Before I could answer, Ronny hustled her out of the bathroom, showering her with concern.

I leaned against the sink, thinking about the information I'd gotten. A woman holding an infant came in. The baby smiled at me and I smiled back, getting ready to comment on how cute it was. I searched for something indicating it was a boy or a girl so I could add the appropriate "he" or "she" to the "cute" comment. I thought of the conversation I'd overheard earlier about the tradition of colors for baby blankets. The baby's white onesie had a tiny pink flower. That had to mean it was a girl, right? My mind started to click and it was like magic. All the pieces that had meant nothing by themselves suddenly began to fall into place. All along I'd thought Nicole had some damaging information about Burton, but now I knew I'd been all wrong. The information wasn't on him; it was on something he wanted.

But here was the problem: It was all just conjecture. There was no proof, but what if he thought there was?

26

PEOPLE WERE LINED UP OUTSIDE THE SEAFOAM
dining hall, waiting for the dinner bell to ring. There was a
buzz of excitement. Not only would Sammy be doing his
magic, but afterward there would be a movie in Hummingbird
Hall. Needless to say the Delacorte sisters and Burton weren't
in the line. Not even Ronny Fiore. Once the dining hall
opened they would go in a side door and sit at the owners'
table. I found Lucinda waiting with some of the people in our
group. I gestured for her to get out of line.

When we were out of earshot, I laid out the favor I needed.
All she had to do was make sure Burton Fiore overheard her
say that I'd figured out what Nicole was doing and I was going
to her shop to get the proof while everyone was in the movie.
"If he's innocent, which I don't believe, then it won't mean
anything. But if Nicole was blackmailing him, he won't be
able to resist," I said.

Lucinda seemed wary. "Are you sure it's such a good idea

to do this when you're there all alone? If he killed Nicole, what's to stop him from trying to get rid of you, too?" my friend said. She glanced over the crowd just as Burton Fiore came in, holding Cora close. "By the way, what is it you figured out?"

"It's better if you don't know. Then you don't have to worry about saying too much."

"Are you sure it's safe for you?" Lucinda repeated. "The Blue Door can't lose its number one baker, and I'd be lost if something happened to you."

"Don't worry. I'm going to have my finger over 911. At the first sound of someone coming in, I'll hit it. The police station is two blocks away. Even if they walked, they'd get there in time."

We synchronized our watches and she went back to her spot in line. I hung back, looking for Sammy, knowing he was lurking somewhere and probably a nervous wreck. I found him behind a Monterey cypress tree.

"Case, over here," he said in a stage whisper. I joined him and noticed that he was sweating profusely. I tried to reassure him he'd do great. I didn't have the heart to tell him I had to slip out early. I also didn't want him asking why.

When the line was all inside, I gave him a kiss on the check for luck and went to join the others. I can't even say what the dinner entrée was. I think I ate some of it, but I was too busy thinking about the trap I was setting.

Kevin St. John seemed to be hovering around the owners' table and left it only when he went to the center of the room and introduced the Amazing Dr. Sammy. Sammy stood frozen to the spot for a moment and I worried he wasn't going to move, but then his stage fright disappeared and his love of magic kicked in.

The plan was that he would go around the room, doing a

mini-show for each table. I held my breath as he got to the first table, but there was no reason to worry. He was all smiles now as he removed quarters from people's ears, made watches mysteriously disappear from people's wrists and performed elaborate card tricks. I tracked his progress around the dining hall. I had to laugh when he got to the yoga table. He threw in a few yoga poses and instead of quarters from people's ears, he produced meditation beads.

I'm afraid I neglected my group, but Lucinda, with her restaurant hostess skills, stepped in for me. When Sammy got to the owners' table, it was time for me to go. It turned out to be easy. Since everyone was watching him, nobody saw me disappear.

Outside it was getting dark as I ran through the grounds and across the street. I realized now the dress was a bad choice, but then when I'd chosen it, I didn't know I was going to be setting a trap. At least it was black.

I was in the main part of town in less than five minutes. I parked my car far away from Nicole's shop and walked up the block quickly, telling my heart to stop beating so fast.

I figured that as soon as Burton heard Lucinda's conversation, he'd find a way to separate himself from Cora and Madeleine and come to the shop to lie in wait for me. I checked the back door and the lock was as easy to open as before. And then I hid. The last of the daylight disappeared and I saw the streetlights come on. I had 911 ready on my phone. All I had to do was hit send.

Time seemed to be crawling by and I began to wonder if something had gone wrong. Or the obvious—that I was wrong about Burton Fiore being blackmailed. I looked at my watch and figured they all had to be in Hummingbird Hall by now watching the movie. I was deciding how much longer I'd wait when I heard a car door slam and footsteps outside the place. I had my finger on the send button on my phone. There was no reason to wait until he opened the back door. I pressed the button. When the dispatcher answered, I said someone was breaking in and gave the address. A moment later I heard another car door slam and more footsteps.

My heart was leaping into my throat as I heard someone fiddling with the back door. I saw a shaft of light as the back door opened and someone came inside. How long would it take the Cadbury PD to arrive? I didn't want to show my cards too early.

I heard noise at the back door again and another shaft of light. Did Burton have an accomplice? Just as I heard the whine of a siren, I jumped up and flipped on the lights. Someone else was coming in the back door.

I did a quick scan of the former bank and was surprised at what I saw. Burton Fiore was standing in the middle of the place. But what was Cora doing there? And Ronny Fiore? And Kevin St. John?

I saw the flashing lights of the cruiser as it pulled into the alley. A moment later Dane came rushing in the back door with his gun drawn and yelled, "Freeze!" before he'd processed the situation.

"We got a call there was a robbery in process," he said, looking from face to face.

27

IT'S AMAZING WHAT HAVING A GUN POINTED IN YOUR general direction will do. The fiancé, the bride-to-be, the manager of Vista Del Mar, and the fiancé's daughter all stood like statues. I have to admit, I did the same. Dane looked over the crowd, and after a moment shook his head with disbelief before holstering his weapon. His gaze had stopped on me.

"Do you want to tell me what's going on?" he said.

"Why don't you ask him," I said, pointing a finger accusingly at Burton Fiore. "He came here looking to find what Nicole Welton was using to blackmail him with and that's why he killed her."

"Killed her?" Burton Fiore said in shock. "Are you crazy?" It was like he suddenly saw Cora. "What are *you* doing here?" he demanded. I guess for the moment the role of swooning fiancé was over.

"I saw you rushing off somewhere and I wanted to see what you were up to." Cora glanced around at the rest of us. "I'm not as foolish as you all think. Or as helpless. I commandeered the Vista Del Mar van." Her eyes stopped on Ronny Fiore. "Missy, what are you doing here?"

Ronny hemmed and hawed. "I don't understand. I thought I was the only one paying Nicole." Her father snapped at her not to say anything more.

Kevin St. John seemed to be trying to recede into the shadows, but we all turned toward him. He appeared a little less the lord of the manor. "I wouldn't call what I was doing blackmail. I'd just been giving Nicole a few bucks to help her out since her business seemed to be struggling." I don't think anybody bought his story.

"Did anyone actually break in here?" Dane said, looking around the group.

"They all did," I said. "I'm the only one with a key and permission to be in here. But it's not about robbing this place. I think one of them killed Nicole."

They all started talking at once, insisting they had nothing to do with her death. Dane put his hands up to stop them. Then he turned to me. There was no flirting. He was all business, or almost. "Okay, Casey, how about you tell me the whole story."

"Yeah, why don't you. I heard you found some things that Nicole had. Let's see what you've got," Burton Fiore said. I realized that he was being cagey, not giving away the reason for the blackmail, no doubt hoping that I had nothing concrete and it would all go away.

I saw his face drop as I pulled the big envelope out of my bag. I'd done some checking earlier and then made a pit stop on my way to pick up some items from the box of moldy stuff sitting in my converted garage. I emptied the contents on a beautifully refinished table. The envelope with the baby photo floated down, but the locket and the hairbrush landed with a clunk. The key made a ping.

"But I thought . . ." Burton caught himself and stopped talking.

"You thought it was the hair jewelry pieces Nicole had in the glass case," I said, finishing what I was pretty sure he had started to say. "So that's why you took them."

His eyes flashed with anger. "Don't be absurd."

I ignored his comment. "The only piece that meant anything wasn't even there."

"Mother's locket," Cora said, reaching for the brown heart pendant. She retracted her hand as she got a whiff of the moldy smell. "That explains it. Nicole asked me about mourning jewelry and asked if I'd ever seen a locket with woven hair on the outside. I said my mother had had one. She never mentioned that she had it."

Dane looked over the items and then back to me. There was a little sparkle in his dark eyes. "I can't wait to hear what you have to say."

I had their attention and I felt like I was in an Agatha Christie mystery during the big reveal. And maybe I was a little caught up with my own cleverness.

I took a moment to explain how I had found the box of moldy clothes and remembered something Nicole had said about hiding things where no one would look. I glanced around at the assembled group. "The box was here up until a day ago. So, whoever broke in here before must have gone right past it." Judging from the scowl on Burton Fiore's face, I was guessing it was he. "Now then, I might as well cut to the chase and explain what it all means." I waited a beat to begin as I organized my thoughts.

"First, I should explain that Nicole bought a dresser at a garage sale, which I now realize was from the former Delacorte family home." There was no need to mention that Sammy's comment about his living arrangements had made me put it together. I remembered that Will had said the garage sale was to clear out a storage area so that it could be made into a studio apartment. And then Sammy had talked about the B and B where he was living doing exactly that. There was a plaque in front of the B and B that said it had been the home of Antonia and Rudolph Delacorte until Antonia's death.

"I think Nicole bought it with the idea of refinishing it and putting it in her shop. Just like she bought the old locket at the same sale, planning to fix it up and add it to her collection of hair jewelry." I'd made a call to the B and B owner and they had verified that along with the dresser, the locket had been part of the odds and ends in the sale. "Nicole might have had it in mind to refurbish the textiles when she emptied the dresser, but I think her plans changed after she realized the real meaning of what she found."

I held up the silver hairbrush. Before I could speak, Cora called out, "That looks like Edmund's." She seemed to choke a little on her words and then explained they'd all had hairbrushes just like it, even mentioning that she still had hers. I nodded and turned it over to display the *ED* engraved in the filigree decoration on the back. Cora reached out to touch it, then seemed a little disconcerted by the handful of hair still clinging to the bristles.

I looked down at the longish dark hairs with the hint of white on the end stuck in the brush. "I think those hairs were the point, but I'll get to that later." I set the brush down and held up the locket and flipped it open. They all leaned forward to get a better view of the tiny black-and-white photograph of a baby.

"That's my brother, Edmund," Cora said. "Mother was so distraught when he died she had the locket made from his hair and the baby photo inserted."

I held up the envelope and photo that had been inside and again Cora spoke. "Is that Edmund?" She seemed puzzled, pointing out that the two baby faces seemed almost identical. She shook her head as a realization came to her. "Of course not. That must be of James, Edmund's son." She lowered her head as she explained that Edmund's only child had died in an accident with his mother barely a year after her brother had died. "Where did that photo come from?"

I repeated the story about the dresser and now added that Madeleine had confirmed it had been her brother's and that it must have been left at the family home after he died.

"But you're missing what I didn't see at first, either. I think it is Edmund's child, but not James." I pointed to the baby's shirt. "The color is distorted, but I'd bet anything it's pink. But the sure giveaway that it's a girl is the bow in her hair." I held out the photo and pointed to the tiny hair ornament. I said a silent thank-you to the woman talking about the baby blanket and the infant I'd seen in the restroom. If it hadn't been for them, I never would have realized that the baby in the picture was a girl, although I'd heard that Edmund had a son.

Cora's eyes were as big as saucers. "She looks just like my brother did as a baby."

I nodded as the meaning began to sink in. "So it seems your brother had another child. A secret child," I said. I showed off the back of the envelope that had *Our Baby* written in blue fountain pen. I heard Kevin swallow so hard he almost choked. "And from what I have heard, your brother was very specific in his will that Vista Del Mar was to go to his children."

The real impact hit Cora. "So then this baby would inherit Vista Del Mar and be entitled to Edmund's portion of the family's estate? Who is she?"

Instead of answering her question, I picked up the small key. "If you notice, it has a number on it. I don't know how Nicole figured it out. Maybe when she was ripping out the pages of those old ledgers to put in the fireplace, she realized they were sign-in sheets for the safety-deposit boxes. Then when she found the number on the key, put it together with the signatures." I turned to Cora. "The key goes to your brother's safety-deposit box."

Everyone glanced back toward the vault and I explained

the locks were all removed and the boxes empty. "Your brother came in the bank every Friday and went into his safety-deposit box. A little while later, someone else came into the bank and accessed the same box."

"It sounds like a money drop for a payoff, probably to the mother to keep her quiet," Dane said. I was surprised at his comment and realized he was listening intently.

"That's a crude way to put it. I'm sure Edmund could have been leaving money for the mother or the child's caretaker. He was a wonderful person and responsible," Cora said. "It was a different time . . ." Her voice trailed off.

"And he wanted to run for governor," I said, repeating what Tag had told me. "Even now a love child can capsize a political career. But that's all old news and not what this is about. It's just about Vista Del Mar and who it really belongs to, isn't it?" I glared at Burton, Ronny and Kevin.

"This is all conjecture," Burton Fiore said impatiently.

"Not really," Dane said, nodding in recognition. He pointed to the hairbrush sitting on the table. "Casey, are you going to explain or should I?"

"I can do it," I said, trying to find a way to explain it so it wasn't complicated. I mentioned that Nicole was interested in the origins of things and had a bunch of books on the history of textiles and fibers. "Hair was just another fiber to her. When she was doing her research it probably came up that you can extract DNA from hair. Well, not really the hair. You need to have the root." I picked up the brush and pointed out the tiny white bulb on the end of a strand of hair. "And if there was any doubt that the hairs in the brush were Edmund's, the strands could be matched with those in the locket, which was known to have been made from his hair. And with his DNA, you can do a paternity test."

Kevin St. John finally spoke up from the back. "You're forgetting one thing. You need to know the baby's identity to get a DNA sample to do a paternity test. Unless you have something with the baby's name on it, there's no way to know who that baby was or what became of her."

Ronny broke free of the group and grabbed one of the ledgers. "It's empty." She went through the rest and saw they were all the same. "They're all empty."

Cora seemed a little confused. "What exactly is the point of all of this?"

"Nicole had figured out a way to increase her income through blackmailing assorted people by dangling the idea that she had proof that Edmund had another child who could inherit Vista Del Mar," I said.

Then Cora got it. "But Vista Del Mar has been ours for years. You mean someone could show up and claim it as theirs?"

"The secret baby is probably in her fifties now and she probably has no idea who she really is," I said.

Cora seemed emphatic. "You need to understand why Vista Del Mar meant so much to Edmund. He was ashamed of what our family's sardine cannery did to the bay. Ashamed that our fleet of boats had fished until the sardines were gone. It was his way of paying back. It wasn't so much about making money as preserving the historic buildings from the old camp and saving the natural quality of the land. My sister and I know how he felt about it and we want to keep it as Edmund would have wanted it. Who knows what some new person might do to it."

She surveyed the group and shook her head in dismay. "I'm sorry, but all this is taking a while to sink in. Let me understand this. You were paying Nicole to keep quiet about all this so Vista Del Mar wouldn't change ownership." She focused on Burton. "Now I get it. Of course you wouldn't want someone else to step up and claim Vista Del Mar." She smiled sweetly. "I've seen you looking around the grounds as if you were making plans and I've heard your suggestions. But, Burton dear, did you really think I was going to hand over the running of it to you and your daughter?" They both did a great act of looking shocked.

"I loved all the attention you both gave me, but I wasn't born yesterday." She looked at Burton's stunned expression. "My goodness, you did more than make up plans in your head, didn't you? I hope you didn't lay out too much of your money." She turned to Ronny. "And, dear, you better not quit that job of yours, because we have a manager and that isn't going to change."

Kevin St. John was her next target. Before she could speak, he started to talk.

"I didn't want anything to change for you or for me," he said. "But this seems to be a big fuss about nothing. There is nothing with the identity of the mother. There's no way to know who that baby was or what became of her," he repeated, trying to reassure Cora.

"Except for this." I put down all the other props and picked up a folded sheet from the ledger, and I heard a gasp go through the crowd.

"Then you do know the mother's name?" Dane said.

I unfolded the sheet and they all saw part of it was missing. "Not exactly. But I can tell you her name starts with an *M*. Someone came in here and shredded what was left in the ledgers." I looked from face to face to see if any of them flinched. Either they were great actors or none of them had.

Kevin gave me a dirty look. "So then what was the point of this charade?"

"To find Nicole's killer," I said and they all began to talk and basically say what a ridiculous statement that was. Even Dane said Nicole's death had been ruled a suicide.

In the midst of it all, Madeleine Delacorte walked in and looked around. "I didn't know you were having a party."

28

"DON'T FEEL BAD," DANE SAID. WE WERE THE ONLY ones left inside The Bank. "I'm impressed at what you figured out. One of them could have killed Nicole if it wasn't suicide and it didn't turn out that they all had alibis for the time when she died." He put his hand on my arm in a supportive manner.

I hung my head, reliving what had happened after the group had seen the torn ledger sheet. "I've made a terrible mess of everything." In my mind's eye I saw Ronny begin to argue with her father. Apparently he'd made it seem like a done deal that he would be taking over Vista Del Mar as soon as the wedding was over. I got the feeling it wasn't the first time he'd made promises he couldn't keep. Burton's mustache had started to twitch from a tic in his face as Cora stepped in. Cora had turned out to be anything but a silly older woman in love. She loved the romance of it all and had simply not wanted to spoil things by bringing up anything like a prenup. Her plan all along was that they would make a life together on equal footing, each of them responsible for half the bill. He'd given the impression that he was such a big shot in real estate, she was sure he'd have no problem going halves with her on one of the cute cottages near the park downtown.

"I'm sure Cora will blame me for the end of her engagement."

Dane sighed. "I think it was going to end one way or the other as soon as he found out Cora wasn't going to support him."

"If only that was all." I let out my breath in a tired sigh. "I've had a troubled relationship with Kevin St. John all along and now it's even worse. He's angry that I stirred everything up even if there is no way to identify Edmund's mystery heir. I know you don't agree, but I still don't think that Nicole's death was a suicide."

"I hate to bring this up, but we need more than your thinking it's not suicide," Dane said.

I noticed that his hand was still resting on my arm. The spot had become increasingly warm, and I had to admit I liked it. It seemed pretty obvious it could escalate into something more really fast. But I couldn't let it happen. I stared at his hand and he seemed to get the message, retracting it quickly as he straightened up.

We walked to the back door and Dane made sure the lock was secure. "At least we solved the mystery of the break-ins. And I don't think there will be any more."

My mood was really descending. I'd been so sure I'd figured out who had killed Nicole. Who would have figured she was blackmailing Burton, his daughter and Kevin. And I began to think of the retreat again and how Wanda had just taken off when the spinning was done and she'd realized how little yarn the group had made.

Dane noticed my expression. Maybe I looked like I was

about to cry. As we walked toward the front of the store he started to put his hand on my shoulder but didn't. "Don't take it so hard. It's not like a killer is going free."

"I'm glad you were the one who answered the call," I said. "It would have been even more embarrassing if it had been someone else. And thank you for not bringing out the troops."

"I figured we wouldn't need the SWAT team for a break-in at an antiques store," he said as his serious face slipped into a grin. "Don't worry. I'll just write up a report that it was a mistake. Lieutenant Borgnine never has to know anything about what went on." When we got outside we stopped at his cruiser.

"I'm assuming that Nicole did figure out the identity of the mother. She must have tipped her hand about the sheets in the ledger to one of them and they came in here and destroyed them." He was thoughtful for a moment. "Maybe it's just as well. It would certainly change things if there was a different owner of Vista Del Mar." He gestured beyond the quiet downtown street to the houses built up the slope on the side streets. "Someone out there, probably asleep by now, could be the Delacorte heir. By now the woman probably has grown children of her own. Maybe it's best to let sleeping dogs lie."

"Maybe it is," I said, "but there is a part of me that thinks whoever that woman is ought to get what she's entitled to."

Dane lightened the mood and started to tease me about being some kind of muffin-baking superhero who wanted to right all the wrongs in Cadbury.

"Isn't that what *you* do?" I said.

"I'm more about keeping the peace," he said. I didn't agree and pointed out how he was trying to help every messed-up kid in town get on the right path.

"It's no big deal," he said. "The garage was just sitting

there. And working with them helps me keep in shape." To show off what he meant he did a few karate moves. "Anytime you want to, join us for a lesson," he said. In the streetlight I could see the crinkles around his eyes when he smiled.

"I don't want to keep you," I said. "It's Saturday night or what's left of it. You must be off duty now and I'm sure you have plans." I thought of the woman I'd seen sitting in his kitchen.

"You're right about me being off duty. If you want I could stop by your place."

I shook my head. "You've got somebody waiting for you."

"Right," he said with a nod. All the teasing was gone. Obviously he'd gotten himself into an awkward position. But it was none of my business.

JULIUS MUST HAVE HEARD THE SOUND OF THE kitchen door as I returned. When I flipped on the light, he came sauntering into the room. He stopped to stretch and give his paw a cleaning before he stared up at me with those yellow eyes of his.

"I certainly made a mess of things," I said. I recounted the disaster with the yarn and my big sting operation. Then I laughed at my confession. Even though I'd never had one, I knew that dogs were like confidants. They knew when you were down and rushed to lick your face to cheer you up. I looked at Julius and wondered if he had any idea I was upset, or even cared. "This is really about stink fish, isn't it?" I said with a sigh. But Julius surprised me. He didn't make a run for his bowl. At least not right away. He blinked a few times and then jumped into my arms and began to purr. I think that was a cat version of licking your face.

"Wherever I go, you're coming, too," I said, petting his fluffy black fur.

I HAD A TROUBLED NIGHT. IT WASN'T SO MUCH worry that the retreaters would be angry or ask for refunds. It was that I felt I'd let them down. I had promised sheep to shawl and gotten nowhere close.

I hoped things would seem more promising in the morning. They didn't. I had a feeling of complete doom when I thought about the last session with the retreat group. No matter what Crystal and her mother cobbled together, it wasn't going to be handspun yarn.

I was dragging my feet getting ready when of course my mother called.

"How is the retreat going?" my mother asked. I recognized it as a setup. She knew me well enough to know that there was bound to be a problem. I tried to say that it was going just fine, but she was an expert at dissecting my tone of voice and saw through it.

"What's wrong?" she said with that knowing sound.

"Nothing," I said, trying to add a cheerful bounce to the word. But my voice was already warbling at the "ing" and I started to spill my guts—at least as far as the retreat was concerned. The words just came tumbling out before I could stop them. No sheep shearing, a dead workshop leader who hadn't thought through the reality of what could be done in the time they had, my group of yarn crafters who'd ended up with only a handful of spun yarn to knit a whole shawl and finally a replacement leader who'd run off in the middle of things.

"Is that all?" my mother said with just enough of a laugh to let me know she was being facetious. "So, maybe you're ready to accept this retreat business isn't for you." I girded for the speech in which she'd tell me to cut my losses and move on to cooking school. But that wasn't at all what she said.

"Casey, you've still got today to fix things with your group," she began. "As much as you've gone from one thing to another, you've never been a quitter. I mean, quit in the middle of something. You finished the semester with good grades before you decided that law school wasn't for you. You stayed with the substitute teaching until the school year was up. Have you ever stopped in the middle of baking a cake? No," she said, answering her own question. "I have every confidence that you will find a way to finish on a high note with your yarn people."

I was dumbstruck. Was my mother encouraging me? Then I told her about Sammy's performance.

"That's the worst thing that could happen," she said when she heard he'd been a success. "Next he'll be dropping his practice and doing magic full-time."

Her comment made me laugh and she wanted to know what was so funny.

"Sammy would take your comment as a compliment. He's trying very hard to become a bad boy." Now my mother laughed.

"Sammy, a bad boy? Not in this lifetime." She wished me well for the day and asked me to let her know how things went.

I looked out the window to see if any pigs were flying by. Because I thought that was as likely as the phone call I'd just had with my mother.

There was no more time for stalling. I dressed in my most confident outfit, wound a royal blue scarf around my neck in my best attempt at a nonchalant style and headed outside. I remembered only at the last minute about Maggie's messages and my plan to talk to her in person. With all that had happened, it wasn't surprising that I'd forgotten. I figured even if she was busy this morning, she could take a moment to tell me her big revelation. I got into my car and headed out onto the street.

This early on Sunday morning, I had the streets to myself. The restaurants and coffee places in Cadbury were already open, but the shops were still closed up tight. As I looked up the street toward the Coffee Shop, I felt my heartbeat go crazy. Two blue-and-white cruisers were stopped in front of the Victorian storefront, and worse, a red rescue ambulance had its lights flashing as it pulled away and took off down the street. I parked and ran.

29

THE DOOR TO THE COFFEE SHOP WAS BLOCKED OFF
with yellow tape. I looked through the uniforms to see if Dane
was among them, but he wasn't. Lieutenant Borgnine was just
getting out of his car, and his expression was grim. I was able
to get a glimpse inside the shop before one of the uniforms
shooed me away. All I saw was a pool of blood and one of
the wool combs. There seemed to be red droplets on the sharp
tines.

I recognized Carol, Maggie's helper, talking to the officers
as Lieutenant Borgnine joined them and she began her story
again. The flat light of the white sky only made her look paler.

"Maggie always comes in early. She leaves the front door
locked until I get here," she said. "When I got here, I knocked
on the front door and when I looked in I saw she was"—the
girl stopped and swallowed before she continued—"on the
ground, right there." She used the back of her hand to point
inside as if she didn't want to look in there again. "I ran

around to the back. The door was open and I went inside."
She choked on her words a little as she said she'd called 911
right away.

One of the officers told Lieutenant Borgnine that the paramedics said Maggie had been attacked with something sharp
they'd found on the floor and there was a blunt-force trauma
injury to her head. I was relieved to hear she was still alive,
though in very bad shape.

I didn't know what to do. Should I tell them the sharp thing
was a wool comb and possibly related to my yarn retreat and
that I'd come to talk to Maggie because I thought she knew
something about Nicole's death? Or was it better to let them
think I'd just happened by for a morning coffee? It couldn't
possibly be coincidental that Maggie knew something and
now she was clinging to life. Two things struck me. If Maggie
was attacked because she had figured out something about
Nicole's death, didn't that prove that it wasn't suicide? And
maybe if I hadn't meddled in the whole thing, Maggie would
be behind the counter handing out drinks and good cheer. I
heard the cops talking and they seemed to think robbery was
the motive, but I knew better.

"You need to get some kind of protection for Maggie, so
whoever attacked her doesn't try to finish the job," I said.
Lieutenant Borgnine acknowledged my presence for the first
time with an unfriendly grunt.

"And why is it we should do that?" he said in a condescend-
ing tone.

I thought fast. If I brought up that I felt all this was connected to Nicole's death, he'd tune me out right then. But they
needed to realize Maggie could still be in danger. "Whoever
was trying to rob the place probably thinks they killed her,
but if they hear she's alive they'll realize she might be able
to finger them." Lieutenant Borgnine's eyes went skyward

and he mumbled something about my choice of words, saying they sounded like they came out of some PI's mouth in a cheap novel.

"I mean she might identify them," I said, irritated at myself for changing my words to please him.

"We've got it covered," he said with a dismissive wave of his hand. "You can run along now. I believe you have a retreat going this weekend and I'm sure all those knitters need you."

I started to walk away, but when he thought I was out of earshot, I heard him tell one of the uniforms to go down to the hospital and keep watch on Maggie. At least I'd done that.

And I'd thought the morning was rocky before. Still, this was no time to feel sorry for myself or dwell on how guilty I felt. I had to pull myself together for my yarn people. What my mother hadn't quite understood was I really cared about the retreaters. It wasn't just about finishing the retreat. I didn't want to let them down.

I was back on the Vista Del Mar grounds in no time. It seemed everyone was still at breakfast and it felt very quiet. My first stop was the original meeting room we'd used. It was the last place I'd seen the wool combs. I wasn't sure what I expected to find. When Wanda had taken off, she had probably stopped to pick up what she'd left there.

The room was swept clean and the tables neatly folded against the wall. The bins were still in the corner. I opened the lid of hers, feeling my heart race. The bag of salad spinners covered only part of the bottom. The pair of wool combs had been next to it. Now there was only one, with the tines pointed ominously up toward anyone who reached in. I thought over who had access to the bin—it seemed like everybody on the Vista Del Mar grounds.

As I approached the Lodge, breakfast was ending and the crowd was filtering out of the dining hall. There was a different feeling on Sunday morning. For most of the guests, the yoga group and my retreaters, their stay at Vista Del Mar was coming to a close. They moved at a more leisurely pace than earlier in the weekend, savoring the last of their time on the wild grounds. I wished I could share their peace.

I saw Lucinda coming toward me. Though she smiled, her eyes seemed concerned as they locked on to my face. "What's wrong?" she asked when she reached me.

"Is it that obvious?" I said, fidgeting with my scarf as if moving it around would make me appear less worried. Lucinda moved my hand, took the scarf off and changed the arrangement of it, which I was sure was an improvement.

"You were a no-show at breakfast and your brows are knit together," she said. There was no point in keeping the news about Maggie from Lucinda. So as we walked toward the meeting room on the ground floor of the Sandpiper building, I told her all of it, including how I felt it was my fault.

She did her best to try to make me feel better, reminding me that I hadn't merely been trying to stir things up, but was trying to find a killer. "Maggie will be okay. You'll see," she said. Just before we went inside, she started to pull away. "I better call Tag and tell him what happened." She looked back in the direction of the Lodge. "I suppose there's a line for the pay phones."

I handed her the keys to my place and told her it would be faster.

I went on into the lobbylike room. Will must have been by; the lights were on and the fire lit. I forced myself to have an upbeat expression as I stood waiting for everyone to arrive. Folks started to come in groups of twos and threes. They all seemed to have tentative expressions as they came in, as if they weren't quite sure what to expect. Who could blame them? Bree, Olivia and Scott came in together and then spread out.

They knew all the roadblocks of the weekend and I watched as they tried to generate some enthusiasm in the group. I wanted to hug them all and thank them. The one person who didn't show up was Ronny Fiore. No surprise.

I tried not to be obvious, but I kept glancing toward the door looking for Crystal and her mother and the replacement yarn. I was relieved when I saw the two of them pulling a stack of bins up the path. It would probably cost me a lot of my profit, but at least they would all have yarn for the shawlette.

I held the door for them and they wheeled the bins inside and went up to the front of the room. "I'm afraid we had to sort of mix and match," Crystal said as she opened the top bin on her stack. There was a cornucopia of colors and the yarn had more of a uniform thickness than real handspun, but there appeared to be plenty of it. We were trying to work out the logistics of handing it out when the door opened and two women pulling red wagons rushed inside.

"I'm sorry we're late," the first woman said.

I did a double take. "Wanda?"

"You sound surprised," the short golf pro/spinning expert said. It was then she took in Crystal and Gwen's bins of yarns. "What's going on? Why did they bring all that yarn?"

Just then Lucinda came in. She looked over the group of us in the front of the room with a puzzled expression and then slipped in with the rest of the retreaters.

It was then that I noticed that the red wagon Wanda had pulled in was heaped with balls of thick natural-colored yarn. The other woman's wagon was filled with the same.

When we'd been discussing the whole retreat concept, Nicole had shown me an example of handspun yarn. Wanda's load matched up with what I'd seen.

"You just sort of left yesterday," I said. I waved at the still spinning wheels. I dropped my voice so no one else would hear. "I thought you bailed when you realized how there was no way they'd have enough yarn to make a shawl." I nodded toward Crystal and Gwen. "They brought some yarn that looks sort of handspun."

" 'Sort of' isn't the real thing. I left you a note on the message board saying we'd be here," Wanda said. The younger woman with her nodded in agreement and for the first time I really looked at her. She resembled Wanda and yet how could the same features on two women be so different? I was sure this must be the sister I had heard about. I instantly felt for my spinning instructor and could understand how she'd been outshone by her sibling. The sister was lovely with a tall graceful build and a different manner than Wanda's. Wanda marched, while her sister had almost danced in.

Wanda did her teapot pose. "I can't believe you thought I would do that. You certainly don't know me then."

I looked at the wagonloads of yarn. "Where did these come from?" I asked. Instead of answering me, Wanda turned to the group and told them they'd each need two balls and it was 100 percent handspun. In an instant the mood had lifted and they all seemed excited. Lucinda looked over at me with a bright smile. Bree and Olivia took it upon themselves to start handing out yarn from one of the wagons, while Scott and Lucinda worked the other one.

"This is my sister, Angelina," Wanda said, introducing the younger woman. Wanda noticed my eyes flitting back and forth between the two women, comparing their looks. She seemed to be used to the reaction and spoke what I was thinking. "I know you can't believe we're sisters, but we are," she said. Wanda left it at that. Now I understood what the travel agent had said about Wanda being upstaged by her sister. Angelina smiled and nodded during the introduction, but then she turned toward the door.

"I'm going to look for Will." Angelina turned back and made eye contact with me. "This has to be such a hard time for him. I just want to let him know I—er, we're here for him." I wondered why she felt the need to explain.

Gwen and Crystal had listened to the whole interchange. I apologized for their trouble and they started to leave, saying the yarn would be available in the gift shop.

My group was totally immersed in the yarn and everywhere I looked, they were casting on stitches and beginning to knit. Wanda watched them with a pleased smile.

I asked her again about the appearance of the yarn. Wanda did her teapot pose again. "Anybody with any sense would have realized Nicole's plan was flawed. I tried to tell her, but she wouldn't listen. She knew better. She had a fancy degree and that artistic shop." Wanda rolled her eyes at the absurdity of it. "You don't take a bunch of people who have never spun before and think they're going to be able to learn how and then spin fast enough to make a couple of hundred yards of yarn. Nicole kept talking about some competitions they have at some wool festivals where they go from sheep to shawl in a day, but she didn't bother looking into them enough to understand that it was teams of people working together to make one shawl. And teams of experienced people."

Wanda threw her hands up. "I knew what was going to happen. Maybe Nicole realized she'd gotten herself in over her head and that's why she did what she did. If only she hadn't been so high and mighty about the whole thing, I would have told her my plan."

"You were the one who bought the fleeces, weren't you," I said, remembering how the rancher had mentioned selling a lot of wool.

Wanda nodded. "When I said I was a spinner extraordinaire, I wasn't just tooting my own horn. I love spinning and

I am fast. I figured when Nicole fell on her face, I'd step in and sell her the yarn." As Wanda said it she handed me a receipt for the fleeces and an invoice for her time. "I was going to charge her extra for saving her behind, but since you ended up hiring me, I'm giving you a discount."

At the moment I was so glad to have the yarn to give my people, I didn't care that with all that had gone on, I was barely going to break even. But then I was still learning the business.

"Just one question," I said as Wanda turned to join the crowd. "Why didn't you just tell me about the yarn you had?"

"And ruin the fun?" she said. "Do you think these women would have tried so hard with the wool if they knew it didn't matter?" She reached down and handed me the last two skeins of yarn. "Knock yourself out."

When the wagons were both empty, Wanda picked up both handles and started toward the door.

"You're not leaving?" I said, coming up behind her.

"My work here is done. All I signed on for was turning the wool into yarn. You can handle the rest." And with that she left, rattling the wagons behind her.

I was grateful for the yarn, but I still had to wonder how convenient it was that she had it. Just like the purchase of the salad spinners—as if she knew she was going to be taking over for Nicole. It wasn't as if I'd even looked to Wanda as a replacement. She'd offered her services. Here's the part I was having a hard time swallowing: It was clear she hadn't liked Nicole. Would she really have gone to such trouble to save the day for Nicole, even if she got paid for it?

And now with Maggie being stabbed with the wool comb . . . Maybe what Maggie knew pointed the finger at Wanda.

30

I SAT KNITTING WITH THE GROUP. THE PATTERN WAS simple and with the thick yarn and big needles, the shawl began to work up quickly, even for me, still a novice knitter. Lucinda moved over to sit next to me.

There was a pleasant hum of conversation. One of the nice things about working with yarn in a group was that people tended to talk and friendships developed. I could see it in the group of retreaters. Bree seemed to have become close with the Ginger. The woman had seemed tense and subdued at the beginning of the weekend, but now was talking readily. Olivia was the center of another group and there appeared to be a lively conversation going on. Scott had attracted a group, too.

I thought of my mother's words. She was right. Was I actually even thinking those words? I chuckled to myself. The retreat was going to end on a high note. I had worked things out. One way or another I had actually managed to take the group from sheep to shawl. Did it really matter that Dr.

Sammy had been a stand-in for the sheep or that they hadn't spun all the yarn for their shawls? We had started with piles of wool and they were well on their way to completing the small wraps.

"Tag was upset when I told him about Maggie," Lucinda said, interrupting my good thoughts. Instantly I thought of my friend in the hospital and went back into worry mode.

"He's going to check on her and come here during our break," she said. She smiled at the thought of her husband. "It's kind of sweet the way he's worried about me. He said he just wanted to see me in person to be sure I'm all right."

I had stopped knitting while she talked. I still needed to pay attention to one thing or another. But then I began again, working the garter stitch and watching the shawlette grow a little wider with each row. I might not be able to talk and knit, but I certainly could think and knit. Everything about Nicole began to roll around in my mind. Even with all the alibis and excuses, I wasn't sure that one of the blackmailees wasn't the guilty party in her death. But I didn't have anything to prove they were. My whole sting had fallen flat when too many people showed up. And well, without the name of the mother, all my so-called evidence of what Nicole knew just became conjecture. The thing about DNA evidence was you had to know who to compare it with.

Lucinda had begun talking to the woman on the other side of her and I listened to their conversation. At first they talked about the yarn and I was relieved to hear that it didn't seem to matter to the woman that she hadn't personally spun the yarn she was using. Then she began to talk about Wanda's sister.

"Such a lovely young woman," the woman said. And then she repeated what I'd thought—how amazing it was that while Wanda and her sister resembled each other, the end result in their appearance was so different. "That young woman's eyes just sparkled when she said she was going to go looking for someone," the woman said. "My guess is it was a man and someone she really liked."

The words resonated in my mind. The woman was right. The look on Angelina's face and the tone of her voice had all changed when she said Will's name. I thought back to what I'd heard about him and the young women in town. He was the high school hero type. He'd been the prom king when Angelina had been the prom queen. Something nagged at me there. Hadn't someone said that he'd taken someone else to the prom? Maybe that someone had gotten in the way of their relationship then and it had happened again with Nicole. With her out of the way, Will was available. And an entirely new motive for murder showed up.

The whole while I was knitting, I played around with the idea in my mind and by the time we took our break I wanted to go talk to Will. As we headed outside, I thought of going off to look for him, but Lucinda came up next to me and put her arm through mine as I zipped up my fleece jacket against the cool morning air.

"I told Tag we'd meet him in the café. He should have some news about Maggie," she said.

Finding out about my friend who favored red won out and I changed my plans, going with Lucinda. The café was packed and the crowd spilled out into the main room of the Lodge hall. There was a lot of activity between people checking out and grouping by the door to wait for the van to take them to the airport.

Lucinda went on ahead to find Tag, while I stopped in the main room with several of the retreaters who needed help arranging for transportation to the airport. I was surprised to see Liz Buckley and her daughter, Stacey, but then realized they were there in their professional capacity as travel agents picking up a group for a local tour when I saw the daughter holding a sign that said WINE TOUR.

"Greetings," Virgil Scarantino said in a cheerful voice as I passed. "I'm gathering folks for a wildflower hike. Any of your people want to join?"

I nodded a hello. "My group is still busy." Someone squeezed between us, interrupting. "This must be like a family reunion for you," I said to the distinguished-looking former banker as I pointed out his daughter and granddaughter surrounded by the wine tasters.

"Being tour guides must be in our genes," he said with a little laugh.

I was about to explain we were just taking a break from our last workshop, when Kevin St. John made his way across the cavernous room. I was going to duck away quickly, figuring I was really a persona non grata after the whole gathering of blackmailees at The Bank, but Kevin stopped right in front of me before I could disappear.

"Ms. Feldstein," he said in his formal managerial tone with a nod of greeting, "I wanted to speak to you." I was glad when Virgil interrupted and said he had a quick question for Kevin St. John. Anything to take the spotlight off me. I edged away as Virgil mentioned the hike and wanted to know if the boardwalk was still blocked off. Kevin St. John said the bench was to be removed in the afternoon, but for now the area was still off-limits. Then Kevin put his hand on my arm, stopping my exit.

Here it comes, I thought, *he's got me trapped so he can dump on the reproach.* Even as Virgil moved away, the manager held on to my arm.

Rather than waiting, I finally just looked him in the eye. "Okay, what is it?"

The moon-faced man smiled at me and I tried to determine the meaning behind it. Was it sinister, triumphant or maybe gloating? Was he about to tell me that he'd gotten the Delacorte sisters to cancel the deal they'd offered me and maybe even ban me from having retreats there? But then I noticed something I'd never seen before in my dealings with him. The clue was in the set of his lips. The smile went all the way up to his eyes. Was he giving me a first-ever genuine smile?

"I wanted to thank you," he said. There was a long pause and I waited for the sarcastic kicker to come. But he said nothing, letting the tension build, probably taking pleasure in making me squirm.

"Okay, you're a master at suspense, but I'm in kind of a hurry. Could you get to the punch line?" I said.

His expression gave in and he began to speak at a regular rate. "This is hard for me to say, but thanks to your efforts at being a detective, Burton Fiore is out of the picture." Kevin St. John seemed to breathe a sigh of relief. "And now if you could just leave everything as it is," he said. The smile had faded and his tone seemed to have a touch of warning to it.

He let go of my arm abruptly and I gave him a little salute as I moved on.

The café was so crowded, I noticed two people working the counter. Lucinda waved me over.

"Tag got drinks for us," she said when I got to the table. Lucinda was holding hers and I realized the one on the table was mine. My friend noticed me staring at it. "You know Tag," she said. "He didn't want your cappuccino to get cold."

Tag went into detail how he'd put another cup over the original one to insulate it and he'd added a lid.

I was more interested in news about Maggie and asked about her before I even sat down. Tag didn't do well at being interrupted. It messed with his sense of order and he had to get out the last part of his efforts to keep my drink hot before he would talk about Maggie. "You need to know all the steps I took," he said. He pointed out the plug in the sip hole and said it had done double duty. It had kept my drink warm and marked it as the cappuccino.

"Tell her about Maggie," Lucinda said, trying to get him to move on.

"She's in critical condition," he said. "The next twelve hours are crucial." It wasn't good, but at least she was still alive.

He stared at my drink and I could see he was getting fidgety. He couldn't help himself, he started gesturing with his whole body for me to try it. I undid all his fixings and in the process managed to slop some liquid out of the cup. I quickly took a sip and told him the temperature was just right.

I heard Tag make a *tsk* sound as he picked up a napkin and began to blot the ring my cup had left.

"I feel better seeing that you're both okay," he said, keeping his voice low. He turned to me. "Lucinda said you didn't think the motive with Maggie was robbery." He gave me all the points in favor of it being robbery, like the cash drawer was open and money was missing.

Tag didn't like my sleuthing, particularly when I included his wife. Even so, I told him I thought Maggie had been attacked because of something she knew—if for no other reason than to make him realize there wasn't a robber on the loose in Cadbury, no matter what Lieutenant Borgnine thought. Tag, with his eye for detail, appreciated how I'd determined by the kind of muffin that had been found with Nicole that it had been purchased on Monday morning, not Tuesday, the day she'd supposedly killed herself. Then he got quiet and I could tell the wheels in his head were spinning.

"You know I take a walk very early every weekday

morning up and down Grand Street," he said. "And you know that I pay attention to everything." He stopped for a moment as if running over something in his mind and then his eyes lit up. "I did notice something odd Monday morning when I passed the Coffee Shop."

He leaned in close and whispered something. I started to dismiss it as the usual kind of useless detail that bothered him, but then I began to think about what he had said. Could it be?

Tag had turned back to his wife and began trying to convince her to leave the retreat now. I tuned him out and stared down at the table, letting things roll through my mind. It was like staring at an anagram and suddenly seeing the word hidden in the mixed-up letters.

There was a slight problem. If I presented what I'd just figured out to Lieutenant Borgnine, he would laugh me out of the police station. I needed some piece of proof to change it from conjecture to fact. And then I thought of something. It was a long shot, but still possible there was a piece of evidence the cops had overlooked.

31

THERE WAS NO WAY I COULD FOLLOW MY HUNCH immediately. It was the last part of the final session of the retreat and I had to be there, so I set a few things in motion before I rushed on ahead, wanting to be in the meeting room when my people all arrived.

I was glad to see Lucinda come in with the group. Tag hadn't won. I did my best to focus on my retreaters and join them in knitting for that last hour, but my mind was elsewhere. I was anxious to check out my theory, particularly after I'd heard about the plan to move the bench.

The workshop ended as the lunch bell rang. I tried to appear calm as they gathered up all their things, but I was finding it almost impossible not to hurry them along so I could take off.

Lucinda saw me edging away and figured something was up. "You're onto something, aren't you?" she said. "Need some help?"

It was thanks to her that all those people had shown up for my blackmail sting even though most of them had heard her tease by accident, and I would have liked some backup, but I was really more concerned that she have lunch with the knitters and act as hostess for their last meal. She agreed and went on ahead, saying she'd left her jacket when we'd met Tag and she'd pick it up on the way.

I took a quick detour, holding out my cell phone. I had already written the text and as soon as I got a signal in the middle of the street, I hit send. I was breathless from running and from anticipation as I got back to the main path in the conference center.

I was going the opposite way as people headed toward the dining hall, while others were pulling suitcases toward their cars. It got quiet when I headed across the grassy area in front of the Lodge and by the time I reached the boardwalk, the only sound was the rhythm of the waves coming from the beach and my footsteps on the boards. I took the turnoff on the planked walkway. I headed up the hilly dune and then saw the barricade up ahead. I stepped around it easily. All that sand absorbed the sound and as I descended into the valley there was an eerie silence. The tall bushes were just ahead and I hoped that Kevin St. John hadn't jumped the gun and had the bench removed already. If there was any evidence still there, the moving of the bench would be sure to trample it and disperse it forever in the shifting sand.

I had to get all the way to the space between the bushes before I could tell the bench was still there. The yellow police tape was gone, but had been replaced by a large blue tarp draped across the open space and held in place by rope tied to the greenery. It was easy to peek over the tarp and see the bench behind it. When I lifted the tarp to climb under it, the ropes came loose and the whole thing fell to the ground.

There were clumps of native plants on either end of the seat and underneath it. I got on my hands and knees and began to poke through the stalks under one end of the bench. I checked the other end and came up empty. My last shot was the row of plants just below the seat. And then I saw it. No wonder the cops missed it. It was green, just like the stems of the plants, and blended right in.

I was considering what to do as I stood up. I felt something prickle my back and I turned quickly.

"Good, you found it," Jane said. She held the other wool comb toward me with the tines out in a threatening manner. "Lucky for me I asked where you were when your friend came to pick up her jacket. Easy as anything she said you were off looking for some evidence." With the sharp metal tines of the wool comb resting against my arm, she leaned down and looked under the bench. I tried to step away, but as she stood, she pressed the weapon harder against my skin. I could feel the tines beginning to cut into my arm.

"Why couldn't you have just stayed out of it? Everyone bought Nicole's death as suicide. The case was closed. Nobody was going to look for any more evidence and once the bench was gone, the whole episode would be smoothed over, just like the sand."

"It was all about Will, wasn't it?" I said. "I asked Stacey Buckley and she said you were the person Will took to the prom." I left off what else she'd said, that it was a pity date.

A wisp of her pale brown hair blew across her face, she raked it back with her hand and I was surprised to see her expression. The only word to describe it was *fierce*. "Yes," she said. "It was wonderful. I had to take care of my mother and I never got to go to many school things. It was like a dream. He said I looked like a princess. That's when I knew that Will and I were meant to be together." The hair flew in front of her face again and she moved it away from her eyes with her free hand. I was relieved that she had stopped pressing the wool comb against my arm, but she still held it as a threat.

"He seemed to be so understanding that I had to be there to take care of my mother. Never pushing for us to get together or anything, but whenever he saw me, we'd talk and he'd remind me of the prom and say what a special night it had been." She stopped and shook her head. "I was sure it was some kind of mistake when Will got engaged to Nicole. I suppose she used some of those sophisticated tricks she learned in San Francisco."

Jane sounded angry as she described what a rough time it had been for her. Her mother had died shortly after Will and Nicole's wedding and Jane had fallen into a depression, working at several stores in downtown Cadbury. "But when I got the job at the café, everything changed. Will stopped in all the time and he'd talk to me. I could tell he wasn't happy with Nicole anymore, and then when he confided in me that she was involved with something that could mess up the whole town . . ." Her voice trailed off. "I did it for Will. I couldn't let her ruin his life." I considered trying to make a run for it, but she sensed it and moved the wool comb against my arm again. The tines were sharp as tiny swords and I could feel them prick at my skin.

She looked me in the eye. "And now we're going to be together. I know I'm right about that. Look at how fast he came back to work. He did it so we could spend time together and it wouldn't look strange."

"Why did you have to hurt Maggie?" I said. "Everybody loves her. She's wonderful to everyone, probably even to you."

Jane looked down. "It's really your fault. Everyone wanted to accept that Nicole killed herself. Nobody liked her very well. She thought she could just come into town and take over."

Her head lifted and she glared at me. "Just like you. We don't need any amateur investigators. You should have paid attention to that note I left in your bag when you came in with Wanda. If you hadn't kept talking to Maggie and then brought up that stupid muffin . . ." Jane shook her head. "I thought bringing the muffin with the coffee would make my meeting with Nicole seem more friendly." She had a determined expression and I had a bad feeling.

"Well," she said. Again I glanced at the path. Anything she had in mind for me seemed to include pain, so I did my best to stall her.

I got her to talk about Maggie. She'd figured there might be something sharp with the knitting tools and found the wool comb, though it had ended up being mostly for show. She'd slipped in behind Maggie and gotten the coffeepot off the shelf before Maggie knew what was going on. I had a hard time listening to Jane describe hitting Maggie over the head repeatedly. She'd heard Carol at the front door and quickly grabbed a handful of money to make it look like a robbery and then rushed out the back door.

Jane appeared as if she'd just thought of something. "If you didn't talk to Maggie, how—"

"Did I figure it out?" I said. Great. It was another chance to stall. "It all really came together a little while ago," I began. And then I told her what Tag had whispered. "Tag Thornkill mentioned seeing you in Maggie's on Monday. He thought it seemed strange that a person who worked in a place selling coffee would stop for a cup at another place. It made me start thinking and putting things together. Like the delivery guy saying you weren't there to sign for the order on Tuesday morning. And when I stared at the lengths Tag had gone to to keep my coffee warm and then saw the ring on the table from my cup, it reminded me there had been one on the bench when I

saw Nicole. It was clearly far away from where she'd been sitting and indicated there had been someone else there also with
a drink. And then I came up with a scenario."

"Oh yeah," she said with almost a dare in her voice. "I bet
you don't know how I did it."

"I admit it was very clever," I began and Jane's eyes widened at the praise. And then I laid it out. She'd gone to Maggie's on Monday morning and asked for a coffee, and waited
until Maggie had pulled off one of the paper cups before Jane
had requested it be double cupped. That way, Maggie's fingerprints would be on the inner cup, but not Jane's. She had picked
up the muffin at the same time. She'd either drunk the coffee
or dumped it. Either way, it was immaterial. Then on Tuesday,
she'd brought the cups and muffin to work with her. Getting
the insecticide was no problem since the shed was left open.
I imagined that she'd used gloves to separate the cups, making
sure to use the inner one for Nicole's poison-laced latte.

It was obvious by Jane's expression that I had gotten it
right. She seemed a little miffed that I'd figured it out and
took over telling me how she'd done the rest, adding more
details as she did. I had wondered how she'd gotten Nicole to
meet her. It wasn't as if they were friends. Jane had asked
Nicole's advice for making over her appearance. Jane had
asked her not to tell anyone about their meeting because she
was embarrassed to have to ask for help. Apparently Nicole
had fallen for it completely.

"I used the outer cup for a coffee for me," she said. I put
lids on them and fit them in one of those cardboard carriers
we have. That way I could offer it to Nicole without ever having to touch the cup. I even told her I'd gotten the coffees from
the Coffee Shop because I knew she liked their drinks the
best." I noticed Jane stopped there because she'd gotten to her
one slipup.

"But it must have occurred to you that the cups looked the same and you wanted to make sure she took the right one. So you marked it by putting one of the green plugs in the sip hole."

Jane's features tightened. "I don't know how I forgot about it," she said. "Everything else went according to plan. I waited until the poison began to take effect, which only took a few minutes. Then I wrote the note on her phone and wiped off the screen. I grabbed my coffee cup and the cardboard holder and walked away."

Jane let out a sigh. "But it wasn't really such a bad mistake." Pressing the sharp metal against my arm, she bent down quickly and plucked the green plug off the ground. She broke it into pieces with her free hand and threw them off into the wild blue yonder, where they would be sure to be lost forever.

"Just like that, evidence gone." She looked down at the weapon in her hand. "I read up on these. Saint Somebody got killed with one. It was quite painful, the skin ripped from his body. I learned some medical stuff when I was taking care of my mother." She looked at my wrists. "A few punctures in the right place and it would be just like slashing your wrists."

I took another look at the path and there was no one coming. I made a last attempt at a stall and brought up Maggie. Jane was convinced she wasn't going to make it and on the slight chance she did, would probably have no memory of anything. There was a shift in her demeanor and I realized I was now completely out of time.

Jane started to move closer as my eyes focused right in front of me and I flinched at something flying by, swiping my free hand at it.

"What are you doing?" she snapped. "Don't move."

I swished the air with the back of my hand. "It's a bee," I said, ducking my head back to miss it. "Look out, it's headed for you." Jane's eyes moved over the air in front of her and I reached out, swatting my hand in front of her nose to shoo it away. Jane moved her head as I waved my hand again.

I heard the rhythm of footsteps and then a voice called out. "Hey, what's going on?" Dane said as he rushed down the boardwalk from the other direction. From that side, the bench and all that was going on was clearly visible.

"Don't come any closer." Jane's voice sounded threatening as she lifted her hand to move the wool comb close to my face. "I'll slash her cheek." But when she looked at her hand, she was surprised to see it was empty and horrified when she saw the wooden comb was in my possession now.

"It's all in the wrists," I said to her in a snarky manner. "I learned it from the Amazing Dr. Sammy. People have a tiny area of focus and their eyes are captured by movement. You were so busy watching me swat that imaginary bee, you didn't even feel my other hand take the wool comb out of yours."

I unloaded the whole story on Dane, who wisely chose to handcuff her. She gave me a dirty look as I got to the end of the tale.

"Except there's nothing to prove it," she said with a shrug.

"Maybe there is," I said. I looked at her directly. The plug you picked up was the one I brought along to poke through the plants. No way did I want to touch any evidence. The real one is still there." I pointed out the clump of greenery under the bench.

While we were waiting for the troops to come, Will and another man came by to pick up the bench.

"I did it for you," Jane said, looking lovingly at Will. "So we could be together. Nicole was going to ruin everything for you. You even said she was causing a problem."

Will looked horrified. "Jane, I was just letting off steam to you. You were a friendly ear. Someone to talk to. I didn't mean for you to do anything."

Lieutenant Borgnine wasn't happy to see me or hear that he'd been wrong, though by now Jane had changed her story and was saying I'd come after her with the wool comb. I pointed out the green plug under the bench. "I'm sure you'll find residue of the poisoned-laced latte and even if you don't find Jane's fingerprints on it, it begs the question what something from the Vista Del Mar café was doing stuck in a drink from Maggie's place."

"I know what to look for," the bulldog-shaped cop said in a terse tone. He glared at Jane. "And I'll be checking if her fingerprints match the ones we found at the Coffee Shop."

As Lieutenant Borgnine and the uniforms who'd come with him started to take Jane away, Dane hung back.

"Pretty clever how you got me here," he said, back to his teasing flirty ways. I shrugged with a smile. I'd just used my ex-boss Frank's perennial advice—flirt with a cop. I knew he was referring to the text message I'd sent him. It had said that I'd reconsidered what I'd said about being the other woman and it sounded exciting. I'd suggested we meet ASAP to discuss and told him where.

"You didn't mean it, did you?" he said.

"Nope," I answered, punctuating it with a shake of my head.

32

LUNCH WAS ENDING AS I WALKED OFF THE END OF
the boardwalk back into the heart of the Vista Del Mar grounds.
The officers and Lieutenant Borgnine had taken Jane away
without going through the hotel and conference center. I was
sure none of the people filtering toward the Lodge had any idea
what had just gone on. I found Lucinda and filled her in.

"I'm so sorry," she said when she realized she'd tipped
Jane off.

"It all turned out," I said and she brightened.

"I can't wait to tell Tag that he had the crucial bit of
information."

We went up the stairs to the deck outside the Lodge and
joined my retreat group, who were milling around. I found the
three early birds and pulled them aside. They'd been there
when Nicole died and deserved to know the outcome.

Bree's blond fluff of curls bobbed with animation as she
heard the news. The young mother reminded everyone that

she'd been the one to find Nicole. Olivia was relieved it was settled and that she'd never been a suspect. Scott was impressed by my sleuthing skills.

"But did you have a good time at the retreat?" I said, hopeful. Before they had a chance to answer, the woman I'd called the Ginger came by and hugged Bree.

"I don't know what I would have done without you," she said, almost tearful. "The first time being away from my kids and no cell phone or Internet . . . You got me through it." The woman turned to me. "The retreat turned out a little different than I'd expected, but it was a great experience."

One of the guests who hadn't been part of the retreat put her hand on Olivia's arm. "I just wanted to give you this." The woman handed Olivia a finished square. "Thank you for letting me sneak into your knitting circle." The woman looked at me and seemed to understand I was the retreat director. "I didn't know there were yarn retreats here." She slipped me a business card. "Please let me know when you have the next one."

Scott was actually knitting as he was standing there. He looked over at a small group of people with their suitcases, standing near the door. A man with thick black hair nodded in Scott's direction as he saluted him with a pair of big red plastic knitting needles.

"That's two guys I turned on to knitting," my retreater said with a satisfied smile. He told the group the other man was the one from the business group that had left on Friday.

"Have you started planning the next retreat yet?" Olivia asked.

I didn't want to tell them I'd been on the fence about going forward with my aunt's business. I didn't want to bring up everything that had gone wrong. But now that I was being asked directly, I rethought the whole thing. Quickly.

I had made a lot of mistakes, but I was learning from them. One major one was the idea that I could handle it alone.

"I'd like to offer you four a proposition," I said. I asked Lucinda if she would act as host at the meals. She was saying yes before I got the last word out. Bree seemed to have a knack with first-time retreaters having a hard time. Would she act as a buddy for anyone who seemed a little lost?

I got a hearty yes in response.

I asked Olivia if she would host square-making activities that outside guests would be welcome to participate in. Like the other two, she accepted with enthusiasm.

"I know what you're going to ask me to do," Scott said as I turned in his direction. "Of course, I'd be happy to teach any guy who wants to learn how to knit. Or any kid, or woman, too."

"I just need to check something," I said. I saw Cora Delacorte come into the cavernous room. There was no Burton hanging all over her or his daughter running up to call her "Mother." I suspected the pair had left the area. Madeleine trailed behind her. As usual, they were overdressed, carrying their handbags Queen Elizabeth style.

I excused myself from my group and made my way to the two women. Instead of waiting for their response, I decided to be proactive.

"I'm so sorry," I said to Cora.

"You should be," she said. "You ruined my good time and the inevitable happened sooner than I wanted," she added. "Casey, I had a prenuptial agreement all drawn up. I was just waiting to give it to him. Once he realized I wasn't going to hand him the keys to the castle, I was pretty sure that would be the end of it. But I was so enjoying being romanced."

Madeleine rolled her eyes.

"I wanted to tell you some ideas I have for the retreat

business," I said. I launched into them quickly, afraid that
Cora was going to say they'd rethought the whole thing and
I was out. I deliberately didn't bring up anything about Nicole,
figuring any connection with a dead body wasn't going to
help my case.

"I was thinking it would be nice if some of the other guests
could take part in some of our activities." I gave the example
of the square-making project. "I'm going to have helpers and
they could teach the basics of knitting." I mentioned that Madeleine had expressed an interest in working with yarn and
said she would be welcome to join in.

While Cora seemed to be mulling it over, Madeleine
stepped in. "I say it's a go," she said forcefully. I'm not sure
who was more surprised at Madeleine's gutsy move.

I went back to my group with a look of relief and said I'd
be doing a mailing soon to announce the next retreat. The
retreaters began to disperse. Some pulled their suitcases
toward cars and others stayed with the early birds, waiting
for the airport transport. Lucinda and I stood with them until
the Vista Del Mar van pulled in front of the Lodge.

There were a lot of hugs and good-byes before the doors
to the van closed and it pulled away, leaving Lucinda and me
waving.

"Tag expects me to help with dinner at the Blue Door," she
said with a wistful sigh. "I better go." It was hardly a good-bye
for a long time, but we hugged anyway before she went toward
her car.

I stood there for a moment letting it all sink in. I was surprised to see Wanda coming toward me. "I came back to pick
up my stuff." She was pulling the bin from the meeting room.
She opened it and pointed out the salad spinners. I promised
to pay her for them and then asked how was it that she'd
bought them in advance.

"I was going to get them to Will. I knew that he'd be handling all the water and thought he could add them to the supplies. I was going to have him tell Nicole about them, figuring she'd take it better from him." She looked up at me. "I don't think you understand. I was really on your side all along. I wanted the retreat to work out. But there was only so much I could do."

She closed the top of the bin and seemed ready to go, but she stopped and reached out for me. "I'm not really one of those huggy people." Her embrace was awkward, but seemed genuine. And then she moved on.

Life was certainly full of surprises. Who would have ever thought Wanda and I might end up as friends? I finally made my way across the street. I expected some kind of greeting from Julius when I went inside, but he wasn't in the kitchen. I checked the rest of the house and couldn't find him anywhere. I went back outside and walked around the perimeter of the house and there was no cat.

He was always in one of those places, and I suddenly got worried. I went out to the street and started walking down it, looking for him. I saw a woman up ahead with electric blue hair and a tight-fitting gray tracksuit with something written across the butt.

I recognized Dane's sister, Chloe, even though the last time I'd seen her hanging around her brother's house, her hair was cherry red. I caught up with her and asked if she'd seen a black cat.

"No," she said, looking at the ground around her and then shrugging. I turned back to continue my search, but she came after me.

"Hey," she said, trying to get my attention. "I got a question. What is it—you don't like men or something?"

"Huh?" I answered, confused.

"What's with you and my brother—or really, what's *not* with you and my brother?"

I just wanted to shrug it off and not explain, but she wouldn't let it go.

"I know he likes you. So what gives?" She looked at me and I realized I was going to have to lay it out for her.

"I don't do the 'other woman' thing," I said. "Whether he likes me or not is immaterial. He's got somebody living with him. You're probably here to meet her," I said.

Chloe's red-lipsticked mouth fell open and she seemed confused, then a look of understanding came over her face.

"He didn't tell you?" she said. "It figures. He's always trying to protect her. The woman is our mother. Dane likes to describe her problem as substance abuse, but she's a drunk. And has been since we were kids.

"He put on a pretty good act hanging out with a bunch of bikers and thug types, but at home he took care of everything. Do you know how embarrassing it is to have your brother take you to buy your first bra?" She didn't wait for me to even acknowledge her comment. I don't know what I would have said anyway; my mind was reeling as she continued on.

"He won't give up on Dolores. He gets her in rehab and then some sober-living place. She messes up, gets tossed out and he takes her in until he finds another place for her and it starts all over again."

Chloe looked at me and her expression was clearly unhappy. "You're right though. I am here to see her. He wanted us to have a family dinner before she goes to her new setup."

I heard a meow and Julius came crawling out of the bushes and rubbed against my leg.

I thought of everything I'd said to Dane and realized I had egg on my face again.

33

I WAS STILL PROCESSING THE WHOLE STORY WITH
Dane when Sammy showed up at my front door holding a bottle
of red wine, a cheese plate and a couple of plastic glasses.

"The thank-you drink," he prompted when I seemed totally
surprised at his arrival. "You offered it when I appeared as
your stand-in sheep. It was going to be a toast to both of our
successes at the end of the retreat."

It came back to me and I invited him in. "Case, the magic
was a huge success. I'm going to be a regular. An every-
weekend regular." He was still standing in the doorway. "I
thought the beach was a more appropriate place." He held up
his offering. I grabbed a jacket and joined him outside.

He eyed the guesthouse as we walked to the street. "Have
you thought about renting it?"

My eyes going skyward were my answer, knowing who
he had in mind as a tenant.

Unfortunately, the sunset happened off camera behind a

wall of white. It was chilly, we got sand in the cheese, and the wine turned out to be from a very bad year, but we had fun anyway. Sammy wanted to prolong the evening, but it was business as usual for me, or baking as usual, and he reluctantly left.

I packed up the Mini Cooper with my muffin supplies and something more. There was no reason to keep the box of moldy fabric with the extras mixed in. I would leave it where I found it at The Bank. It was the last loose end to tie up. Tag had called with an update. He'd heard that Jane was going to be charged with first-degree murder of Nicole and maybe an attempted murder charge for Maggie, since it looked like she was going to pull through. I was relieved to hear about Maggie and hoped she'd be back dispensing coffee soon. I couldn't help but feel sad for Jane even though she'd threatened me.

I parked the Mini Cooper in front of The Bank. I'd planned to put the box back where I'd found it and get going. As I walked through the shop I thought of all the times I'd been there in the last few days and all that had gone on.

It was never pursued who had taken the hair jewelry pieces, even though I was sure it was Burton Fiore. Oddly enough, someone had found them in a paper sack left on the end table in the Lodge. I was pretty sure Will was going to donate them to the historical society along with an old quilt Nicole had found locally and refurbished.

As the cops were leading Jane away, Will had broken down and told me that he had shredded the ledger sheets. Nicole had never told him everything she knew, just that she'd figured out something that could make her some money. He knew the ledger sheets were connected and just wanted to make the whole thing go away.

I got to the cubicle back by the vault and went to set the box down. I looked at the open metal door and a thought kept going through my mind. What Nicole had said about locks being like a red flag that there was something valuable inside. I rummaged through the smelly fabric until I found the key. The number was clearly marked on it. I was probably wrong, but I had to check anyway.

The interior of the vault felt claustrophobic and I looked around at the metal wall made of the safety-deposit boxes. They all had holes where the locks had once been. I had to use the meditation table as a step stool to reach the box. I pulled it out and stepped down. The top of the box was closed tight.

I could feel my pulse rate go up as I took the box into the cubicle that had been built for this purpose. I set it on the built-in shelf and took a deep breath before grabbing the latch and pulling it back. I waited a beat and looked down.

The box wasn't empty. There were some photographs, a few envelopes and a folded sheet of paper. I recognized the baby from the other picture, but this time she was holding a knitted teddy bear. I looked at the envelopes. One was marked *Edmund's Hair*. The other one was old and appeared to have been sealed. The ink that said *Edmund* appeared faded, but the ink that said *Mother's DNA* on the flap appeared quite fresh. I unfolded the sheet last, already pretty sure what it was. This ledger sheet was complete. I saw Edmund's name and then a few lines down, a repeat of the box number. The *M* was for Mary and the last name was Jones. Everything together was enough to find the Delacorte heir and prove the relationship.

It would shake up the town and I wondered what I should do. Should I destroy it or follow through?

Patterns

Handspun Shawlette

Easy to make

12 ounces (340 g) handspun wool
Size 13 (9.00 mm) circular knitting needles
Tapestry needle

Gauge is not important for this project.

Dimensions: approximately 48" × 18".

Note: Shawlette is worked from the bottom up.

Cast on 20 stitches.

Row 1: Knit into the front and back of the first stitch (1 increase made), knit across.

Rows 2–33: Repeat row 1 until there are 53 stitches on the needle.

Row 34: Knit into the front and back of the first stitch (1 increase made), knit across until the last stitch, knit into the front and back of the last stitch (1 increase made).

Repeat Row 34 until the shawlette measures 18" from the middle of the top to the bottom.

Bind off loosely and weave in the ends with the tapestry needle.

If-You-Don't-Have-Handspun Shawlette

Easy to make

1 skein Lion Brand Homespun Thick & Quick, Super Bulky #6, 88% acrylic 12% polyester (160 yd/146 m/8oz/227g)
Size 13 (9.00) circular knitting needles
Tapestry needle

Gauge is not important for this project.

Dimensions: approximately 52" × 18".

Note: Shawlette is worked from the bottom up.

Cast on 20 stitches.

Row 1: Knit into the front and back of the first stitch (1 increase made), knit across.

Rows 2–33: Repeat row 1 until there are 53 stitches on the needle.

Row 34: Knit into the front and back of the first stitch (1 increase made), knit across until the last stitch, knit into the front and back of the last stitch (1 increase made).

Repeat Row 34 until the shawlette measures 18" from the middle of the top to the bottom.

Bind off and weave in the ends with the tapestry needle.

Recipes

Ebony and Ivory Muffins

EBONY

⅞ cup unbleached all-purpose flour
¼ teaspoon salt
½ cup organic sugar
½ cup unsweetened cocoa powder
1 teaspoon double-acting baking powder
1 large egg
⅓ cup plus 3 tablespoons milk
2 tablespoons butter, melted

Combine flour, salt, sugar, cocoa powder and baking powder; sift.

In a separate bowl beat egg. Combine milk and melted butter. Add to egg and mix.

Add dry ingredients to egg, milk and butter mixture. Stir until just blended. There will be lumps.

IVORY

⅞ cup unbleached all-purpose flour
¼ teaspoon salt
½ cup organic sugar
1 teaspoon double-acting baking powder
1 large egg
⅓ cup plus 3 tablespoons milk
2 tablespoons butter, melted
1 teaspoon vanilla extract

Combine flour, salt, sugar and baking powder; sift.

In a separate bowl beat egg. Combine milk, melted butter and vanilla. Add to egg and mix.

Add dry ingredients to egg, milk, butter and vanilla mixture. Stir until just blended. There will be lumps.

Line muffin tin with paper inserts and preheat oven to 400 degrees.

Fill inserts ⅓ full with Ivory mixture, then another ⅓ full with Ebony mixture.

Bake for 15–20 minutes, or until a toothpick comes out clean. Cool. Makes 12 3" muffins.

Moment's Notice
Butter Cookies

1 cup butter, room temperature
⅔ cup sugar
1 large egg
2 teaspoons vanilla

2½ cups sifted unbleached all-purpose flour
½ teaspoon salt

Cream butter and sugar. Add egg and vanilla and mix.
Combine salt with flour and gradually add to the butter,
sugar, egg and vanilla mixture, mixing until blended.
Form into logs about 2" in diameter, wrap in wax paper
and chill for at least 4 hours. Can be kept in refrigerator
for about a week. When ready to bake, preheat oven to
350 degrees. Slice and arrange on a cookie sheet. Bake
for 8–10 minutes, or until slightly colored. Cool on rack.

Cookies can be garnished before baking with things
like colored sugar, almond slices, chocolate chips, or dried
fruit.

Makes about sixty 2" cookies.

Turn the page for a preview of Betty Hechtman's
next Crochet Mystery . . .

Available in hardcover from Berkley Prime Crime!

YOU KNOW THAT SAYING ABOUT BEING CAREFUL what you wish for . . . ? My name is Molly Pink and I can tell you it is one hundred percent true. Ever since my husband Charlie died, I've been saying that I wanted to try flying solo. To live without having to answer to anyone. You know, I could wear sweat pants with a hole in them and eat ice cream for dinner. I could be the captain of my own ship.

I thought I was heading that way. I'd worked through my grief and had started a new chapter in my life by getting the job at Shedd & Royal Books and More as the event coordinator/community relations person. But then I met Barry Greenberg and we had a relationship. Okay, maybe he was my boyfriend. It's hard for me to even say that word. It just sounds so ridiculous, since Barry is a homicide detective and in his fifties.

You might notice I said *had* a relationship. Really it was off and on again, and off again and on again. You get the picture. But now it was finally off forever.

Then there was my friendship with Mason Fields. Friendship was all it ever was, though he really wanted it be more.
When things ended with Barry for the last time, they did with
Mason as well. It hadn't been deliberate on my part. I had
gotten so involved with work. I guess there were missed phone
calls and messages I didn't answer, and then just silence. My
social life had gone dark.

Assorted people had stayed with me for various reasons,
but that had all ended as well.

The final step came when my son Samuel moved out—
well, in with his girlfriend. Though he didn't take his cats.

And suddenly there I was alone. At least almost alone. I
had the two cats and my two dogs—my terrier mix Blondie,
and Cosmo. The little black dog was supposed to be Barry
and his son's dog, but that's another story. So here at last was
my chance to soar on my own wings. Do whatever I wanted.
Answer to no one (except my four-legged friends).

At first I was so busy with the holidays and everything at
the bookstore, I didn't think much about being on my own.
But it was January now and as I looked around my cavernous
living room, it all began to sink in. I walked into the kitchen.
It was just as I'd left it when I went to bed. No dishes in the
sink, no ravaged refrigerator. No one had come knocking at
my door in the middle of the night looking for comfort after
a bad shift with suspects. No one had called and suggested a
fun outing. All the bedrooms but mine were uninhabited.

I made coffee for myself quickly. Did I want to sit around
and revel in all this quiet and independence. No. I couldn't
wait to get to work with the problems, the confusion, and most
of all the people. I'd heard the statement that silence was
deafening and now I understood. I needed some noise. I
needed some upheaval in my life. Yes, I had learned my lesson
about being careful for what I wished for. I'd gotten it in

spades and absolutely hated it. I knew what I had to do to stir up the pot of my life.

I didn't even drink the coffee in my kitchen. I filled a commuter cup, made sure the dry cat food bowl was full and located where the dogs couldn't help themselves. And I left.

It took a bit of doing to zip up my jacket while holding the coffee mug as I crossed the backyard. Even here in Southern California, January days are short and chilly. I probably seemed like a wimp for bringing it up when it was icy and snowy back east, but the dew had frozen on the grass.

The sun had already melted the thin layer of frost on the Greenmobile, as I called my vintage blue-green Mercedes. *Vintage* sounded so much better than *old*. I ran the windshield wipers for a moment and they got rid of the residue of moisture. One negative about my car. No drink holder, which meant I had to hold the commuter mug between my legs. I looked down at my usual khaki slacks and hoped I'd make it to work without any coffee stains.

A few minutes later, I pulled the car into the parking lot behind Shedd & Royal Books and More. Once I was inside, I took a deep breath, inhaling the familiar fragrance of the paper in thousands of books, mixed with the scent of freshly brewed coffee drifting in from the café. Then I nodded a greeting at Rayaad, our chief cashier.

The last of the holiday merchandise was gathered on a front table with a sale sign. Even after all these years it still seemed odd how the same merchandise looked so exciting before the holiday and irrelevant after. I mean, a chocolate Santa was still at its heart chocolate.

Any day we'd start putting up Valentine's Day decorations and sell the same chocolate the Santa was made out of shaped like hearts wrapped in red foil.

As I made my way through the store, I saw the playwright's

group gathered in a tight circle around their facilitator. The yarn department was in the back corner of the store, and along with handling events and community relations, it was my baby. I always liked walking in and seeing the feast of color from the cubbies of yarn. Ever since we'd put up a permanent work table in the middle of the area, it was never empty.

I recognized a few faces of my fellow hookers. That's *hookers* as in crochet. The Tarzana Hookers had been meeting at the bookstore since even before the yarn department had been added.

We exchanged a flurry of greetings just as Dinah Lyons caught up with me. She's my best friend, a fellow hooker and an English instructor at the local community college. She slipped off her loden green boiled wool jacket and dropped it on a chair.

"I need to talk to you," I said as we hugged each other. "I've decided to change my life." Dinah's eyes snapped to attention as she got ready to listen. Then my voice dropped. "It'll have to wait. Mrs. Shedd has just joined us." She was the Shedd in Shedd & Royal and my boss. This wasn't a usual gathering of the crochet group to work on projects. This was a meeting.

"Give me an update," Mrs. Shedd said quickly. She never seemed to change. Her blond hair didn't have a hint of gray even though she was well into her sixties. She'd been wearing it for so long in the soft page boy style, I bet her hair naturally fell into it when she washed it.

She didn't sit and seemed a little nervous, but that seemed to be her default emotion lately. Keeping a bookstore afloat these days wasn't easy. We were surviving, but only by broadening our horizons. Thanks to my efforts, the bookstore had become almost a community center. Besides the playwrights' group, I'd added other writing and book groups. We'd recently taken on hosting crochet-themed parties, which was turning into a nice success. And of course, we had author events.

But what we were attempting this time was really a stretch and required an outlay of cash. "Tell me again why we're doing this," my boss said, looking for reassurance.

Adele Abrams joined us as Mrs. Shedd was speaking. Adele was still dressed in her outfit from story time. I'm just guessing, but I bet she'd read *Good Morning, June*. It was a children's classic written in a different time, when girls wore pinafores like the pink one Adele wore over a puffy sleeved dress. She'd completed the look by forcing her brown hair into tiny little braids. Adele would have stood out even without the outfit. She was tallish and amply built and her voice naturally went toward loud.

Before I could say anything, Adele began. "This is the chance of a lifetime. We are carrying the torch of crochet into the world of knitters." Mrs. Shedd didn't look impressed. Who could blame her? She wasn't interested in us being pioneers as much as doing something that would make a profit and help the bookstore. I was relieved when CeeCee Collins slipped into the chair at the head of the table and took the floor away from Adele.

"I feel responsible for encouraging you to have the booth at the yarn show. But I'm sure it's going to be a big success," CeeCee said to my boss.

CeeCee was the real head of our crochet group, though Adele never quite accepted it. She was also a well-known actor who, after a long history of TV and film appearances, had started a whole new chapter in her career when she began hosting a reality show. Then she'd nabbed the part of Ophelia in the movie based on the super hit series of books about a vampire who crocheted. There was Oscar buzz about her performance since the movie had come out, but now we'd see if there was any truth behind the buzz because the actual Oscar nominations were going to be announced in the next couple of weeks. Needless to say, CeeCee was a little edgy.

As always, CeeCee was dressed to be photographed. She said she'd seen enough celebrities snapped in jeans and T-shirts with their hair sticking up to learn her lesson. But she claimed it was a fine art, not to look too done. Kind of like her reality show. It was supposed to look real, but a lot of editing and planning went into what the audience ended up seeing.

CeeCee noticed the two women at the other end of the table who were not part of the group. They appeared to have no idea what was going on. CeeCee, in her typical gracious manner, explained that we were talking about the bookstore's upcoming booth at the Southern California Knit Style Show.

"This is a very big deal because it is the first year they're including crochet in the show. Before, everything was about knitting. You know, knitting classes, fashion shows of knitted garments, design competitions for knitted pieces. There probably wasn't even a lonely crochet hook for sale in any of the vendors' booths in the marketplace."

CeeCee made a slight bow with her head. "I'd like to think I had something to do with K.D.'s change of heart." She explained to the women that K. D. Kirby put on the show along with being the publisher of a number of knitting magazines. "I was the only crocheter included in an article in *Knit Style* magazine about celebrity yarn crafters. I think hearing about how popular the craft is and seeing what wonderful things you can make made her realize what a mistake it was not to bring crochet into the show."

The women nodded their heads in unison to show they were listening, though I noticed knitting needles sticking out of their tote bags. "So, this year there is going to be a crochet category in the design competition with yours truly as the judge." CeeCee did another little nodding bow before adding that she was also going to be acting as the celebrity face of the show.

One of the women finally spoke. "So you mean you can do more with crochet than just make edging on something or use up scraps of yarn to make one of those afghans full of squares?"

Adele was squirming in her seat at the words. All of the Hookers thought that crochet was the more interesting yarn craft, but Adele took it even further. She thought crochet was superior to knitting, and she wasn't afraid to say it.

CeeCee put her hand on Adele's shoulder. It looked like it was just for reassurance, but I knew it was to hold her in her seat. "Why yes, crochet has become quite a fashion statement. Designers have taken intricate lace patterns that had been used to make doilies and are blowing them out into shrugs." CeeCee had taken her hand off of Adele's shoulder and my bookstore coworker took the opportunity to pop out of her chair and start talking.

"I'm going to be teaching one of the crochet classes," Adele said, doing an imitation of CeeCee's bow. "A stash buster wrap." The women didn't seem to know what to make of Adele's statement and looked back to CeeCee for some kind of reassurance.

CeeCee dropped her voice and spoke directly to Adele. "We need to talk about that."

Since the booth was sort of my baby, I jumped in and told Mrs. Shedd how we'd come up with a plan to bring shoppers to our booth. "We're going to teach people how to make a little granny square pin with some beads for decoration." I was glad I had brought a sample and showed it to my boss and the women.

"That's wonderful," one of them said. "I bet a lot of people will want to make one of those."

It was like music to Mrs. Shedd's ears, and she looked a little less tense. "Bob wants to have us offer some of his treats," I added. Bob was the barista at the bookstore café. He also made fresh baked goods. "The wonderful smell alone will act like a magnet."

Mr. Royal arrived carrying a piece of posterboard with a miniature version of the booth he'd constructed. He laid it on the table in front of us all, as more of our group arrived. We all leaned over and admired it. The two newcomers got up and walked to the head of the table to get a better view.

"It's wonderful," I said. It looked like a little store. There was even a sign across the front announcing the name of the bookstore in big letters.

"There's just one thing missing," Adele said as she scribbled something on a piece of paper and tore off a strip. She attached it to the bookstore sign. It said: Crochet Spoken Here.

Mrs. Shedd seemed a little less worried when she saw the name of the bookstore prominently displayed. "A lot of the people coming to this show are local. We want to make them aware of us. Perhaps you can add something that mentions all the groups we have meeting here."

I reassured Mrs. Shedd that with the hookers helping, we'd make sure the bookstore was well presented.

"I'm depending on you two," Mrs. Shedd said, referring to me and Adele but looking squarely at me. We were the bookstore employees, and no matter what help the others offered, the buck stopped with us, or actually, me.

I'd been hired as the event coordinator and community relations person and Adele had been given the kids' department as sort of a consolation prize, since she thought the job should have been hers. But somehow, with one thing and another, we'd ended up working as sort of a team, putting on the crochet parties and now this booth. Adele balked at being left out of running the yarn department, but she'd cooked her own goose with her feelings about knitters. She didn't even think we should have knitted swatches of the yarn we sold.

Yes, I knew how to knit. The basics, anyway. All those knitted swatches had been done by me. There was no way we could have a yarn department and shut out knitters, even if some yarn stores weren't so happy with crocheters.

"No problem," I said with a smile. We've got it covered. Mrs. Shedd muttered something about hoping so, because if this booth turned out to be a disaster, she wasn't sure what she would do. Then my boss left the area, saying there were things she had to take care of.

"I didn't get a chance to tell her about the kits I'm going to sell," Elise Belmont said. She'd extracted one from her bag and put it on the table. "If she'd seen these, she wouldn't have been so worried. We're going a sell a million of them," then Elise caught herself. "Or at least the whole stock. Do you want to see all the different kinds?" she asked.

Elise was a small woman with wispy brown hair. She seemed a little vague until you knew her and then it was obvious she had a steel core, even if she did look like a good gust of wind could carry her off. The group shook their heads at her offer. We didn't need to see the kits; we knew what they were.

I sometimes wondered what Elise's husband must have thought about her love affair with the character of Anthony, the crocheting vampire. She'd read all the books, seen the movie made from the first book countless times and even gotten CeeCee to get the film's star to sign a life-size cutout. What did Logan Belmont think of having a full-size figure of Hugh Jackman staring at them as they slept?

The kit on the table was the first one she'd made for her vampire scarf. It had black and white stripes with a red tassel, or what she called "traditional vampire colors." The white

was for their pale colorless skin, the black was for their clothing choice, and the red—I'm guessing you can figure that one
out. Her stitch of choice was the half double crochet, which
she insisted looked like a fang.

Rhoda Klein rolled her eyes. She was a matter-of-fact sort
of person with short brown hair and sensible clothes who
couldn't understand an imaginary affair with a literary blood
sucker. "I think Mrs. Shedd would be more interested in the
free crochet lessons we're going to offer."

"Did I miss something?" Eduardo Linnares said as he
joined us at the table. He was holding a garment bag and laid
it on the chair next to him. "I brought what you asked for,"
he said. Dinah suggested he show it to us. Eduardo had been
a cover model until recently. He'd been on countless covers
of romance novels dressed as pirates, wealthy tycoons, cow-
boys, and assorted other hero types. The one thing all the
pictures had in common was that his shirt always seemed to
be unbuttoned down the front. When he started being cast as
the pirate's father and pushed into the background on the
covers, he'd decided it was time to move on and he'd bought
an upscale drugstore in Encino. We were asking him to go
back to the old days for the weekend.

He opened the garment bag and laid a pair of leather pants
and a billowing white shirt on the table. The plan was that
dressed in that outfit, he'd attract a lot of people, well women,
to our booth.

"Anything to help out," he said. Like all of the hookers,
he was grateful to the bookstore for giving us a place to meet.
He'd been a lonely crocheter until he'd found us. The plan
was that he would teach his specialty. It was hard to believe
with his big hands, but he was a master with a small steel
hook and thread. He'd learned Irish crochet, which was really
lace, from his grandmother on his mother's side.

Sheila Altman came in at the end. When she realized she'd missed everything, her brows immediately knit together and she started to go into panic mode. Somebody yelled to get her a hook and some yarn. Sheila was actually much better than she'd been, but she still had relapses, and nothing calmed her better or faster than crocheting. Adele made a length of chain stitches before handing it to Sheila, who immediately began to make single crochets across. She didn't even look at the stitches or care that they were uneven; the point was just to do them and take a few deep breaths. After a few minutes she sank into a chair. "That's what I'm going to teach at the booth," she said with a relieved sigh. "How to relax."

We talked over our plan of action for a few minutes. Who was going to be in the booth when and what they were going to be doing. Sheila put down the crochet hook and took out a zippered plastic bag with a supply of yarn in greens, blues and lavender. "I thought I could sell kits, too, if it's all right." She showed off the directions for a scarf.

Sheila was known for making shawls, blankets and scarves using a combination of those colors. Her pieces came out looking like an impressionist painting. I told her it was fine and it was agreed that the kits would be sold only when the two women were there to oversee them.

With everything agreed upon, we all started working on our projects. The two new women asked if it was okay if they stayed and we all agreed. Adele sucked in her breath when they took out knitting needles and began to cast on stitches with the yarn they'd just bought.

"Calm down," I said to her. "None of us like the way knitters treat us like we're the stepsisters of yarn craft. But we'd be just as bad if we treated knitters the same way."

Adele started to protest, but finally gave in and went back to working on a scarf made out of squares with different motifs.

Dinah moved closer to me. "You said there was something you wanted to talk about?"

I was hoping for a more private situation. Not that I had secrets from the rest of the group. One of the beauties about our group was that we shared our lives with one another. Good, bad, happy and sad. Still, I wasn't quite ready to share my decision with all of them. Not until I saw how it worked out.

Before I could even say this wasn't the best place to talk, CeeCee interrupted. "We need to talk now." She looked around and saw that Mrs. Shedd had gotten all the way to the front of the store. CeeCee moved in closer, making it clear what she was about to say was just between us and probably some sort of problem. "When K.D. decided to bring crochet into the show, she asked my advice about classes and I suggested Adele. All the knitting classes are taught by elite knitters who have written pattern books and traveled around doing workshops. She called them the knitterati." CeeCee turned toward Adele. "She found some master knitters who knew about crochet to teach the crochet classes, but to get to the bottom line, K.D. now has her doubts about having you teaching a class. And to be honest, there haven't been a lot of sign-ups."

I watched the whole group suck in their breath and prepare for Adele's reaction. As predicted, Adele seemed shocked and huffed and puffed that she was more qualified to teach the class than all the famous yarn people. CeeCee put up her hand to stop Adele. "The point is, K.D. would like you to give her a personal demonstration." Before Adele could object, CeeCee added that it wasn't a request, it was a command and that K.D. would just cancel the class otherwise.

Adele absorbed the information and begrudgingly, she said she would do it. There was no way I was going to let Adele go alone. Who knew what she would do? Adele actually seemed relieved when I suggested going along.

"I'm going, too," CeeCee said. "My reputation is at stake, since I am the crochet liaison for the show." She looked from Adele to me. "Did I mention she's expecting Adele tomorrow morning?"

Adele began to sputter about having to audition and the fact she hadn't been consulted about the meeting time, but CeeCee made it clear she had no choice and we agreed to meet at the bookstore and go together. I was grateful there was a few minutes of peaceful yarn work before the group broke up.

As I got up from the table, Dinah linked arms with me.

"Now we can talk."

Yarn to Go

A Yarn Retreat Mystery

Dessert chef Casey Feldstein doesn't know a knitting needle from a crochet hook, but when her aunt dies and leaves
her a yarn retreat business, the sweets baker finds herself
rising to the occasion. When a retreat regular is murdered,
though, she has to unravel whodunit.

Includes a knitting pattern and a recipe!